Champagne &

Presents

Binding
Circumstance

By

Kelley Griffin

This is a work of fiction. The characters, incidents and dialogues in this book are of the author's imagination and are not to be construed as real. Any resemblance to actual events or persons, living or dead, is completely coincidental.

No part of this book may be reproduced or transmitted in any form or by any means, electronic or mechanical, including photocopying, recording, or by any information storage and retrieval system, without permission in writing from the publisher.

Champagne Book Group
www.champagnebooks.com
Copyright 2019 by Kelley Griffin
ISBN 978-1-897445-99-0
August 2019
Cover Art by OliviaProDesign
Produced in the United States of America

Champagne Book Group
2373 NE Evergreen Avenue
Albany OR 97321
USA

Dedication

To God for my abundant blessings. And to my mom, Nancy Lamberson—my first beta reader who encourages and inspires me daily by her loving example and witty comebacks. *I love you, Mama.* And to my other mama, Nancy Griffin—I miss you every day. Thank you for loving me so well for over 29 years.

Dear Reader:

Thank you for purchasing this book! I loved writing this story. After you finish reading, please consider taking thirty seconds to go to a retailer, Goodreads, or other place you like to hang out and give a quick review. It doesn't have to be long. Reviews will encourage others to take a chance on a new author.

THANK YOU for helping me!

XO~
Kelley

Find me on Facebook or Goodreads as Kelley Griffin Author or http://www.kelleygriffinauthor.com IG as @kelleygriffinauthor twitter at https://www.twitter.com/AuthorKTGriffin

Chapter One

The numbers were wrong.

Leslie Carroll's thin fingers ached. She pressed them together, then grasped her frayed, yellow measuring tape and took a third stab. Her stomach fluttered, like always when faced with the prospect of handing over her well-worn ID—albeit fake—to a new HR department. Even if nobody else did, she knew who she was and what she'd done. Her new name, "Leslie," couldn't erase the guilt of her twin sister's death. Anne never slipped far from her mind.

But this was a different kind of nervous.

Leslie's dream job hung in the balance. The one she'd longed for since she was young, but deep down, knew she didn't deserve. Maybe this was why she struggled to read the measurements for the man's waistline.

"You *have* done this before, haven't you, Miss Carroll?" the infamous Mr. Miller crooned in perfect speech reminiscent of a Shakespearean actor. Condescension seeped through his shiny, plastic-looking lips. His phony smile didn't come close to touching the hint of eyeliner below his gray eyes.

"I'm a little nervous," she admitted.

"Well, dear, you'd best thicken your skin. This industry eats young women like you for brunch."

He was right. Designing costumes at Plantation Rock Pictures, the top film production house in Southern California, meant living the dream: sewing fabulous beaded gowns, attending red carpet events, and dressing A-list Hollywood celebrities. She'd even practiced her acceptance speech for Best Costume Designer in her bathroom mirror. But never did she imagine measuring an irritated, impatient executive designer as part of her final job interview.

"There, I'm finished." Leslie printed the last measurement with slow and deliberate care.

Mr. Miller stuck out his hand. When she passed the paper to him, he wrapped long fingers along the edges of the pale-green notecard carefully, so they didn't skim hers.

Did he have touching issues too?

He held the card high near his face as if he was nearsighted. But he was known for having a flair for the dramatic. She sucked in a breath and held it. His cold, gray gaze darted back and forth. She stood tall, feigning confidence, yet picked at her fingernails. Mr. Miller lowered the card and glared. Then he lowered it farther below his chin, and a smirk spread across his lips.

"You have my waistline wrong," he stated plainly, as if he expected an excuse. "You're off by a quarter of an inch."

"Maybe you had a big brunch," she deadpanned, hoping he had some small shred of good humor.

He didn't.

"Miss Carroll, I don't deal well with 'errors'." Tight-lipped, Mr. Miller tossed the note card on the orange suede couch, then snatched her favorite measuring tape from a side table, snapped it taut, and shot her a look. "I've had a twenty-nine-inch waist since before you were born. No amount of charm or ill-placed humor can change that fact." Nimble fingers stretched the tape out to the side, then around his midriff.

Wonderful. The end of the shortest costume career in history. She shuffled from foot to foot, as Mr. Miller let out a quick, frustrated sigh, shook out the kinks in the tape and re-measured. His even-toned cheeks took on a pink hue. A growl told her he'd gotten a similar measurement to hers.

After a moment, his head snapped up as if he'd forgotten she was in the room. He rolled up her worn, yellow tape and tossed it in her direction. It fell short and landed on the plush white carpet between them.

"When you work for me, Miss Carroll, you'll need to bring a *new* measuring tape," he declared. Chin high, he pretended to pull a piece of lint off his pressed, white shirt, rather than meet her eyes again. "Now, make your way back to HR. Get a badge. Finish your paperwork. Meet me on the fourth floor when you're finished."

"Yes, sir." Her voice cracked, but she cleared her throat.

After the door clicked shut, her eyes closed, and she bounced up and down—clapping like her Nate sometimes did when he saw trains. She did it. Landed her dream job. Things were finally looking up. New city, new job, new identity, and new start. Even Nate's new special education teachers were making breakthroughs with him. He'd interacted and talked way more than at his last school.

Maybe this time, she'd plant roots and stay.

Leslie lifted her faithful measuring tape and held it. A slow smile unfolded. "I'd never get rid of you. You're my lucky charm." She wanted to squeal. The smile diminished as she looked around. Other than Nate, who rarely understood her, there was nobody left to tell.

Her father, The Judge, would've told her she should've haggled for a higher salary. That is, if he could remember his own name. What might her sister have said? Would Anne have told her she was proud? That at least one of them lived long enough to go after her dreams?

~ * ~

When Leslie trudged into the HR room, she felt like a dirty penny in a tray of new quarters. Several suited women snapped their heads up and surveyed her, studying her face as if they knew she wasn't who her ID said. She gripped her badge along with a black pen clipped to a non-disclosure agreement and rushed toward an empty cube.

Gazing at the picture on her badge, Leslie smiled. She no longer resembled the selfish college girl who made bad decisions. For once, her skin had color, as if she'd sunbathed at the beach she was too chicken to go to. Her appetite had waned in recent weeks, so her white button-down and gray pants hung loose around her slim frame. Chestnut hair tucked into a smart bun and black rimmed glasses were supposed to make her look trustworthy and responsible. Bologna. She looked like a geeky librarian.

Leslie read through the lawyerly nondisclosure agreement. Since she'd be working on multimillion-dollar movies, they wouldn't want her leaking plotlines or cast secrets. That made sense. She flipped the papers over and signed—careful to use the correct name. New name for her new start.

As if the past never happened.

~ * ~

Clutching her purse and stocked costume pouch like life preservers, Leslie exited the elevator onto the fourth floor to a sea of stares. After a beat, as if someone blew a silent whistle, the jam-packed cubicles roared to life. Obviously, she was *not* who they expected.

The room resembled a deafening circus of jugglers. Papers flew, employees shoved personal items into open drawers, desktops were decluttered, and cell phones were stashed. Several people sat like ice sculptures, looking as if they had rods pasted to their backs. After their initial stares, nobody paid attention to her. Thank God. Her single goal this week was to fly under the radar.

Faint groans of frustration rumbled as the main receptionist whined for everyone to move faster into their places. Leslie stood, fascinated and open-mouthed. A heavyset, bleach-blonde with a bob haircut, strolled toward her. The woman's smile put Leslie to ease at once.

"Miss Carroll?"

Leslie nodded.

"My name is Dana. Dana Godwin. Mr. Miller wants you to shadow me this week." Dana seemed to be the calmest person in the room.

The ding of the elevator caused the room to stop again, as if someone pushed the pause button on a remote. It didn't faze Dana. Air in the room stopped circulating and thickened into stress soup. The noise level died at once. Leslie didn't risk turning or moving. Someone important entered the room behind her.

Mr. Miller strolled between her and Dana and stopped. Like a general inspecting his troops, he surveyed the rows of boxed workspaces. Thick, wavy hair, slicked back off his smooth face, made him seem taller. He held tight to both fashion and his youth. The pungent smell of his black leather shoulder bag and matching Italian shoes filled the air. His eyes were the same gray as his pin striped suit. Blinking twice to make sure, she swore he wore lip-gloss.

Without looking in their direction, he spoke in a low but eloquent voice. "Good morning, Mrs. Godwin, and hello again, Miss Carroll. I trust you completed your paperwork in HR?"

His change of attitude had Leslie struggling to find her voice. "Yes, sir."

He paused. "Well. We have you now, don't we?" A faint smile brushed his lips before he marched toward his glassed-in office. A few employees scurried to look busy as he passed.

Dana glanced at Leslie, rolled her eyes as she shook her head. She walked toward the receptionist's desk, then nodded toward Mr. Miller's office. "Your workspace is the last one on the right, in front of his office. Why don't you get set up, then meet me on the sixth floor? I'll be in workroom number three. Come find me when you're settled."

Leslie nodded.

Dana scooted a heavy-looking box sitting on the reception desk toward her and let out a long sigh. "We've got to measure and fit over two hundred extras today. I'll introduce you to the other two on our team when you come up. Hope you ate breakfast; it promises to be a long day." The older woman placed an apologetic hand on Leslie's shoulder before she hoisted the box as if it were filled with air and walked toward the elevator.

Leslie hoped she didn't feel her flinch.

Chapter Two

"Workroom" was hardly a fitting description for this place. The ceiling stood twenty-five feet tall, and the space was ten times larger than Leslie's new rental in Pomona, easy. The room resembled a football field of concrete. Rows of sewing machines and giant cutting tables lined two sides. Massive fabric bolts of all types and colors stood like guards in one corner. On the other side of the room, lines of actors waited their turn to be measured and fitted. Red curtains swung open and shut at breakneck speed as they tried on their costumes.

Toward the far wall were several large wooden doors, all closed. She spotted Dana next to one of the lines, waving. She jogged over. Dana's wide grin said she appreciated Leslie's enthusiasm.

"Pace yourself, dear," Dana cautioned, blowing her bangs off her face. "This is our busiest day and it happens to be your first. I promise they won't all be like this." She glanced at Leslie's pouch, then pointed. "Oh good, you have your tools. Perfect. Head over to that last fitting line. Angela and Frank, the other two assistants, will show you what to do. Come find me in an hour—we'll take a break, okay?"

"Yes, ma'am," Leslie responded.

Dana trotted off toward the sewing machines while Leslie headed for the far line, where the extras gawked at two people arguing. The sea of faces looked puzzled, as if they were watching a professional ping-pong match on roller skates.

"Angela, you never listen to me," a man—she assumed it was Frank—whined, waving skinny arms. "I told you we're only fitting good-looking men in this line. Women and fugly men need to wait in line five." The tall, gangly man chuckled to himself at his own joke. The extra winced as Frank yanked his tape measure around the man's waist.

"Frank, don't be a prick," Angela bellowed between a female actor's legs as she knelt to measure her inseam, then sat back on her heels. "There's no reason to make anybody go to another line. Regardless of your horrible taste." She shot a nod of camaraderie to Frank's current victim. "We've got their paperwork right here. Stop horning in on all the male extras. We'll measure *everyone* in this line."

Heavily tatted and sporting bleached, spiky hair, Angela stood, took a gulp of her drink and snapped her fingers. Like magic, the next person in line ran to her. Without missing a beat, she knelt and measured the next extra's outer seam.

"Hey, guys." Leslie lowered her shoulders and wrung her hands. "Where do you want me?"

Frank turned and stared. Exasperation laced his face, while his gaze raked Leslie up and down. Manicured eyebrows knitted together while his mouth contorted, as if he tasted something sour.

Angela didn't bother turning around. Instead she shouted over her shoulder, "Run and grab us coffee, would you, honey?"

Was she yanking her chain or serious? Setting her jaw, Leslie opened her mouth to reply with her usual smart-ass comment, deliberated for half a second, then closed it. Rash decisions were the reason she was alone and on the run. The last thing she wanted was trouble on her first day. All the same, she shoved aside what appeared to be Frank's coffee, pulled out her tools, placed them on the table, and snapped her fingers high like Angela had. The next person in line came running to her.

Without glancing either Angela's or Frank's way, Leslie took the actor's measurements and wrote them down on the list along with name and employee ID number. Angela stopped moving and glanced over. She nodded. A slight grin crept up her lips. Frank stared for another beat, then apparently satisfied she knew what she was doing, he continued to measure.

Two hours and countless names, faces, and body types later, Leslie forgot to find Dana. Even worse, she needed a bathroom. Now. Grabbing her bag, she tapped Frank and told him she'd be right back. He waved her off like a gnat.

Shuffling through the masses of extras and costume assistants, she came upon a row of drafting tables covered in drawings. Seated were costume illustrators sketching and consulting with one another. She squinted to catch a glimpse of the mock-ups but couldn't see that far.

As a peon, she wasn't told much. She didn't know what type of film, what costumes were to be made, or even the names of the main actors. Talk among the extras told her it was a knight-in-shining-armor type. She spotted Dana waving over the chaos, near a row of glassed offices.

"I'm so sorry I didn't stop earlier and come find you, dear," Dana called out over the noise. "This might be our biggest project yet.

How's it going over there?" she asked, yet looked away, distracted.

"It's…going well," Leslie fibbed, leaning in so Dana could hear over the noise. "It'd be better if you pointed the way to the restrooms?"

"Oh, dear, I didn't tell you where the bathrooms were? Forgive me." Dana stood on her toes like a prairie dog and pointed toward the other side of the room. "Beyond that last dressing room on the left. I'll grab us something to drink. Tea okay with you?"

"Yes, ma'am—thank you."

Once Leslie navigated the sea of people and made it to the other side of the room, she found only one locked door with the word "storage" stenciled in red. She backtracked a few feet and examined the space. With nobody around to direct her, she hurried down the long row of doors, searching for a sign. No bathroom sign anywhere. Her bladder was now screaming for having had a second cup of coffee.

Had to find a bathroom. Fast. Her head swiveled back and forth as she reversed, searching in the direction Dana pointed. She looked like a lost tourist at Disneyland. She'd misunderstood. Maybe Dana meant the last door on the right. Leslie tried the handle. It turned, so she pushed.

The door was heavy, like shoving a cement-block house. Grunting, she dug in with her feet and thrust with her whole body. As soon as it swung open, she regretted not paying closer attention to Dana's instructions.

Standing a few feet inside the room, wearing only low-slung, faded blue jeans, no shirt, and resembling a Calvin Klein ad in Times Square, was *the* Charles Erickson.

He was only the hottest male actor of the year. Somehow, he seemed taller in real life. Had to be around five eleven. His iconic sandy-blond hair was not perfect like on screen, but messy. And his deep blue eyes were the color of the sea next to a tropical island. Rounded, muscular shoulders contrasted with his sharp jawline, which, she noticed too late, was set in anger. He stared like she had three heads.

When their eyes met, he roared, "Hey! This is a closed dressing room!"

The momentum from pushing the door catapulted Leslie, with zero grace, a few steps inside the room. Then, the stupid door clicked closed on its own. When her mind caught up with her body, she wanted to crawl inside a hole. The command from her brain to move her legs and close her gaping mouth was blissfully ignored.

Finding her voice, she rattled out a quick apology, walking

backward toward the door. One hand fumbled around behind her to find the doorknob to escape.

"I-I'm so sorry. I'm with the costume department—my first day. I was trying to find the—"

Bam! Bam! Bam!

Leslie yelped, covering her mouth as the large door shook.

"Charlie! Are you in there?" An angry voice yelled through the door.

Charles Erickson took two quick, athletic steps toward Leslie. Her breath caught. His famous face was inches from hers. When he stooped to speak, minty breath tickled her cheek.

One arm held out, he whispered, "Hurry, pull your stuff out, and measure me. Maybe she'll get the hint and leave."

Breathe, Leslie.

Minty air swirled around her face in slow motion. He stood too close. By normal-people standards, the distance was fine, but not by hers. He'd invaded her bubble. And yet, her brain didn't register panic. No visions, no smell of burnt flesh, and no cold sweat. Definitely not normal.

Hell, she must be in shock.

She couldn't think, let alone understand what this beautiful man was saying. Her mind sputtered. An impatient blue gaze darted from her to the door and back again. What did he want? Whatever it was, she was in—if only she could make herself move.

"Oh, for Pete's sake, stop looking at me like that. Grab your bag," he ordered.

His tone snapped her back into reality. Moving back to give herself space to breathe, she unzipped her costume bag and pulled out her tools. As she measured the length of his arm, the door flung open.

Christine Langford waltzed into the room with an air of self-importance rivaling the Queen of England. She was every woman's run-of-the-mill nightmare. Besides being a famous leading lady in numerous box office hits and the daughter of two other world-famous actors, she was stunning. Her body looked like a supermodel's—tall and thin with her blonde locks falling in classic waves a little past her shoulders.

The actress was picture perfect in every way, from her expertly painted toes to her flawlessly manicured eyebrows. Her features were small for one so tall, but her skin glowed as if tiny lamps were placed strategically to shine flattering light on specific areas of her face. The woman was maddening to behold, even up close. She eyed Leslie, stalking around her like she was a pile of poop. Then she turned her anger on Mr. Erickson.

"So what *exactly* did that last text mean? Are you breaking up with me? Is that it—one *tiny* mistake and I'm out?" She slithered close, toe to toe with him. Her face, pink and contorted, was inches from his.

Tension crackled in the air between them. His body grew rigid. Leslie wanted to run. Nobody should witness this private moment between these two famous people.

She knelt and rushed through the rest of the measurements. Someone would need these, she was sure. If not, she'd frame them on her wall at home. But right now, she had to finish. And escape.

As if he could read her mind, Mr. Erickson shot down a look of warning as if to say *stay put*, then turned to Christine. His voice was smooth and deep. Quiet, yet menacing. "I meant what I said, Chris. I'm done. You think it was a 'tiny' mistake? That's your problem."

Christine stepped back and bent to pick a magazine off the coffee table. She thumbed through it casually as she shot back, "Oh, get over yourself, Charlie. Everybody's done it. I'm sure this girl here has done it." She motioned to Leslie as she emphasized the word *girl*.

Leslie glanced up as Mr. Erickson scowled toward her as if he was angry with her too. Then, in an instant, his eyes softened and held hers. He surveyed her. A curious look crossed his face. His lips upturned slightly. It was as if he hadn't fully seen her until now. Heat rose up her neck. Caught in his stare, she broke the trance and stared down at her fingers.

When Christine cleared her throat, both their heads jerked back toward her. Regaining his irritation, he stepped toward Christine, lowering his voice. "Screwing your trainer isn't something *everyone* does, and it's not a 'tiny' mistake. I want you and your crap out of my house. I'll stay in a hotel tonight. I'm done."

She spun around and stomped back toward him. "Oh, no sir, we are not done!" Her bellowing, angry voice startled Leslie. "*You* want to break up with *me?* I'm Christine-freaking-Langford, buddy. I was getting big money acting jobs when you were still scraping by on commercials! Your pretty face has gotten you far, Charlie, but it was dating me that got you this gig, and you know it."

She paced in front of him like a caged lion, flailing sculpted arms.

"I'm not doing this now," Charlie said through gritted teeth. He eyed Leslie.

"What?" Christine glared at her but spoke to him. "You don't want to do this in front of the *help?* That's your problem, Charlie. Too worried about what the little people think of you. The craft service people and the mousy seamstress might think you're a bad guy. You're pathetic, you know that?"

She rolled her eyes, flung the magazine back on the table, then stomped toward the door. When her hand hit the doorknob, she turned. "That humble, southern boy thing doesn't work with me, Charlie. You're just as entitled as the rest of us." Then she flashed a devilish grin. "And guess what…you'll call me. You always do."

Christine stomped out, slamming the door behind her.

Mousy? Wait. Bitch was talking about me?

Leslie's thighs were on fire. Crouched during Christine's tirade, Leslie pretended to write his already copied measurements. The muscles in her arms were stiff too. When she stood, her legs jellied, which was in complete contrast to her jaw, now clamped shut. The snobby actress made her feel small. Only one other time in her life had she wanted to pummel another human until they bled.

Unfortunately, her tear ducts and pissed-off-glands were tied together. She had to flee from that room before any of them fell. Away from him. Her face splotched hot. Without looking in his direction, she chucked her measuring tape along with his measurements into her bag.

Charlie let out a long sigh, pulled a T-shirt down over his head, and said to himself, "Good riddance."

Leslie slung her bag over her shoulder and bolted toward the exit. As she turned the handle and yanked on the heavy door, Charlie called out, "Oh, hey…uh, miss? I didn't catch your name."

"Mousy!" she yelled, glaring back as she stormed out of the room. She didn't care if he thought she was rude. She wished the door would slam shut like before to help make her point, but this time, the hinges caught, and it closed at a snail's pace. Figured. Charlie strode toward her. To make herself feel better, she added, "Arrogant, pompous-windbag actor."

As she trotted the length of the hallway leading away from what she now knew were private dressing rooms, her ears filled with the welcome hum of machinery. Her eyes stung with pointless tears while her bladder threatened to release. A tiny bathroom sign hidden by an open door emerged. She glared at it.

Charlie yelled in her direction, "I need your name!"

She ignored the actor and rushed into the bathroom.

When Leslie emerged, her anger remained, although most of it was aimed at herself. She'd let Christine's words get under her skin. Truth was, she had become mousy. In high school, she'd been headstrong, bold, and daring. Then in college, thanks to unwise decisions, unspeakable things happened. Because of those things, she'd become paranoid and cautious. If she was being honest, more than a little mousy.

That was the next item on her bucket list to change.

As she walked back toward the line, the drone of machines had lessened.

Frank's skinny arms flailed around. He looked like a chicken fighting a snake. He spoke to a man, but because of the crowd gathered, the back of his head was the only visible body part. Angela too, appeared wild-eyed and pointing in her direction. Coffee churned in Leslie's stomach. The crowd turned to stare as she trotted up.

Mr. Miller stood like ice. His eyes narrowed. A hush came over the crowd of extras. Folding his arms, he glared.

Great. What now?

She swallowed hard. Mr. Miller cleared his throat and grinned like a cat. Slowly, as if he had nowhere to be, he sauntered toward his prey, ready to pounce. "Miss Carroll," he said, steepling his fingers, "how pleasant of you to join us. Did you have a relaxing break?"

She opened her mouth to explain. He held one finger in the air to silence her, then circled like a shark claiming its lunch. "Did you get autographs from anyone famous? Is that why you're here, dear—to attract an actor? I hired you to do a job, not to *fraternize* with the famed."

The thirty or so extras gaped with delight as the torture unfolded. Frank's face was lined with pretend sympathy yet smug, while Angela's seemed more humbled. Blood drained slowly from Leslie's face, and her fists balled. *Damn.* Her only crime was not finding the bathroom. It wasn't as if she sought out the crazy.

Mr. Miller circled one last time. He strutted a few feet from her, head cocked sideways. A faint smile drifted across his lips. Enjoying his assault, he resumed, "Miss Carroll, please share with the group precisely where you went for *an hour* and what you were doing?"

She opened her mouth to speak, but everything she wanted to say, sounded crazy. Then it hit her. Leslie cleared her throat and forced a smile. "Mr. Miller, I'd love to tell you where I've been, but, you see, I signed a non-disclosure agreement. I'm sure you'll understand, the actors I ran into would appreciate my discretion."

He reeled. Anger rolled off his skin like fog. His nostrils flared as he stomped back toward her. His face was inches from hers. "I had such high hopes for you, Miss Carroll. You came with such recommendation. Now I know you are not a team player, but someone who enjoys the spotlight. I'm afraid, I am going to have to ask you—"

Gasps from the crowd rang out before he finished. She knew. Knew someone walked up and stood behind her. Normal range, but again, too close for her.

"Mr. Miller?" Charlie's familiar voice boomed.

Her back straightened as if someone poked her. Perhaps it was her imagination, but the warmth from his body radiated through the back of her thin shirt. Or she was having a hot flash twenty years too early.

His signature cologne, designed by someone else but stamped with his name, filled the air. A body-awakening musk mixed with a fresh rain. She shuddered. Instinct caused her to whirl around and step to the side, gaining a foot of distance between them. As she did, their eyes locked. Another chill racked her body. If she was lucky, he didn't notice.

One quick look at Charlie's head cocked to the side and the question in his eyes—he'd noticed.

Mr. Miller's demeanor and voice changed, as if someone flipped a switch on his back. "Mr. Erickson, what a pleasure! To what do we owe this visit? Oh, I remember, you were to be measured today, weren't you? Let me get my top assistant, Dana, and we will get that underway right now."

He brushed past Leslie, shooting daggers, when Charlie stopped him.

"Mr. Miller, I've already been fitted by this young lady here." He moved toward her, holding out an arm like an invitation for a side hug.

Great. He was a hugger. When she mirrored his movement, only backward, she crossed her arms and shot him an apologetic nod. Questions arose again in his eyes. But this time, a sign of understanding accompanied it.

Charlie shoved his hands into his pockets and examined her yet spoke to Mr. Miller. "She saved me time and embarrassment today." Charlie's gaze darted from the gawking crowd to Mr. Miller's aggressive stance. Then he added, "I hope she was being commended for her efforts, rather than reprimanded."

Charlie slid a long look at Mr. Miller.

Frank gaped, star struck, while Angela's stare switched from the famous actor to Leslie and back.

Charlie turned toward her. "I didn't realize—wait, did you say today is your first day?" He shook Mr. Miller's hand. "Nice catch. She's an excellent hire."

Mr. Miller stammered, "Why...thank you, Mr. Erickson. That

is generous of you. So Leslie measured you already?" Confusion laced his voice.

"Leslie," Charlie repeated her name.

His slow, smooth voice rumbled with a touch of his southern drawl. Nothing could stop the flaming in her cheeks. Heat spread all the way to her ears. She wanted to disappear under the concrete floor. Her mind logged and registered all the exits. An old survival habit she couldn't break.

Fidgeting, she moved a baby-step farther out of his reach. He'd already made her shudder and his mind-numbing scent mixed with his unwavering stare had her terrified he'd touch her, and yet wanting him to at the same time.

Yes, she was aware a costume professional by design must touch people. But it wasn't her touching others that bothered her. It was not having control of someone else touching her. As long as other people stayed in their bubble, she was fine. But somehow, Charlie seemed unaware of the bubble rule.

"Yes, Leslie did an amazing job of putting up with my shenanigans." He turned toward Mr. Miller. "Could I have a private word?"

Mr. Miller puffed up like a peacock. "Me? Well, of course, you can, Mr. Erickson."

Chin raised a notch, he walked a few feet away from the crowd for their chat. When he returned, he waved his hand in dismissal of the crowd. Frank shrugged and turned. Angela actually smiled toward Leslie. She beamed back. They'd not be getting the better of her today.

Mr. Miller turned. His normal intimidating presence softened. "Miss Carroll, I owe you an apology. It was my understanding you'd gone missing." He glared over at Frank and exhaled. "I should have considered the source. I had no idea you were recording measurements. Will you please accept my request for forgiveness?"

"Of course, sir."

She offered her hand. Mr. Miller shook it as if it might bite him. Letting go, he raised one perfect eyebrow and added, "Interesting first day, wouldn't you say?"

"Yes, sir." She exhaled, deeply grateful to still have a job.

Straightening his suit jacket, he reverted to his more formal speech. "Mr. Erickson requested a private word with you as well. When you are finished, I would like for you to find Mrs. Godwin again and speak to her about your next assignment. That will be all, Miss Carroll."

"Of course, sir."

What does he want now? Leslie made her way from the crowd toward Charlie. He leaned against the edge of a drafting table. Strong arms were folded across his chest, his golden hair still messy, and his legs stretched out. He surveyed her as she came toward him, his eyes questioning, as if figuring out a puzzle. His I-told-you-so smile was enough to make anyone swoon, but she took a deep breath, squared her shoulders, and pressed her eyebrows together as she neared him.

He chuckled. Then in a low, sexy voice he said, "There she is. My elusive friend, Mousy—I mean Leslie."

"Mr. Erickson." She nodded.

"Charlie," he stated, looking her dead in the eyes.

This was a strong-willed chess match she was determined to win. "*Mr. Erickson*—was there something you needed from me?"

"Not a fan, I take it?"

"Fan of what?"

"Me."

She shrugged. "I guess so, why?"

He mimicked her shrug. "Just wondering. I know you're not a fan of being touched."

He'd nailed her in five seconds flat. Her hackles rose. "Did you need something?"

"You're a mystery, that's all. Most people in this town fight to stand next to an actor, name drop, snap pictures, you know the whole not-real fame thing." He slid her a curious look. "But not you. It's refreshing."

She nodded, then raised her eyebrows as if to say, *your point?*

His smile faded, then rebounded as he mouthed the word "lunch."

Her eyes narrowed. She cocked her head to the side as she placed both hands on her hips. "You expect me to fetch your lunch?"

He pushed off the table and took a cautious step toward her. Both hands raised in surrender, he looked hurt. "No, I want to *take* you to lunch. You know, for being discreet and not telling the world about the arrogant, pompous, windbag actor and his lunatic ex-girlfriend."

She bit her lip. She wanted to full-out cackle. An unstoppable grin fought its way through. It radiated across her lips, erupting into giggles she had zero hope of controlling. He lowered his arms. His warm eyes danced with laughter along with her.

"I guess I should apologize for the pompous-windbag comment, eh?"

"No way," he said. "Besides, it was cute."

He examined her—too closely. The heat in his eyes caused

warning bells to clang in her mind. Her laughter faded fast.

Clearing his throat, he continued, "Please let me take you to lunch. Come on, *Slim*, you gotta be hungry." His boyish grin made her smile. "What do you say? They make a mean salad at the Canteen downstairs."

Frank watched them with a mixture of respect and jealousy in his eyes. Perfect. Obviously, he was a fan of Charlie's. Charlie didn't notice. In fact, he didn't seem to notice anything in the room but her. A few short years ago, she would've jumped at the chance to go to lunch with a famous actor.

Not now.

Shaking her head, she backed up. "Sorry. I just can't. We're slammed. Thanks anyway." She turned on her heels toward the sea of human mannequins.

"Hey, wait."

She turned back as he stepped close.

"I'm sorry you had to listen to all that—you know, before with Christine. She's such a…" The struggle between being honest and being kind washed over his face. Charlie tilted his head up as if his answer hung in the rafters. He gave the impression he was searching for the vaguest, yet most correct word in the English language.

"Bitch?" Leslie offered, her lips curved upward.

"Yeah. That's probably the best one."

His wholesome laugh softened his jawline and lit up his eyes. She didn't want to look away. He didn't seem so intimidating or so famous anymore.

Charlie bent toward her. "Listen, can I buy you coffee and a salad to make it up to you? Please?"

She allowed no one except Nate and her father to touch her or be in her space. Charlie had weaseled his body closer to hers. Back inside her bubble. *Breathe.* Tiny beads of sweat trickled around her temple. He was only being polite, she reminded her brain.

"No thanks, I'm more of a peanut butter and jelly type of girl anyway." Leslie backed away, winning and grinning. She spotted Dana waving from the other side of the room. "*Mr. Erickson,* I gotta go." Walking away, she sensed a gaze on her rear. Something about him staring both excited and terrified her.

"Leslie?" he yelled.

She stopped in her tracks and turned, hating how it thrilled her when he called to her. Turning on his Hollywood charm, he declared, "It's Charlie—and I *will* see you around."

Chapter Three

He was dreaming.

Couldn't have been her. Everything in his meticulous, analytical mind told him the girl in the market was *her*. Her cropped cut, shiny and brown, made her look different. The dark didn't suit her. He wanted the strawberry blonde locks, long like he remembered from the night they met.

She recognized him too; her beautiful dark pools widened when she noticed him. But she fled. Why? Why did she run out of the market? Weren't there conversations they needed to have? Like, why she left him in the first place?

He drove to his home, giddy with a renewed sense of purpose. She was alive. He'd show everyone. He could keep a girl like that. Superior. Out of all the ones he'd taken and played with, she was distinct. Gentle and fresh. Innocent. Not the usual pub whore he gravitated toward.

He'd resume his internet search tonight with a bottle of wine to celebrate. He'd bought a few more unauthorized database searches on the black market using a pseudonym. This time, he'd find her if it killed him. Then he'd remind her why she couldn't live without him.

When he got his hands on her this time, he'd make sure she never left him again.

Chapter Four

At eight o'clock, exhausted and sore, Leslie left Plantation Rock Pictures. The muscles in her arms ached from non-stop measuring the last three hours of the day. She shook them out and walked through the garage toward her old Bronco. Self-conscious, she hated the way she had to be hyperalert all the time and the way she swiveled her head back and forth inside parking garages. She felt like a paranoid mess.

Dana walked a few feet ahead of her, toward a shiny red Cadillac, as if she had energy to spare. The woman had to be in her late fifties, and if she was tired, she didn't show it. Too strong to let her weariness break through her pleasant demeanor. Leslie admired her for that.

"Bye, dear," Dana sang out, as she pulled her keys from her purse. "You had a stellar first day." She halted, turned and cocked her head to the side. "You *are* coming back tomorrow, right dear?"

"Of course," Leslie said, with a weak, half-smile. "Wouldn't miss it."

Dana shot her an appreciative look.

Leslie reached for the "oh shit" bar with both hands to haul her body into her truck. She sat with a heavy sigh. She could've curled up and fallen asleep, but she still had to drive to Aunt Reva's house to pick up Nate. For her aunt's sake, she hoped the boy slept.

Leslie rolled down the window, hoping the night air would keep her awake. As she pushed the key into the ignition and glanced up, a brown paper package stared back at her from the hood.

Tiny hairs shot up on the back of her neck. All senses alerted at once.

He'd found her. But how? She'd rented the house in a different name, no phone number listed, and all mail was re-routed to a P.O. box. It'd been weeks since he spotted her in the quickie mart. Thank God, Nate hadn't been with her. Her breathing became ragged, spitting and spurting as sweat poured around her hairline.

Real or imagined, the smell of electricity burning through flesh invaded her nose. She jerked her head side-to-side, searching for any signs inside or outside as she choked and gasped. Nobody around.

Digging fingernails into one arm to bring herself back to the present, she commanded her breathing to slow. Opening the Bronco door, she grabbed the small box as if it were a bomb. With shaky hands, she pulled the package into her lap.

She shut and locked the door, then scolded herself. Exhaustion was no reason to be careless. The window remained open. *Real safe.* She tugged on the handle, and it closed with a squeak.

Turning the package over, she inspected it for markings. Nothing. Taking a deep breath, she pulled back the brown paper. A bright, colored inner box had shapes and cartoon animals on it. Someone left a toy for Nate? That made zero sense. She opened the top of the box to find a sandwich wrapped in butcher paper and an apple juice box.

Folding back the butcher paper, she sighed. Peanut butter and jelly. *Charlie.*

With her forehead resting on her steering wheel, she exhaled deeply, forcing her heartrate to slow. Irrational fears dominated her life.

Wait…how did Charlie know which car she drove? Leslie surveyed the almost empty parking garage and remembered the expensive, shiny cars parked when she arrived. Her indestructible '89 black Bronco with rusty fenders might have stood out.

She was intrigued though. Tossing the box into the passenger seat, she fastened her seat belt, and pulled out of the parking garage. Smiling at the kindness, she devoured the sandwich as she drove away.

Later, with Nate tucked into bed and an empty wine glass next to hers, she considered the events of her day. If she kept Charlie in mind as she drifted off to sleep, would he be enough to ward off the nightmares? She hoped so. They were becoming more vivid, more telling. It was as if the past she blocked out so long ago was warning her.

In truth, she didn't want to dream about anybody. But if she had to dream, she'd make damn sure she dreamt about him. Even if he was exasperating. Her eyes closed. Had Christine Langford moved out or had the witch used her magic, swung her hips, and demanded Charlie take her back? He'd be a fool not to. Any red-blooded man would. Leslie hoped—for his sake, of course—he was stronger than that.

~ * ~

Focus. The drugs were starting to seep from her body. Awareness of her surroundings caused her stomach to hurl. Her sister's low cry crawled down her spine. Padding mostly naked and barefooted down a long dark hallway, she hushed her sister. All the

23

doors were locked. They needed a window. The place was a labyrinth of doors and hallways.

The wood floor creaked upstairs. He was coming. Frantic, she dropped her sister's hand and searched the floor near the cabinets for something—anything—big enough to stop him. She had to give them time to escape.

Leslie woke, as usual, screaming. She headed to the bathroom and splashed water on her face. Without light, she tiptoed to Nate's room. Luckily, he never woke during her bad dreams. Sleep would finally return an hour later, when her eyes were too heavy to stay open.

She focused on Charlie's face, his kind eyes and strong jaw, as she drifted off to sleep.

For once, she slept the rest of the night without nightmares.

Chapter Five

"Damn, you can't drink one beer with an old friend?" Charlie yelled into his phone as he crossed the busy downtown street toward his Maserati. "Jase, they do let attorneys *out* from time to time to have a life, don't they? What if I needed legal advice? Or someone to go mudding with? You'd come running then, wouldn't ya?"

The late afternoon sun stung Charlie's eyes, and the designer sunglasses didn't help. A cheap dollar store pair from home would've worked just fine. The struggle between being the son of a poor farmer and a top earner in the multibillion-dollar film business pulled at him always. He was an imposter in one of them and yet both fit.

Jason Gilreath exhaled into the phone. Charlie knew he was at a legal conference, which is why he whispered.

"Mudding? In your Maserati? Right. You'd end up getting us stuck, like you did on grumpy Mr. Thompson's farm in high school. My fast talking is the only reason he didn't hang us by our balls, and you know it." Jase exhaled. "Fine, Charlie. Jesus—why can't you text me like the rest of the world? You called three times in the last hour. You'd make a horrible stalker."

"So tonight...deal?" Charlie's tone was light. "Somewhere quiet. I wanna sneak in and drink without too much commotion. I'll even let you whip my ass in pool, like in college."

Jase chuckled. "Have you met you? A—you never go anywhere without commotion, and B—you never let me win, pinhead. That was skill." He took a deep breath. "All right, eight o'clock, *sharp.* And I swear if you stand me up again with some sex story about your hot-mean-woman there won't be—"

"The hot-mean-woman is no longer in the picture."

"Right. This makes, what, the fourth time? Nice try. I don't believe you."

"You should talk. The last real relationship you had was...hmm, in college, right?"

"You know I can't date the money-grubbing L.A. girls. And I'm waiting on Sissy. She's the only girl for me."

Their rivalry-turned-friendship began in the seventh grade. All because Charlie's sister caught the eye of the most popular girl in the class, Nicole Davenport. Most seventh-grade boys crushed on Nicole, with her long red hair and pretty face, but she had a mean streak. One day in the hall, she and her followers were making fun of the mentally challenged class and especially one heavy-set girl, who wore a too-tight pink shirt and polka-dotted knee socks. Sissy.

Charlie strolled up from class, took one look at his sister's face and pushed through the crowd to defend her. Only someone else got there first. A new kid in school, Jase. He'd stood nose to nose with Nicole, hands balled into fists, and told her off in front of everyone. The volatile kid had sheer hatred plastered on his face. Nicole looked terrified. Nobody picked on Sissy again, and Jase became the class pariah and Charlie's best friend in the process.

It was only later in high school when Charlie's family took Jase in, that he became aware of Jase's hot temper and his distrust of anyone who resembled his mother.

"You're one to talk," Jason continued. "I don't know of any relationship you've had, other than Christine...oh, and the *freshman*."

Charlie winced. He deserved that one. One hormonal decision junior year that almost ruined their friendship and could've stopped his career before it started. Jason had never forgotten or, he suspected, forgiven him either.

With Jase, everything was a competition. From challenging each other in sports, to eating contests, to racing toward who could have the best career, they pushed each other to be the best. But junior year, Charlie had taken it too far.

"I gotta go, fucker," Jase's tone was clipped.

"Fine, hotshot, go learn. See you tonight." Charlie parked his blacked-out Ghibli in the last spot at Plantation Rock Pictures. He wiped a hand across the plush interior as Rachel's face drifted into his mind. Jase had been crazy about her, but she wanted Charlie. They'd both been so young. Even though she'd been two years younger, she was lightyears faster than both boys put together.

They hadn't been careful. He'd found out too late she terminated the baby. It was a regret he'd carry the rest of his life. He spent the last of high school with one goal—get a job, settle down, and start a family. He became baby crazy like one of those desperate forty-two-year-old single women without a date.

Then fame came knocking.

According to social media, Rachel was now happily married to a Marine, lived in Charleston, and had three little boys. She was happy.

Her life turned out like she wanted. Past forgotten. He shook the memory from his mind.

Ambling toward the elevators, he breathed in the warm L.A. air. So far today, he'd met with his trainer and gotten his ass handed to him, deleted Christine's number from his phone, and had his security codes changed.

His agent pitched a new script and spoke of possible A-list costars. Now, he was back at the studio to go through pre-production creative meetings regarding his current script. He was content for the first time in forever.

It'd be the perfect opportunity to call his parents, except they'd bitch because he hadn't come home last Christmas. Tennessee was worlds away. Yes, they weren't getting any younger. And he was sure the barn needed a coat of paint, the stalls needed a repair, and Sissy was probably driving them crazy. But he couldn't get away.

He could always pay to have those jobs done, but they wouldn't hear of it. They wanted him home.

All the same, going home always made him doubt L.A. life. Like it was wrong for him. His dream had been to build a house and a horse barn on his parent's property and settle down. Start a family. Rachel's decisions, without his knowledge, had pushed him toward fame. Fame derailed his small dream. Today, though, he wouldn't change a thing.

Today was his opportunity to drop in and glimpse the hot, smart-mouthed costume designer who smelled like laundry detergent. She reminded him of his Smoky Mountains after a rainfall. He'd dreamt of soft chestnut hair and a glorious rear end all night. There was something about the way she noticed him, at first, like a movie star. Frozen in place by the sight of him—he got that a lot—but later, as she walked, head high and confident toward him, he knew. She cut through the BS celebrity to the real him.

When he found her, she'd have to thank him for the sandwich, and he could stand in front of her and breathe her in. Without touching her, of course. Yet.

~ * ~

Leslie, in her newly appointed cubicle with tan fabric walls, skimmed pages of names and measurements. She understood when Dana mentioned that neatness, in Mr. Miller's eyes, was the defining factor between a good costume designer and an outstanding one.

PRP was massive, but so far easy to navigate, even with her less than stellar sense of direction. The fourth floor housed the costume offices, fifth floor the stitching rooms, and the entire sixth floor was slated for workrooms. She called the tenth floor the "stuck-up" floor. This was where the big dogs worked. Highly paid actors, actresses, producers, and directors had meetings on the ultra-shiny tenth floor.

Mr. Miller placed her in the empty cubicle closest to his office on purpose. She was sure of it. At the front of the class, as if he wanted to catch her passing a note. Nobody would have a neater cube, she'd make sure of it. In this, she wanted to stand out and not settle in with the pack.

The shrill ring of her desk phone made her jump. The incoming line read: Ext. 115.

"Costume, this is Leslie." She clicked on an incoming email.

"Leslie, this is Dana. How're you this morning, dear?"

She breathed a sigh of relief. "I'm fine, Dana. How are you?"

"Not well, dear. I've got a slight problem. I'm due to run up to the executive floor today in Mr. Miller's absence. He's with the scouting team getting a feel for how the costumes will look on our next film location. But I ...." Dana paused then continued, "fell last night in the shower. I'm clumsy, dear. Anyway, I'm supposed to be up there in ten minutes, but my eye is turning blacker and now a touch of purple too. Without Mr. Miller here to ask, well...I think you should go in my place."

Leslie stammered, "Of course, but—" she searched, frantic for words, "—but Dana, don't you want to send someone more experienced? I mean this is only my second day and—"

Dana cut her off. "Yes, yes, I know, but I need someone who can be professional. The others aren't exactly...well, you're the best candidate. Oh, and Mr. Erickson needs to try on the final mock-up costume, and he requested you."

Leslie swallowed hard. *Damn him.* She didn't need to be thrown into the deep end on her second day of work. Her hands shook.

Dana's voice interrupted her panic, "You still there, dear? Anyway, good luck, take your bag, be polite and professional, and you'll do fine. You have ten minutes. Room 1014. They're expecting you, and thank you, dear!" The line went dead.

Leslie's stomach did a summersault. She stood like a robot and grabbed her purse from inside a drawer. Long, quick strides got her to the bathroom in seconds. She pushed open the door and instinctively looked under the stalls. Empty.

Dragging her brush through her hair, she sprayed it and added lip gloss with a shaky hand. Thank God she'd chosen to look professional today. She paused to glance at her reflection. Her pale arms hung down, too skinny, out of her navy, sleeveless dress. Without her smart glasses, her eyes appeared sunken in and too dark. She pushed her shoulders back. Her colored hair and dark eyes were supposed to help her seem more professional and help her to be taken seriously, right?

She rounded the last corner toward her cube to drop her purse and pick up her pouch before heading for the elevator. A man sat in her chair, staring at her computer. Damn contacts blurred, but it didn't take a rocket scientist to know who invaded her space. Hot anger pulsed through her. She picked up the pace. As she got closer to her desk, the man's face came into focus.

"Erickson, what do you think you're doing?"

Spinning around in her chair, Charlie leaned back. He wore a black T-shirt, faded jeans, and a frustratingly sexy smile. A trace of his cologne hung in the air. The scent alone caused good but distracting tingles to make their way up her body. This infuriated her even more.

"I'm waiting for you to stop primping, so we can get to the tenth floor. You look beautiful, by the way." He grinned and reached for her hand, but at the last second, changed his trajectory to swipe at his hair. She tossed her purse inside a drawer and slammed it shut. When their eyes met, he nodded toward her computer screen. His unwavering stare didn't change as he ignored her anger.

"Who's the dark-eyed boy on the screensaver?" His face was innocent, as if he had no idea he was trespassing.

See if this slows you down, Pompous. "He's my son," she stated confidently.

Charlie didn't hesitate. "He's cute. Looks a lot like his mama." He smiled, a canned Hollywood grin, no doubt.

"Look, Erickson, I don't need a tour guide. I can find it all by myself."

"Not if yesterday was any indication of your navigational skills." His half-cocked grin made him look like a teenager instead of his late twenties.

"Erickson, I'm—" she sputtered, pinching the bridge of her nose.

Charlie cut her off. "Come on, an elevator ride won't kill you." He stood, then sidestepped out of her way, arms up like he was being robbed. He nodded toward her bag.

Leslie shook her head, let out a frustrated sigh, then snatched it. She walked as fast as she could to the elevators while the entire damn office gawked at them. This wasn't the attention she needed. She needed to be invisible. Blend in, damn it. When she reached the elevators, she was so rattled she forgot to push the button. He leaned around, invading her space again, to push "UP."

He whispered close by her ear, "They're all staring at you."

She glared, which only made his grin widen. Stomping into the elevator, she squashed the number "10," hard. On purpose, she placed her bag on the shoulder closest to him, like a small brick wall between them.

Without warning, he grabbed her left hand. "No ring, hmm. No boyfriend, then?"

She pulled her hand back, but he gripped it tighter, staring into her eyes. He expected an answer she wouldn't give. His habit of invading her personal space ticked her off. It only added to her nervousness, yet somehow, it was flattering, too. She yanked her hand from his grip.

"You know, I'm from the south, right?" he said, one eyebrow cocked.

"So?"

"We're huggers. And we like to touch people when we talk."

"Your point?"

Charlie grinned. "You don't like me touching you, do you?"

"No. I don't." Frustration made her enunciate each word. "But for some strange reason, you continue to do it."

"Bad manners, I guess." Charlie ran a hand through his hair, eyes pinning her in place. "Or maybe—I like touching you."

Her breath caught. Strange, damn little butterflies fluttered in her belly. She cleared her throat and played it off. "I think you enjoy annoying me and making me uncomfortable."

His eyebrows danced in laughter, as he stalked closer. "Oh, I make you uncomfortable, do I?"

"Stop." The tremble in her own voice pissed her off. Underlying panic hung in the air. She walked backward, one hand outstretched toward him, then added with a smaller, but steadier voice, "Please, stop."

Charlie shoved both hands into his pockets and eyed her, then shrugged. "You're sure?"

"Yeah," Leslie's brows furrowed. "I'm sure."

"I tell you what, cute girl. I promise I won't touch you again until you ask me to." His voice took on a self-assured tone as he glanced up at the elevator numbers. "I can wait."

Her eyes widened, then narrowed. She balled both fists. "Erickson—were you born this arrogant or were you raised by snobs?"

Charlie turned, crossed his arms, and fired back. "I was raised by loving parents. Farmers. Poor farmers. They're not snobby. And I'm confident, Leslie, not arrogant. There's a difference. You may not realize it now, but…" His voice trailed off as the doors opened on the eighth floor, and two suited men entered the elevator.

She'd hit a nerve. He didn't like to be called snobby. Maybe the Hollywood in him wasn't as prevalent as the southern boy, which came out in his speech when he was mad.

The men glanced from Leslie to Charlie, then turned in unison to face the door. No doubt they sensed the tension in the air. She examined Charlie out of the corner of her eye. He stared right back from across the elevator. No matter how hard she squeezed them together, her knees still knocked from when he stalked toward her.

Slowest damn elevator on the planet. She stared at the climbing numbers wishing she had superpowers to open the doors to the tenth floor. Now.

The red "10" illuminated, and the elevator jerked to a stop. No way would she look over at him. When the doors opened, she bolted between the three men, running into the lobby like she was coming up for air. She didn't care what they thought. Didn't care if they thought she was rude or a lunatic, she needed space. Away from *him*. He'd crawled into her world and under her skin. She needed to escape his stare and focus if she wanted to excel in this industry. Better plan— ignore Mr. Erickson like he wasn't there.

Chapter Six

Leslie could afford no mistakes—not on this floor. Mentally, she recalled all the names and faces of upper management she'd studied from the website.

Giant marble columns flanked a sleek reception area. A curved, black counter encircled four model-looking women, typing on shiny laptops and wearing stylish headsets. Did everyone have to look like a supermodel? Light flooded in from floor-to-ceiling windows. It gave the illusion of a warm and friendly company. Make no mistake, she was inside the snake pit. One of the model-receptionists stood and glided toward her.

"Miss Carroll? Please come with me, and I'll show you..." She stopped mid-sentence. "Oh, *hello*, Charlie," she cooed.

"Hi, Julia," Charlie muttered, sounding unaffected. He'd strolled up and stood in Leslie's bubble, then declared, "I'll show her the way."

A vein throbbed in Leslie's forehead. To make a good impression, she'd need to use her wits, be sharp and on time, and navigate the labyrinth of shiny, bright identical hallways leading away from the reception area. It looked like a confusing wagon wheel. This would require help. But not from him.

Leslie leaned toward Julia. "I can find it on my own. Can you tell me which hallway I use to reach 1014?"

Polite, but sounding bored, Julia gave Leslie a three-part direction: go through the vestibule, to the third hallway, turn right at the first opening, and the room was the fifth one on the left past the bathrooms.

She repeated the directions in her mind but went blank after "vestibule." Damn it. Charlie spun on his heels and appeared to be heading in the right direction, so she thanked Julia, squared her shoulders, then followed him.

When they reached the door, Charlie hesitated before opening it and whispered, "You'll do fine in here. Keep that backbone intact, okay?"

Forcing her shoulders to relax, she took a breath and nodded.

Even though it seemed Charlie's personal mission was to annoy her, she was witnessing his kind side. Being southern, she rationalized, he probably didn't even realize he was breaking the bubble rule. She'd give him the benefit of the doubt—for now.

The oval mahogany conference room table could've seated fourteen people comfortably. Three well-dressed men sat along one side, arguing among a throng of papers, while a woman with a man's haircut sat alone on the near side playing on her phone, ignoring them. She glanced up with a crooked smile, nodded toward the men and rolled her eyes, then motioned for Charlie to sit by her. Charlie hugged her, then whispered in her ear.

Leslie took a seat, shaking off the quick pang of jealousy running through her. She chose a seat with at least one chair between herself and Charlie. He frowned.

"How could she back out at the last minute? We're supposed to start shooting next week. Where's her contract?" one gray-headed man spat toward another.

"She hadn't signed the contract yet, Phil," a man with slicked, jet-black hair chimed in. "We'll have to find someone to replace her."

Their raised voices masked Charlie's when he leaned over the empty chair and muttered, "I knew it wouldn't work. That actress signed on to do an action flick two weeks before they proposed this one. She thought she could do both. I guess she figured out it'd be too hard." Then Charlie nodded toward the men. "Those two are producers. That dark-skinned man is the corporate attorney. Kat here on my right is my agent. She's a lesbian." His eyebrows flickered like Groucho Marx in an old movie.

Kat leaned in and shot Leslie a huge toothy grin. Leslie liked her immediately.

As soon as they noticed extra people in the room, the men stopped arguing. Standing, a man reached out a stubby hand to Charlie and then to Leslie, introducing himself as Phil Jones, executive producer. He was heavyset with thick, gray hair, and his worn face was covered with worry. The other two men followed. Kat and Leslie shook hands.

Phil stood. "Charlie, don't take offense, but it was the combination of your box office power and hers that we hoped would take this film to the numbers we needed. Casting needs to secure someone with enough firepower to bring in the masses."

"And someone who isn't working on a film right now," the other producer chimed in, tapping his pencil on the table.

Christine Langford's face popped into Leslie's mind. Had she and Charlie ever done a film together? If she had time to have an affair with her trainer, she had time to be in this film. Leslie pushed the thought out, not wanting to envision Christine and Charlie in an old-world romance. Especially now, since she couldn't get Charlie out of her dreams.

Charlie leaned forward. "Phil, I appreciate your faith in me. Kat and I can put out feelers within our circles."

The corporate attorney chimed in, "What about Miss Langford? You two are still a couple, right? She'd have the right amount of draw, wouldn't she?"

This kick-started the three men arguing again. A puzzling look crossed Charlie's face. Her heart sank. He was still in love with her.

Charlie's jaw tightened. "No. We're no longer a couple. Hiring her might, shall we say, negatively play into the chemistry."

The men looked stunned. Kat, Charlie's agent, glanced up from her phone, leaned in and stared pointedly at the three men, and then Leslie. "That information stays in this room."

The group nodded.

The second producer flipped through a notebook, then sorted stacks of papers with handwritten notes all over them. He appeared unaffected by the banter in the room. He stood, as Phil and the attorney discussed possible replacement actresses, then pulled out a large, brown box from under the table.

Mr. Miller's scrolled handwriting was on the side. He opened the box and motioned for Leslie to join him. She walked behind Charlie and Kat. Charlie scooted his chair out as she passed, like a middle schooler flirting. She never broke stride. When she rounded the last corner of the conference table, she caught a glimpse of a richly colored burgundy fabric peeking out of the edge of the cardboard.

The producer bent toward Leslie, lowering his voice. "Take Mr. Erickson next door to try on this rough-cut knight costume." He glanced up at Charlie, adding, "You'll need to spot alter it." He then waved her off like a child, muttering under his breath, "Would've been better if we'd had the leading lady here, too."

"Yes, sir." She gathered the box and placed her small bag on top. She stopped behind Charlie's chair and said, "Come with me."

Charlie smiled, as smug as if he'd won the lottery. "Be right back, gentlemen. I've got to follow this pretty lady." He puffed out his chest when he stood. He was making a joke, but Phil's watchful gaze homed in on Leslie and Charlie as they strolled out. If the look on his face was any indication, he wasn't amused.

No sooner had the door shut behind them then Leslie shoved

the costume box into his chest, hard, and lit into him. "Is it impossible for you be serious for one minute?"

Charlie opened his mouth, no doubt to roll off a smart-ass comment, but her glare stopped him cold. "You might not take anything in your life seriously, but I fought hard to get this job. I'm not about to let an arrogant, flippant actor make me look like a joke."

She hooked her bag on her wrist and yanked the lanyard from around her neck, then shoved the key into the door lock. She twisted and pulled, but the lock wouldn't disengage. And now the key was stuck. She drew the knob toward her as she turned the key, then tried pushing the knob and twisting it. It still wouldn't budge. New tactic: gentle fingers guiding it to the left then right, as slowly as ketchup from a glass bottle. She spun the handle. The door remained locked. Grabbing the knob, she shook it as if she belonged in a straitjacket.

Charlie didn't move. When she cut her gaze up at him, quick and frustrated, he squeezed his lips together, shooting no doubt for a serious look. And failing. Then, in one swift move, he set the costume box on the floor and moved in. He shot her a knowing look and nodded toward the key. She moved her hand away. He eased the key out of the lock with careful hands, then back in and turned it with grace. Magically he unlocked the door then pushed it open.

She leveled a look at him. Charlie grinned, then shrugged before scooping up the box. Stomping into the room, she pulled the key out and slapped the light switch. God, he was infuriating.

The abandoned office was immaculate and shiny. A clean smell of lemon permeated the room. One lonely, polished, L-shaped desk begged to have papers and computer equipment thrown on it. The matching file cabinet stood like a shiny knight protecting his forgotten queen.

She spotted an alcove at the corner of the room. Sensing Charlie's gaze following her every move, she placed the box down on the desk and pushed the empty filing cabinet in front of the alcove. When he came toward her to help, she waved him off. Didn't need Mr. Pompous getting dirty. She required a spot where he could change, protected if someone barged in, like the day before. Wait, had it only been one day?

She shook her head like an Etch A Sketch to erase the question, then pulled out each costume piece and arranged them on the desk. She strolled toward the door and without turning, said, "Open the door when you're dressed."

"Yes, Ma—"

She shut it before he could finish.

In the hallway, five slow minutes went by. When Charlie turned the handle and yanked open the door, she jumped. Her nerves were on edge. She followed him back into the room. When he turned around, she slapped one hand to her mouth.

The burgundy tunic and dark gray knickers clung to his body perfectly. Her gaze lingered on his chest longer than was polite, but then snapped back to the heavy armored pieces, which hung in reverse. Based on his perplexed look and angry, pink cheeks, he hadn't done it on purpose.

"What the hell is *this* thing?" He pointed to a scaly three-piece breastplate smaller than his frame. It was more the size of a child's kneepad than something that should go across his muscular chest. The shoulder pads hung off his back, making him look like Quasimodo.

"It's fine," Leslie said, stifling a giggle. "Don't worry, I'll fix it all."

She stood on tiptoes and placed the pads on top of his shoulders. They gave the illusion his already broad shoulders were even wider. She steadied herself as she reset the breastplate, but still didn't like the looks of it, so she took it off and twisted until it fit.

As she adjusted the thick armor, tugging here and there, she was acutely aware of Charlie's body language. He stilled when she placed her hand on the chest plate to steady herself, then flattened a cockeyed shoulder piece. His gaze followed her every move. Was he holding his breath? She sure was. At one point, his hands twitched toward touching her, then dropped back down.

"You've got nice hands," he stated, looking straight ahead. Then he cleared his throat. She searched his face to see if he was joking, then scoffed. As she narrowed her eyes, the edges of her mouth curved up.

"You are an awkward compliment-giver." She chuckled as she tucked a piece of the silver tunic back inside the armor.

He laughed. "You got me. I got most-likely-to-be-awkward for senior superlatives in high school."

"I don't doubt it." She grinned wide. "Guess what I got?" She placed a pin in her mouth as she struggled to keep a flap of material in place.

"I'm gonna go out on a limb and say friendliest?" Charlie stood like an uncomfortable crossing-guard as she pinned. She lowered his arms to his sides and turned to pack up her things.

Rolling her eyes, she answered. "Nope, but close...Biggest Flirt."

Thoughtful, he quieted. "I didn't see that one coming."

"People rarely do." She looked down then motioned for him to exit. He hesitated, shot her a curious look, then walked through toward the hallway. Leslie locked the door behind them.

Chapter Seven

Charlie grinned like a damn idiot. Leslie had told him something personal and true. The grin couldn't be erased, not even with a jackhammer. Pulling his shoulders back, he willed the corners of his mouth to straighten as he waltzed back into the conference room.

Three new executives had arrived. Two men and a woman, all dressed in suits. The men fidgeted, but not the woman. She wore no makeup except bright red lipstick and looked calm. Too calm. Back straight and chin high, she was unaffected by the sense of calamity of the room. Kat even sat up straighter, eyeing the woman as if she tasted a rotten egg.

Were they sent by the studio to deliver bad news? Maybe the studio wanted to replace him since the leading lady bailed. Even more likely, someone finally concluded he was a shitty actor.

The two men stared, star struck, as he sat. With Leslie two seats away, he felt like a phony. He glanced toward her. Her face gave nothing away. Good. Maybe she hadn't noticed the way they looked at him. *Focus, Charlie.*

"…but we have the location," one producer argued. "The perfect spot, the good old Bible Belt in the South. The builders, electricians, and prop crew are all flying out today."

Phil piped up, "Exactly how do you expect us to stick to a grueling four-week timeline without a lead actress?"

The woman with red lips spoke. "The studio has found an actress to take her place. The contract is pending, so we are under orders not to divulge her identity. We will inform you once everything is signed."

Phil looked pissed. Obviously, Charlie hadn't been the only one left out of the loop.

Kat's head snapped up. She eyeballed the woman. "So, who is she?"

The woman turned to Kat, never cracking a smile. "I'm not at liberty to say." Miss Red Lips was smug, as if she got great pleasure withholding this information from Kat.

Kat didn't even blink. Anger rolled off her. She announced through gritted teeth, "Mr. Erickson's contract clearly indicates he has a caveat to opt out if the lead isn't compatible."

Phil stood, raising his hands. "I'm sure whoever she is, the studio will conduct the proper screen testing to ensure a suitable fit." Then to Charlie, "You know they wouldn't pair you up with someone incompatible." Phil sat, flipping a piece of paper over before turning to one of the other producers. "So the rest of this week is props and setup. Monday through Thursday next week, we shoot actors with extras for the armies in Knoxville. Friday's shoot will be retakes of any close-ups. The following Monday we shoot studio work. Back to Knoxville for week three and back here for final shoots on week four, correct?"

Charlie's thoughts drowned out the rest of the conversation. Going on location, which normally excited him, depressed him. He shrugged it off. If he was in Knoxville, he'd make time to go home. The upside would be that his parents would stop sending him snarky emails about how they'd be dead long before he came to visit again.

His lips twitched up as a plan hatched. He could request Leslie be assigned to go on location. She'd get to know the real him. With his family, he could let his guard down and be normal. They didn't treat him like a star back home. Well, except for Sissy. She'd always acted as if he had superpowers. But this could work. He might break through that damn wall of Leslie's, too.

Charlie glanced around the room, drawn out of his thoughts. Everyone at the table stared, including the dark-eyed beauty he couldn't get out of his mind. "What? What'd I miss?"

The female producer stood. "We need you to stand over here for costume mockup pictures."

"Oh, sure...sorry."

The female producer then turned to Leslie. "Miss?"

"Yes, ma'am?" Leslie sprang from her chair.

"I wonder if you'd be so kind as to drape the female lead dress on and stand next to him, so we can get an idea of the design?"

Leslie stammered, "Ah, sure, of course, but the dress was sewn to the actress's exact dimensions, and if memory serves, she's much taller than me. You wouldn't have a true picture of the beauty of this dress." She took the dress in her arms and held it high in front of her. "I can hang it next to Mr. Erickson. You could get a good visual of the colors together for the picture. Would that work?"

The female producer cocked her head to one side, squinting at Leslie as if she was at an MLB game in the nosebleed section. She wasn't buying it. Leslie shot a look to Kat for help. Kat was even shorter than Leslie, but beefier. She merely grinned back. Leslie turned her eyes to Charlie, pleading. The one thing he knew for sure; she *needed* to try on this dress.

Clamping his mouth shut, he shook his head then cleared his throat. "It's beneficial to see it on a person rather than on a hanger. And it'll give them the picture they need for their storyboards, even if it's a little long."

After a deadly scowl toward Charlie, Leslie pulled the costume out in front of her and began to step into it. The female producer stopped her. "Would you care to go into another room and put it on," she clarified, "instead of over your clothing?"

"Ah, sure." Most in the room probably didn't catch the shudder in Leslie's voice, but he did.

A few minutes later, the door handle turned, and Leslie swept back into the conference room.

All chattering ceased. Charlie held his breath. Honest to God, she looked like a Disney princess. The dress itself glittered as if it was surrounded by pixie dust. The embroidered golden material had a maroon swirl embedded into it. It flowed down from a fitted V-necked bodice that made his mouth water. It fit her like a glove. The sleeves were made of lace and reminded him of intricate, woven spider webs that glittered off his parents' barn at sunrise. Breathtaking. She was flippin' breathtaking. An unfamiliar pang pierced his chest.

The dress was too long, but Leslie held it up. Her jaw was locked tight, and yet somehow she managed to exude confidence. She marched through the room, striking and beautiful. She'd unselfishly tied her hair up into a soft bun, so the producers could view more of the dress.

She was gorgeous before, but visions of Leslie in this dress would haunt him long after today. He couldn't imagine anyone else wearing it. Kat elbowed him, hard. Charlie glanced at her, then looked about the room. Everyone stared again as if he was supposed to answer a question he hadn't heard. Kat pulled on the back of his shirt to urge him to stand. He ambled toward Leslie, shaking his head. What a chump. He was like a newbie actor on his first day. Could she tell how nervous he was? The air thickened the second they stood next to each other.

Phil's face took on an odd half smile. After working on two movies together, Charlie knew him well enough to recognize that look. The wheels in Phil's mind were turning. He inspected Leslie, but not with an eye of lust. Never had he witnessed Phil so intense. Charlie glared. The primal need to protect Leslie caught him off guard.

Maybe the casting director would offer her a screen test. Phil leaned toward the producer with the camera and muttered something in his ear, "Okay, you two, stand a little closer," he called out. "Wonderful. Now can you turn toward each other and hold hands? I know it's awkward. I'm sorry, but we need a solid picture."

They turned to face one another. Leslie's face softened. She shot him a reassuring half smile. Remembering his promise, he didn't grab her hands. She looked down, shook her head and took both his hands in hers. The room got hot. Instantly hot. Charlie blew upward toward his tousled hair to give his forehead a breeze.

"Hey," Leslie said in a low voice, "You're touching me without permission." Her eyebrows raised as she lifted her chin toward him.

"Technically, you touched me." When he leaned toward her out of habit, her body angled away. He straightened and shot her an apologetic look, then added, "I have to tell you; I've never seen anything so beautiful in my life."

Leslie glanced at the dress, then back at him. "It's gorgeous, isn't it?"

Looking over her head, he whispered, "I didn't mean the dress."

His gaze locked on hers. Her cheeks turned a quick shade of pink. The photographer said something, but for all Charlie knew it was in Latin. Leslie's grip tightened. "Charlie? Leslie? We're finished. Thank you for being such troopers."

Leslie dropped his hands. Fast. She faced the suits and cleared her throat. "No problem. Glad to help."

Her face was still flushed pink as she bee-lined toward the door. Charlie wanted to go with her. He needed to change out of his costume, too. But something in her mannerisms told him to stay put.

A few minutes later, she reappeared in her own dress, the golden one folded and tucked under one arm. She laid the dress into its box and slipped out of the room before anyone, except Charlie, noticed her. He stood to change, hoping to catch her in the hallway. When he opened the door, the hallway was empty. She'd left the dressing room office open. His clothes were folded neatly and stacked on the desk.

He changed back into his street clothes. A stab of disappointment picked at him. He wanted to talk to her. Hell, he'd be happy merely standing next to her. Had she noticed the same surge of heat he did? She was casting a powerful spell on him. He wanted to think of an excuse to visit her floor but couldn't. He trudged back into the conference room as the meeting ended. He shook hands then spoke to Kat in private.

That's when inspiration stopped him in his tracks. *Yes!* He'd stroll down to HR and sweet talk those ladies out of personal information on a certain exhilarating woman.

Chapter Eight

If ever there was ever a night to drink, it was Tuesday. After getting thrown into the lion's den on her second day, putting on a gorgeous gown, and holding hands with the man she couldn't seem to shake, the rest of her day was even more taxing. Her shoulders ached from spending hours sorting costumes according to location and scene. After boxing them up, Leslie returned to her desk to send a scrutinized list to Mr. Miller. The day left her drained.

The clock chimed at four-thirty on the dot. She grabbed her purse and bag, along with costume notes for the next day, then headed to the parking garage. When she was within sight of her Bronco, she noticed something stuck under her windshield wiper. Panic squeezed her throat. Her head swiveled side -to-side as she trudged toward it. A note. Had to be the work of the pompous actor again, right? She pulled the paper off the truck and read it.

Leslie,

Hope you had an outstanding second day. Wondered if you and Nate would go to dinner with me tonight? I'll pick you up at 6:30.

—Charlie

Fury bubbled in her chest. "Of all the..." She crumpled the note, climbed into the Bronco, then threw it into the back seat. Shoving her key in the ignition she backed out, squealing tires. "He assumes everyone does what he wants—well, guess what? I won't be home at six-thirty, idiot." Perfect. He'd reduced her to talking to herself. "How does he know where I live?"

This answer came quick and easy. He could charm the pants off anyone, especially the HR girls. They were star struck. No doubt, Charlie waltzed in there, gave them one of his dazzling Hollywood smiles and they handed over her identity.

Not her real identity, of course, but he didn't know that.

If she didn't put a stop to this, he could screw things up for her. A wicked plan took shape. After grabbing Nate from aftercare and learning about his day, they went home to change for his baseball game. Leslie grumbled out loud the whole way, which, Nate commented, was hilarious.

Tuesday nights were her favorite because she coached Challenger League baseball. Kids like Nate, with all types of developmental delays, played while a college fast-pitch softball team helped. She tugged on Nate's white uniform shirt with navy lettering. He pulled his hat down over his sandy-brown hair, then smiled up like always with a cheesy grin as if to say, *how do I look?*

"You are one handsome young man. Now go. Finish your chicken while I get dressed and then we'll leave a little early, okay?"

"Umm hmm, Mama," came Nate's stock answer. He trotted over to the table, popped a piece of chicken in his mouth then scurried onto a chair to eat. Within seconds he was engrossed in *Thomas the Train.*

Leslie jogged to her closet to change clothes, grab her stuff, and get the heck out of there. She'd be long gone before Charlie arrived. The nerve. Showing up *assuming* she'd go on a date. She pulled on her coach's shirt then stepped into her comfortable stretch jeans. Brushing out her hair with a rubber band in her mouth, she waffled over whether to wear the team hat. Might be a good night to take the top off the Bronco, but then they'd be exposed. They might be recognized.

That was silly. It was an hour's drive away from her old hometown. New name, new place and hopefully *he* hadn't noticed her Bronco when she ducked out of the quickie mart. Brave. She'd promised herself this was her year to be brave. She shook her head. She'd take the hat and make the decision when they walked outside.

Leslie tucked it under her arm, pulled her hair back into a ponytail, then freshened her makeup. Almost giddy at leaving before Charlie got there, she grinned at the image in the mirror. The last of her makeup applied, she padded back toward her closet to retrieve her shoes. A faint knock caught her attention. She froze. With a past like hers, a knock at the door was never easy. But this was a new panic. *It's only 6:05, Please, God, say that's not him.*

She laid the cap on her bed and crept to the door. Standing on tip toes and holding her breath, she gazed through the peephole. A tanned finger covered her view. Instinctively, she glanced down. The rusty deadbolt was locked tight. It always was. She glanced behind her from side-to-side, both guns hidden out of view. She moved back from the door and took a breath. *Calm down.*

In her strongest voice, she called through the door, "Go away."

The chuckle on the other side was Charlie's. "Somehow I knew you'd say that. Hey, I'm early…because I figured you'd bolt if you got the chance."

He paused, waiting she assumed, for laughter. Laughter that didn't come. A muffled shuffling sound drifted through the thin door, and she envisioned him moving from one foot to the other with his hands shoved into his pockets. "Can I come in?"

Leslie stood with her back against the door and surveyed her living room. Not too messy. Only a few things out of place but picked up and decent. She glanced at Nate. Placing him at risk by introducing a stranger didn't seem like the best of ideas. Her eyes closed as she exhaled. "No."

"No?"

"No," she repeated.

"Even if I tell you I brought you something?"

She smiled despite herself. Then turned her head and called through the door, "That would depend on what it is."

His deep voice sounded closer. "You'll have to open the door to see."

She shuddered. It wasn't the first time he made that happen today. She took a deep breath, turned back toward her living room and stared at Nate. What would he think of Nate? Might make him run. Unlocking the deadbolt, she opened the door.

He could've been in a Cartier watch commercial. Sunlight filtered through perfect, messy hair, while his dark jeans slung low around his waist, and a thin white T-shirt defined every muscle in his chest and abs. He stood stock still, one hand behind his back. He appeared apprehensive, as if he was gauging her mood. She stood in the threshold and stared. He stepped closer, as if tiptoeing up to a sleeping bear. Too close, invading her space again. He hitched an eyebrow, expectantly. She hadn't consciously meant to, but her body blocked his way inside.

She moved back. He glided past, handing her a bouquet of daisies. She took them but kept a close eye on him as he noticed Nate. Charlie wasn't a foot inside when he produced two small Matchbox cars from his back pocket, a shiny red one and a sporty yellow one.

"Hi." Charlie squatted as if he was giving a treat to a puppy. "I'm Charlie. What's your name?"

Nate hopped down from his chair and ran to Charlie, not looking him in the eye. A trait of his autism. His big smile said it all as he snagged the cars from Charlie's outstretched palm. "Nate." He made car sounds and ran the wheels across Charlie's knee.

"Nice to meet you, Nate."

Nate echoed, "Nice to meet you, Nate."

Leslie's mouth gaped open, and for once she didn't care. She choked back an emotion that had never stirred before. Out of long habit, she shut her front door, double locked it, then remembering her manners, she moved toward them with a polite smile. "Nate, can you say thank you to Charlie?"

"Thank you to Charlie," Nate said, again without looking up.

Charlie took Nate's hat off his head and examined it as he stood. Nate didn't seem to mind. He bolted toward the living room rug and lay on the ground to track the wheels going back and forth.

Charlie turned to Leslie, "Baseball, eh? That's where we're headed? Perfect. Hey, you got another cap I can borrow?" When Leslie didn't answer he continued, "So people won't recognize me?"

Her brain kicked in as she rattled out, "Wait. No. *We* are headed to Nate's baseball game, but—"

Charlie interrupted, "Yeah, I know. I need something to hide behind, to be incognito?" He winked as he inspected her house and helped himself to a tour of her kitchen.

"I don't think that's a good idea," she said, scrambling behind him. "It's not a *real* baseball game and..." She stopped short and stared.

Nate stood, then walked into her bedroom. Without a word he grabbed the baseball cap from her bed and strolled back in. He held it up for Charlie.

"Well, thanks, Nate," Charlie said, grinning like an idiot.

Leslie stared at Nate as if he was an alien. Never. Never had he done anything like that without direction and prodding. Big tears watered her vision.

Charlie loosened the back of the cap and put it on. He placed it high on the top of his head. Like an idiot, she took the bait.

"Whoa, stop. That looks ridiculous." She walked over to fix it.

Up on her tiptoes, Leslie cinched the hat on Charlie's head. To complete the look, she pushed a stray lock of hair out of his eyes, and he stilled. Only afterward did she notice his crooked grin and realize he'd done it on purpose. His hands came around as if he wanted to place them on her, but at the last minute, he shoved them deep into his pockets. Struggle washed across his face. He was doing his best not to touch her. And she was filled with gratitude.

She shot him a kind smile as warm tingles ran up her spine.

Then she backed up. "Listen, please, you don't have to go to this game and…" She hesitated, lowering her voice as she said, "we're not going out on a date, okay?"

"Not yet." He scratched at his chin. "But someday…" Charlie leaned back against her kitchen counter as a faint smile tugged at his lips. "See, I know where you live now, so I can bug you anytime I want."

Panic pinched the bottom of her stomach. She inhaled, too sharp. He was kidding. She knew that, but her insides locked up just the same.

Charlie raised his hands in surrender, back-pedaling as if he sensed her terror. "Of course—I won't, but I could…you know, if you needed someone to cook a meal or get something from the store. I'm kind of handy to have around." He glanced down at his watch before she could say another word. "Oh, wow, shouldn't we be going? Come on, Nate, we gotta get you to baseball."

Nate ran past the kitchen table, stuffing another piece of chicken in, before heading for the door. She sprinted around Charlie and grabbed hold of Nate before he made it there. "Hold on, buddy." She let out a defeated breath. "Let's get your baseball bag out of the closet." She opened the closet door and handed him a backpack with a small bat sticking out of the top.

Charlie's clear blue eyes widened. She followed his line of sight to the shotgun propped up inside the top of the closet. She closed the door and ignored the questioning look. There had to be a believable reason a normal twenty-five-year-old woman kept a shotgun in her front closet. Though, she hadn't quite thought one up yet.

She grabbed her keys and sunglasses from the counter before looking back up at Charlie who pointed at her naked feet. "Ugh!" she muttered and ran back to her closet to shove her feet into her shoes.

He's an irritating man. A self-centered, arrogant, irritating man. Pulling on her shoes, Leslie exhaled. That wasn't fair. He'd brought flowers. And he was kind to Nate where most people only stared as if he was a bug.

"Mama, hurry," Nate yelled.

Leslie froze. That was independent thought. She crept back to the living room.

Charlie was squatting, teaching him to say it. "Say, 'Mama, hurry up!'" He held the boy's hand.

"Mama, hurry up!" Nate repeated, smiling.

Chapter Nine

Insisting on driving, Leslie pulled into the ballpark. She glanced over at Charlie. He was the very picture of a GQ model sitting in the front seat of her dirty Bronco. This was ridiculous. What was she doing? She couldn't go out with anyone, let alone someone famous like him. People gaped at them at every red light between her house and the ball field.

"Interesting driving," he said peeling his fingers off the "Oh Shit" bar. "Is NASCAR aware that you drive around on city streets like that?"

"Ha… funny guy. I had to get us here on time since we had a *distraction* at home." She unbuckled Nate's seatbelt, grabbed his backpack and pulled it over his shoulders, then held him firmly by the hand.

Nate was a runner. If she didn't hold him tight, he'd run straight into traffic and not think twice about it. And he was fast. Most kids like him were harnessed or leashed for their own safety. But she believed good old-fashioned handholding did the trick. No matter how distracted, she'd never let him go.

"My main goal, Miss Carroll, is to be a distraction in your life." Charlie said it with complete sincerity, walking around to her side of the Bronco.

"You're pretty good at it, Mr. Erickson."

He narrowed his eyes playfully as Leslie smiled. She held Nate's hand and jogged toward the gate. Charlie followed alongside.

Every Tuesday, two crusty old sports announcers sat in the press box and called the game. Parents brought kids from all over Pomona. All disabilities were welcome to play: kids in wheelchairs, with walkers, with mental disabilities, and even a few that were blind or deaf. Each child had varying disabilities, and all were encouraged just the same.

When they rounded the corner toward the field, she turned and walked in reverse then threw her keys and sunglasses to Charlie. "Run up there and sit with the old guys in the press box. You won't be recognized, and it's the best seat in the house. I know how you're used to being pampered."

She shot him a cheeky smile which he volleyed back. Shaking his head, he turned and ran up the stadium stairs toward the press box. She walked backward, all the while staring at his muscular legs. At one point, she remembered to close her mouth and head for the field.

~ * ~

At the top, Charlie bent over to catch his breath. He knew she was watching him. He'd wanted to show off his agility, but damn, his heart was pounding out of his chest. When his breathing slowed, he reminded himself not to look straight down. Nobody needed to know how much he hated heights.

He ambled toward the open door of the press box, then stopped short. A wooden leg was thrust out the open door, adorned with a short, black sock and bright, white tennis shoe. A shiny brown cane reached out and whacked the leg twice. It sounded like a wooden bat smacking a fast pitch.

Two men cackled. Charlie stood at the threshold of the door and peered inside.

"Got him," one wrinkled man said to another, still laughing.

"Didn't even need a line and a pole. Hooked him right in," hollered the other, larger man with one wooden leg. Both papery-skinned men howled with laughter.

"What?" the first one said.

"You are deafer than a doorknob, is what I said, Leo. Turn up your hearing aid."

"Piss off, Fred. Just 'cause you mumble, don't mean I'm deaf." Fred rolled his eyes toward Charlie and mouthed, "He's deaf and dumb."

Charlie cracked up.

"Who are you, muscles?" Fred tilted his head back, eyeing Charlie. "You're new."

But before Charlie could answer, Leo chimed in, "He walked in with your girl, Fred. Must be a beau, and by the looks of him, he could outrun you." Leo laughed as Fred glared.

Grunting, Fred took a full minute to stand and when he did, he was a house of a man—if that house was as wide as it was tall. His head was as slick as a bowling ball, with kind eyes nestled in a stern face. Fred had to be in his mid-seventies, and stretching as hard as he could, he wasn't even close to being as tall as Charlie. As Fred struggled to crane his neck higher, Charlie involuntarily straightened.

"Humph," Fred grumbled. Then, turning to Leo, he yelled, "I

thought she was a lesbian?"

Leslie emerged magically at the doorway, panting and growling. Angry faced, she bared her teeth as she rounded the corner, running smack into Charlie.

He caught her around the shoulders. "Whoa, where's the fire?"

She huffed and pushed past him. Rushing between the two older men, she leaned across the soundboard and smacked a button, turning it from green to red.

"Gentlemen!" she scolded. "Could we please turn off the mic before announcing I'm a lesbian? Which. I. Am. Not!" Without turning around, she warned, "Fred, don't even think about it."

Fred stared at Leslie's backside with his hand up, about to strike. The old man froze, as if he had no idea how she could've known. Funny old fart.

She straightened, caught her breath, and adjusted her shirt. "Now, Leo and Fred, this is my *friend*, Charlie. Charlie, these are my friends Leo and Fred." She placed her hands on her hips and breathed deep. "They've been play callers for our Challenger games since I got involved. They're outstanding at making each kid feel special."

She lowered her voice and spoke only to Charlie. "Careful, they're wicked jokesters."

Fred lifted his cane. Leo fist-pounded it.

Charlie grinned. "I'll be fine. You sure I can't help you out there? I played baseball in high school, ya know."

Leslie scrunched up her face and shrugged. "The women's softball team would recognize you. And if not them, most of the parents. You wouldn't be incognito for long."

His chest deflated. Disappointment must've shown on his face.

She stared for half a beat, then added, "How about toward the end, you come down and help? With my driving abilities, I'll be able to get you out of here fast, right?"

She was giving a little of herself, and he was sure this was way out of her comfort zone. He moved to touch her arm, out of habit.

She moved back. A tight, apologetic smile crossed her face. "Until then, keep these two in line, okay?"

Leslie tossed the handwritten lineups for each team between Leo and Fred, then mouthed, "be nice" to both men. She turned on her heel and ran back down the bleachers for the start of the game. Charlie noticed how gracefully she moved. The tug at his heart made him shudder. He was way out of his league with this one. He had to be careful, but he couldn't make his heart listen to his head.

When he turned back toward the men, they grinned, devious,

like they knew something he didn't. "What?"

"You got it bad, boy. Worse than old Fred here," Leo said.

"I'll step aside in the name of love, but you better reel that lovesick look back in," Fred said, stretching his legs out.

Charlie pulled up a chair. "What do you mean?"

"Boy, take it from me, quickest way to run off a woman like that is to let her know you care. It's too soon. You'll spook her. She's like a doe in the woods, and she'll hear you cock your gun. She'll be paralyzed with fear for a split second before she leaps into the air and disappears."

"You're the first man she's brought here in the time we've known her," Leo piped up. "Never even mentioned a man, which is why we entertained the idea she was a lesbian. Ever asked where Nate's dad was? She'll tell you she got artificially...shit, what's that called, Fred?"

"Inseminated," Fred said.

"Right, but then last week, she told us Nate had his father's skin, but her eyes."

Curious, Charlie surveyed the field. He found Leslie running the dugout for Nate's team. She was outfitting a young girl with a pink bat and a pink helmet. Why would she need to tell people she used a sperm donor? The thought perplexed him. As he stared down, lost in his thoughts, she waved up to the box. He almost mirrored it until it dawned on him—she was giving them a signal to start the game.

Fred turned the mic back on and cleared his throat. Out came a smooth, deep, announcer voice: "Welcome to the Challenger Game. Please give a warm welcome to our volunteer helpers today, the softball team from Mt. San Antonio College." The crowd cheered. Most of the college players ran out onto the field to help the outfielders, while a few stayed behind the plate to help batters.

"First up," Fred continued, "is the beautiful and talented number twenty-three, Katie Baskin."

A girl of about six or seven with a curly red ponytail cascading below her shoulders limped toward home plate. A T-ball stand was placed in front of her. Katie swung, missed, swung again, and connected. The ball rolled a few feet. Katie squealed and ran with a stilted gait to first base.

A dark-skinned boy with a walker wore a T-shirt that read, "I don't have Cerebral Palsy, I'm drunk." He was closest to the ball and made a beeline for it, then held it high in the air, helped by his MSAC player. The play stopped. Fred and Leo chirped and whooped making it sound as if it was the game-winning home run. The smile on the young girl's face was infectious. Charlie stood in awe of them.

He searched the field for Nate but couldn't find him. Must be in the dugout. He couldn't find Leslie either. Charlie wanted to show her how familiar he was with kids with disabilities and prove he could handle this. But the pandemonium that would arise if the people in the stands recognized him would stop the game. It'd happened once before at his sister's basketball game, when someone recognized him, and he'd gotten roped into giving autographs. The line was too much of a distraction to the players; he'd left and didn't get to see her play. He didn't want that for Nate.

"Next up, Nate Carroll, the hard-hitting, fast-running number seven."

Leslie and Nate lined up at the plate to hit. A blonde MSAC player stood a few feet in front of him and lobbed the ball. Nate and Leslie swung on the first one and missed. A robust girl behind the plate threw the ball back to the pitcher. Nate readied himself again, pushing Leslie away to swing the bat by himself. She stood off to the side, waiting with a smile. The pitch came in slow and arching. Nate reared back and hit it hard, then flung the bat, and ran.

Leslie ran alongside Nate, steering him toward second as the outfield scrambled to get the ball. It dropped into the outfield between second and third, but the players out there weren't close to it. Nate was almost faster than Leslie. She directed him around second heading for third, right as the ball was picked up and thrown toward second. This gave Leslie and Nate an opening to run from third to home. The announcers went wild.

Charlie jumped outside the press box and yelled. "Go, Nate! Run!" he cheered, louder than he meant to. Nate stopped in his tracks a few feet away from home plate and turned, waving at Charlie. Then turned back and ran, jumping on home plate. Charlie waved back. Leslie patted the boy on the back, then stared up at the box.

Toward the top of the third inning, the old guys broke into a round of "Take Me Out to the Ball Game," loud and off key. They'd grabbed him after the first round and made him join in. He spotted Leslie smiling wide at them. The three men swayed side-to-side, arm in arm, while the crowd clapped and roared.

Man, his dad would've loved this. Hands down, the most fun he had in years. And for the first time since hitting it big, he got to act like a normal guy.

Challenger games were as short as the kid's attention spans. Before the fourth inning, Charlie said farewell to the two men. They fist-bumped him and slapped him hard on the back, wishing him luck.

Leslie and Nate stood in the outfield.

On the drive over, she had mentioned the outfield was the one place Nate wouldn't run. If his attention was good, he could catch fly balls too, but often, he wasn't paying attention.

Her silky, dark hair blew in the breeze. He trotted down toward them with Leslie's sunglasses on, hiding his eyes. Her smile, as she spotted him, switched from a straight line into a sexy half-smile.

He returned it. They gazed at each other for seconds longer than usual. Unspoken yet familiar, like the bond between them was growing.

~ * ~

"Hey guys," Charlie said, stopping next to Nate.

"Hi Charlie," Nate replied without looking up.

She raised her chin. "Nice singing. Now I know why you don't do musicals."

The edges of his mouth twitched up. "Thanks. I'm a better singer after a few beers. We should go do karaoke on one of our dates."

She leveled a look at him. Obviously, he wasn't taking the hint about the one date thing. She ignored his comment. "You look ridiculous in my sunglasses."

"No, I don't. I make these look good." His Hollywood smile confirmed it.

"Keep thinking that, hotshot."

Charlie crouched next to Nate, who was counting blades of grass. He touched his shoulder. "Hey buddy, where's your glove?"

"Where's your glove?" Nate repeated, then pointed toward his mom's feet. Charlie strolled over, grabbed the glove, swatted Leslie's right foot with it, then turned to run back.

"Here you go, buddy. Let's put this on."

Nate rose and pushed both hands toward Charlie. Leslie smiled. He never could remember which hand went into the glove. Charlie tugged Nate's glove on him, straightened his hat then brought him closer to stand between them.

"Okay, so stand like this with your legs apart and your knees bent." When Nate didn't move, Charlie situated Nate's limbs until he looked like a real baseball player. He giggled every time Charlie grabbed a knee or elbow. Charlie fussing over Nate caused little cracks to open in her heart.

Charlie began, "Keep your elbows resting on your knees and your glove ready so when the ball comes, you can run and catch it, okay?"

Nate answered, "I run fast, Charlie."

"Yes, you do, buddy." Charlie glanced over the top of Nate's head toward Leslie. She held a hand to her heart. If she could've reached over and brushed his arm, she would've. Happy tears brimmed her eyes. Charlie grinned ear to ear.

The crack of the bat turned their attention to home plate. One of the bigger, more coordinated kids had hit the ball. It headed straight for Nate. Both Charlie and Leslie glanced from the ball to Nate and back a few times. The struggle of whether to let him catch it spread across their faces.

Charlie yelled, "Nate! Look up! Catch the ball!"

Nate did as he was instructed and tilted his head up but forgot to lift his glove. At the last second both Charlie and Leslie reached out before the ball could hit Nate. It bounced from Charlie's hands to Leslie's glove, then from Leslie's glove into the bare hand of Nate.

"You're outta here!" Fred said into the mic. "Third out and ballgame! Great save made by the Carrolls and the famous Hollywood star, Charlie Erickson."

Charlie froze and cut his gaze toward Leslie. Crap. Sneaking him out of the ballpark would be impossible now. Leslie turned to Charlie and scooped Nate up into her arms. "I'm sorry. I didn't think they'd recognize you. What do you want me to do?"

The team and part of the crowd filtered onto the field. "Can you stand by me for a few minutes? I can sign autographs and take photos, and then you can say we need to go?"

A multitude of people walked toward them, phones in hand ready to snap pictures. She took one look then pulled her sunglasses off his face and put them on hers. He shot her an odd look. She couldn't afford to be caught in a single picture. She'd be exposed. Pulling Nate's hat down over his face she turned toward Charlie.

"Sure, we can," she said lightly. Then as the crowd pulled his attention, she walked in reverse.

Away from the limelight.

Chapter Ten

After thirty minutes of autographs and pictures, Charlie glanced over at Leslie. His eyebrows rose as if to say 'help'. She'd been so intrigued seeing him interact with his fans, she forgot she was supposed to rescue him. The large crowd agitated Nate, which gave her the perfect excuse to get distance away from all the cameras. Instantaneous social media was the enemy of someone in hiding.

Charlie laughed, joked, and hugged every person who stood in line. He was kind and genuine. Not like the pompous windbag she'd called him the day before. He'd started to grow on her like a slow-moving vine, making her dormant heart feel alien.

She scooped Nate up, then strolled over, off to the side and cleared her throat. "Friends, I promised to have Mr. Erickson back at a decent hour, so we need to wrap this up." She didn't stand near Charlie until they left the stadium and were walking toward the parking lot.

Charlie snagged Nate from her a few feet from the Bronco and swung him high, then caught him. He was giddy, and Nate roared with laughter. She wrung her hands. Trusting Nate with someone she barely knew wasn't easy.

The boy could give a seasoned prison guard the slip. One mistake and he'd be running into a busy parking lot. But Nate never attempted to wriggle away. Charlie buckled him into his seat, then skulked around to the passenger side, skimming a hand along the top of her Bronco as if petting a puppy. "You're really not gonna let me drive this thing?"

Leslie climbed in, shoved the key into the ignition and smiled. "He's a classic, and you have to be gentle with him. I'm not sure you know how."

Charlie hoisted himself in and turned toward her, leaning close, his voice low and seductive. "I think you'd be surprised at how gentle I can be."

Her face burned hot in three point two seconds.

Charlie let out a hearty laugh. "You blush like a ginger. You sure that dark hair is real?"

"Shut it, Erickson," she said through gritted teeth. "You're not driving my truck."

He scooted back, buckled his seatbelt, then raised both hands in defeat. "Touchy, touchy. Sheesh." Charlie pulled out his phone and groaned.

"What's wrong?" she asked, backing out of the parking space.

"Confession time. I just remembered I was supposed to meet an old friend downtown five minutes ago."

"No problem." Her voice was even and stiff. He was ready to ditch her. Fine. His mere presence put them at risk, anyway.

"Give me a raincheck on the rest of our date. I gotta make sure he doesn't hate me for standing him up. I've done it too many times. What if I take you on a real date this weekend?"

She exhaled. "Listen, I had fun tonight, but I can't go out with you. I can't afford any distractions right now. I need to focus on my career and Nate. And there's not room for anything else."

Charlie listened to every word, although by the look of him, none of it sunk in. "Head to Garey Avenue and 2nd Street; there's a sports bar with a glass front on the corner. Drop me there and I'll pick up my car later," he rattled off, pointing.

"Okay, but did you hear me?" Leslie squinted. Pleading didn't seem to help, either. His confident, not-about-to-give-up-that-easy kind of smile lit all the way to his eyes.

Charlie placed his hand on hers on top of the gearshift. Then stared down at it, wide eyed, like he hadn't meant to do it, as if his hand moved of its own volition. His gaze darted to hers, and he winced, shooting her an apology with his eyes. A part of her wanted to yank it away, but it was high time, to let platonic touches be a part of her world again. She mouthed, "It's okay." He relaxed.

Charlie spoke. "Listen, I get it. But you can't deny there's something here. I know you feel it, too. One real date, then you can tell me to go to hell if you want, deal? And I swear, nothing physical."

She bit her lip. Her insides jittered. She was just beginning to be able to withstand touching, so how was she going to manage a date? When she didn't answer, he tilted his head to one side like a dog hearing a whistle. He must've thought she was pretty screwed up if going on a real date caused this much anxiety.

When she glanced over, he stuck his tongue out. Piercing eyes, boyish face and a pleading look—she couldn't hold back her smile. She nodded. Maybe navigating one real date wouldn't kill her.

One peek down at the speedometer made her realize she was pegging eighty. Charlie lifted his hand and leaned over to check it out as well. "You in a hurry to get rid of me?" One eyebrow cocked; his question was serious.

She nodded. "Yep. And Nate'll be a terror in the morning. I gotta get him home."

"He's one heck of a baseball player." Charlie glanced at the boy in the back seat and touched him on the leg.

"He definitely doesn't get that ability from me."

"Oh, yeah? What was his dad like?"

Leslie gripped the steering wheel, pondering the question. *Evil, controlling...*

"No idea." She looked anywhere but at him. "Sperm donor."

Well, technically...it wasn't a lie.

Eyes narrowed, Charlie's face told her he knew something wasn't right with her story. Before he could ask any more annoying questions, she announced, "We're here."

She parked the Bronco next to the curb outside Plato's Sports Bar. Nate's soft, rhythmic snore broke the silence. "Bye, buddy," Charlie whispered. "I had a great time with you today."

Nate didn't stir. Charlie twisted back then whipped out his phone. She really noticed it this time. It was the shiniest, newest piece of phone technology on the planet. That phone version hadn't been released to the public yet. Spoiled man. He held it, gazed at her, and tapped a finger—expecting information.

She deliberated for half a second. She could slip him the wrong number. No, that wouldn't work, he'd be smart enough to try it before the night was out. And his car was still parked at her house. He might knock late at night or want to come in. Ah, no, that wouldn't do. Exhaling, she rattled off her digits.

Why did this all seem so normal? Together, they weren't normal. He was famous, and she drove a rusty Bronco, for crying out loud. Charlie shoved his phone back into his pocket and leaned toward her in the car. She stilled, not breathing.

"I had fun today." He was genuine and sincere. Not like his famous persona, but him. "Thanks for sharing Nate with me. I know that wasn't easy." Soft as a butterfly landing, he touched her hand again, gazed into her eyes, then sprinted into the bar.

Leslie sat curbside, frozen, until her heart jumped back into rhythm. Pulling out into traffic, she smiled.

And smiled the entire drive home.

Chapter Eleven

Through the bar window, Charlie quick-counted three empty rum and coke glasses perched on Jason Gilreath's otherwise empty table. Jesus. He hadn't been *that* late.

A pretty waitress stood at Jase's table laughing at something he said. Even in high school, Jase was slick with the women. Made perfect sense. He began his career handling higher-end divorce settlements, and his clientele had been mostly women. But now, he was part of the DA's team prosecuting organized crime lords.

He downed the drinks. Charlie felt bad. He'd been a shitty friend and stood him up too many times. It'd become their norm. Usually, it was because of the now ex-hot-angry-girlfriend. But not anymore. That was the old Charlie.

Jase lifted one of the empty glasses to finish off the last drops. Charlie flung open the door, causing a vacuum of air that sent his hair flying. "Well, look who we have here," Jase, a little wobbly, proclaimed to the bar.

Charlie grinned and embraced his old friend. "What'cha drinkin' there?"

"The usual, a whole lot of rum and a splash of Coke. You want?"

Charlie nodded and sat. Jase raised his empty glass for the waitress to notice. She trotted over. "Yes, sir?"

"Two more please and make his a double—he's gotta catch up." Jase grinned, raising eyebrows at Charlie. The waitress nodded then ambled off to get their drinks.

Charlie turned back toward Jase. "Sorry I'm late."

"Yeah, I bet. How's Christine?"

"I told you. Broken up."

"Not a chance. Hundred bucks says you'll be back together within a week. Why don't you hurry up and marry her and squeeze out a few pretentious, well-dressed hellions?"

Charlie laughed. Jase had wanted to wager a bet every day since he'd won ten bucks off him in middle school. He'd dared him to jump off the cliffs into the lake back home, knowing Charlie's fear of heights. Jase craned his neck toward the bar.

Charlie's eyebrows rose. "Keep your pants on, Gilreath. You remember the last time you were impatient with a waitress, right?" He strained to keep a straight face.

Jase pointed and bellowed, "I don't care what you say, pinhead, that girl spat in my drink. I was not about to let that go quiet."

"Nobody would ever accuse you of being quiet, Jase. Hell, we almost got thrown in jail."

"No, we didn't. I had that off-duty officer shaking in his boots." Jase ran a hand through his mop of black wavy hair. He resembled a good-looking, dark-skinned Q-tip.

Charlie scoffed. "He wasn't afraid of us, dumbass, he was annoyed. Like we were gnats buzzing around his face. He threatened to call reinforcements before we were escorted out."

"Well, I wasn't going to jail. I could talk my way outta hell, and you know it."

Charlie nodded as the waitress arrived with their drinks. Jase smiled as he took his drink from the tray.

They bantered like brothers, which made perfect sense since Jase had lived at Charlie's house throughout high school. "The drunken whore," as Jase called his own mother, had skipped from rehab to rehab, leaving him and his dad broke in more ways than one. When his dad neglected his own health to pay for her habits, Charlie's parents offered to take Jase in.

He'd given Charlie's parents a run for their money, too. His reputation of being reckless and impulsive in high school was well earned. He was damn fun to be around. Always a fast talker and a competitive arguer, he'd chattered their way out of several scrapes when they were stupid teenagers.

Charlie had trusted Jase with his life more than once. Now, he used his unpredictability as an advantage against opposing counsel and won more cases than most attorneys his age. Everything with Jase was a competition. Always had been.

"So what's new with you, boy?" Charlie volleyed, changing the subject. "Last we talked you'd won the Torres case, and they were thinking of making you partner." He took a swig of his drink, noticing a small group of women staring.

"They made me partner three weeks ago. I left you a voicemail," Jase said, following Charlie's line of sight to the same gaggle of women.

"Well, that's good, right?" Charlie turned back to him.

"I guess…if you consider I'm working double the hours to keep up with my case load, plus more travel, conference calls and partner meetings. There's no room for anything else." Jase raised his glass and tilted it toward Charlie, "And I can't seem to get a date with a woman who doesn't find out I'm an attorney and latch on. It's like a witch hunt in reverse." Jase took a long draw on his drink.

Charlie leaned in. "I'm guessing that last lead in finding her didn't pan out, huh?"

Jase shook his head.

He'd been looking for this one girl from his last year of college. According to him, she was the one. Beautiful, funny, and vibrant. He couldn't seem to get over her. They had a whirlwind romance of a week, and then she disappeared. No note, no warning. Gone. For years he was convinced someone kidnapped her. He searched for her in his down time, hoping she'd come back.

"So what happened this time with your woman?" Jase asked, taking another swig of his drink.

"Christine?" Saying her name again seemed odd. If he was honest, it'd been a long time since he'd been crazy about her. "I don't know what she's up to. We broke up. She moved out yesterday, or at least she was supposed to."

Charlie texted his housekeeper, Elaine, to give him an update. He'd forgotten to check, but he wanted to stretch out in his own bed tonight, not a hotel.

"Charlie…what the hell is wrong with you? The woman is rich, famous, and has an amazing body. You're an idiot."

Charlie took a sip of his drink then lifted it toward Jase. "She screwed her trainer." He let that sentence linger for a moment before finishing, "And you know as well as I do her popularity and amazing body is exactly where her good traits end. She's a total bitch. Plus—" he waited until Jase's eyes met his, "—I met someone else. A real girl, who doesn't seem affected by the whole made-up fame thing."

Jase's face softened, and Charlie continued, "She's smart and puts me in my place. The first time we met she called me a 'pompous windbag.'" He chuckled. "She's got spunk and character and a sweet son. He's a great kid."

Jase cut him off. "A kid? Whoa, whoa, whoa. She's got a kid? Are you insane? You don't want to take on another man's brat! Have your own kids, Charlie. You'd be the dreaded stepdad. He's gonna end up hating you."

"No way," Charlie said, as his phone dinged. It was Elaine. It read: *"Nope. Still here. Wants to talk to you."*

Charlie set his jaw and shook his head while his fingers tap danced on his phone. *"Nope. She's out by five tomorrow or my attorney will call hers. Thanks E."*

"Yes, sir," came the reply.

As he tossed his phone on the table, a young couple walked over. "I hate to interrupt, but could we get a picture with you?" the girl asked.

Jase raised an eyebrow, making fun of Charlie. He shot his friend a glare then agreed, asking the waitress to take the picture. Years of PR training made him position himself so the rum and coke wouldn't show—or social media would label him a drunk.

Both their glasses were empty. Jase asked the waitress for another round. Charlie made a mental note to call his driver to take them home. Well, Charlie to Leslie's to pick up his car, then to the hotel.

Charlie followed Jase's stare toward a young red-headed girl. She'd apparently caught his eye in the group playing pool. He licked his lips. "Hey, hotshot," he said toward Charlie, still ogling the girls. "Go use your 'made-up fame' and bring those cuties over here."

Charlie crinkled up his nose. Why did he always go for the super young ones? They barely seemed of age. One girl couldn't have been old enough to drink. Charlie shook his head. "Uh no, I'd rather not see the inside of a cell tonight, thanks. They don't even look old enough to be here."

"Dude, it's a sports bar. You can even bring kids in here."

"Yeah? And they did. Looks like they're babysitting—in a bar." Charlie shook his head again at Jase's pleading face and repeated a second, firm, "No."

The waitress darted past, dropping off their drinks. Jase touched her hand before she could escape again. "Hey, can you let that group know Charlie Erickson's over here, and if they want to get a picture with him, he'd be happy to oblige?"

"Sure," she said and walked straight over to the cluster of girls. Charlie took another drink and glared at Jase. "Jase, I'm texting Jimmy. He'll be here with the car in thirty minutes, whether you've finished hitting on the middle school girls or not."

"Relax, Erickson. One drink and conversation." Jase stood and buttoned his suit jacket as the girls made their way toward the table.

Noise doubled in the bar with the nervous giggles of college girls. It rattled Charlie's ears. They must've called everyone in the sorority house because within ten minutes, the bar was full. They'd snapped too many pictures. He excused himself to use the bathroom. A balding, stocky college prick with a goatee stood next to him and struck up an awkward conversation while he was pissing. The guy followed him out of the bathroom, still talking.

Charlie grabbed the last lonely bar stool and ordered a water. He checked his watch. Ten fifteen. She'd still be awake. He pulled out his phone and texted Leslie, *"I had fun tonight on our date."*

Her reply buzzed back. *"It wasn't a date. I don't date."*

Smiling, he typed, *"I know, but it was fun anyway. Thanks for letting me meet Nate."*

"He liked you."

"Do you?" he held his breath then stared at his phone like a bomb. Her reply took forever.

"Nope."

He shook his head, grinning like an idiot, then typed, *"I like you enough for both of us."*

"You're distracting me from my video game."

Charlie snickered. *"A gamer? Wow, you're a woman of many talents."*

"Nate loves to watch Minecraft, so I build him worlds and video in it while he sleeps."

"Ur a good mom."

"Not really, but thanks."

Laughter rang out, and Charlie turned. A few girls had gone back to their pool game, but several remained at the table. The one Jase had his eye on was trapped, sitting next to him. She appeared uncomfortable yet laughed with the others. Several minutes later, finishing his water, Charlie paid the tab and meandered back to the table. "Hate to break the party up, but my boy Jase and I have to leave."

"Aww," came the collective sound of the young women.

Charlie stood tall over Jase, expecting him to stagger outside to the waiting black sedan. Jase stood, and swayed as he announced to the table they'd be back next week to play pool. Charlie rolled his eyes and helped his drunken friend navigate around tables to the door.

The ride back to Jase's house was quiet except for a few unintelligible words his friend mumbled right before passing out. Big Jimmy tilted his head in the rearview mirror, smiling when Jase finally shut up.

Charlie stared out at the lights and hustle of L.A. What would life have been like if he wasn't famous? Maybe he would've worked as an electrician or even helped his dad run cattle. Probably would've married, finished out school, and still been a die-hard, head-to-Neyland-Stadium-every-Saturday kind of fan. Work all day and play all night. He knew one thing for sure, he'd be a dad by now.

His mind drifted to Leslie. The way she loved Nate and protected him. God, if she'd only trust him enough to tell Charlie where the touching issue stemmed from. He shuddered. Maybe he didn't want to know. Hopefully, she'd trust him more on location, at home where he could show her he was genuine.

She'd love Tennessee, though. The lush green mountains of summer and, in the fall, the overnight invasion of reds, oranges, and yellows because of the crisp air. His family would adore her. She and Sissy would be fast friends, and his mom would dote on her.

His dad would probably make ridiculous, corny jokes and embarrass her, but maybe she'd love them, too. He hadn't entertained the idea of bringing anyone home before. He nodded at his reflection in the window.

Big Jimmy stopped the car in front of the guard shack that anchored the gated community where Jase lived. Charlie wrestled a half-comatose Jase, pulling his card out of his wallet to show the guard.

Around the last turn toward Jase's house, a line of unmarked police cars, no lights on, sat in front of Jase's house. Charlie asked Jimmy to slow down and shook his friend awake. They pulled up about twenty yards behind one of the police vehicles and parked.

In a split second the car was surrounded by officers, weapons drawn. They shouted orders to shut off the engine and everyone to get out of the car, hands up. Big Jimmy did as he was told and threw the keys into the street, then opened the door and put his hands in the air.

Jase and Charlie got out of opposite doors with hands over their heads. Each lay face down on the street in front of the sedan as they'd been instructed. All three were roughly cuffed, searched, relieved of all personal belongings and pulled to their feet.

"What's going on?" Charlie demanded toward the larger of the two male officers holding him.

Per his name tag, Officer Clarke on his left spoke first. "Sir, this is a crime scene. I need your silence and cooperation." The officer outweighed Charlie by a good fifty pounds, spoke like a college professor, and looked as agile as a cat.

Jase's terrified, high-pitched voice cut through the darkness as he made his argument. "Why are we being detained?" The officer holding Jase said nothing, glared, and held him in place. The wheels of the stretcher made a clicking sound as three paramedics emerged from his house with a young, redheaded woman strapped down.

Charlie held his breath. *Oh, God.* He couldn't tell if she was unconscious or dead. Two men carried the gurney as one smaller female paramedic, perched on top, performed CPR. Three plain-clothes agents walked out behind them carrying pieces of electrical equipment and a computer, loading them into a van.

A petite, blonde detective in a gray pants suit with a crisp white button-down, walked over and spoke harshly to Jase. Charlie strained to listen to the conversation. He couldn't make out much except the words, 'kidnapped, beaten, tied up, and electrical shock.'

This was like living in Bizzaroland. Jase was a good-looking, successful partner in a firm. He would no more kidnap and hurt a woman than Charlie would. And why would the police need his computer?

Jase's voice was quick as he spoke to the detective. "This was all planted, don't you see? I don't even know that girl. Hell, I wasn't here. I've been traveling for the last week. This must be in retaliation for the verdict in the Torres case. Call my office and they'll corroborate. His relatives have threatened me since the case began. It's documented. And I wasn't even here tonight. I was with Charlie Erickson. How can you place me at the scene at six, when I met my friend then?"

Charlie was at Leslie's house at six, and not with Jase, but he shrugged it off. Officer Clarke tugged on Charlie's arm, "Mr. Erickson, Detective Majors would like to speak to you next, in the car."

They walked over to a black, unmarked sedan. Officer Clarke opened the door. Charlie scooted onto the plastic seat with Officer Clarke scurrying in right beside him. Charlie was still handcuffed and finding it impossible to sit up straight.

As Charlie fidgeted to find a comfortable position in the stuffy squad car, officers roped off Jase's house, then stuffed him into a cruiser and left. The female detective opened the door and sat in the front passenger seat. Her bobbed hair was pulled back and from Charlie's angle he could tell she had a tattoo down the back of her neck. Something with wings, but he couldn't tell what it was, because of her collar.

"Mr. Erickson, I'm Detective Michelle Majors." And then to the officer, "Jerome, please take the cuffs off Mr. Erickson." Officer Clarke leaned over as Charlie turned to give him access. Once the cuffs were off, he rubbed his wrists.

"Better?"

Something in her voice pissed him off. She spoke to him like a child. "No," he spat. "An unconscious woman was pulled out of my best friend's house, and I've been forced to lie on a street then handcuffed. Two things I didn't expect to happen when I woke up this morning. So no, detective, it's not better." He glared into pale, blue, steadfast eyes. Clearly, she was not intimidated by him or his speech.

"I need to ask a few questions. We can do it right here or drive you to HQ. Up to you." The detective nodded toward the back window. Charlie turned. A gaggle of paparazzi gathered outside the guard gate.

"Here is fine," Charlie said, tight lipped. "But I want answers, too."

Detective Majors didn't respond. She read his Miranda rights, then pulled out a paper and her phone and set it to record. "Beginning with waking up, give me your complete timeline for today."

Charlie complied.

"Leslie Carroll?" She stopped him and repeated. "And how do you know her?"

"She's a friend who works at PRP, where we're in pre-production for my next film. We took her son to a baseball game, then she dropped me off at the bar to meet Jase.

"What time?"

"Around 8:20 tonight."

"So will Miss Carroll corroborate this?" she asked without looking up.

"Yes."

Charlie answered all her questions. As she wrote notes, three uniform cops carried more boxes out of Jase's house. When she gathered her things, he finally spoke, "Detective, tell me what's going on." She leveled a look at Officer Clarke, then back to Charlie. Yes, he probably sounded like the spoiled Hollywood type who expected answers, but he didn't care.

"Mr. Erickson, I'm not at liberty to say, but you and your driver are free to go."

She opened her door and swung her legs to get out. He needed to show her his other side. The compassionate southern part of his personality.

"Ma'am, wait, please. Jase and I grew up together in Tennessee. We've been friends since the seventh grade. Can you at least tell me—is the woman gonna be okay?"

The detective took a long breath as if she hadn't slept in a week. "Officer, give us a moment?"

Officer Clarke excused himself and stood like a guard outside the car. She didn't strike Charlie as a woman who fancied men, but something must have broken through that tough exterior. She stared for a long moment, as if deciding what to say then began. "Do you read the papers, Mr. Erickson?"

"Every day."

"Remember a story last week about a high-profile real estate mogul and her nineteen-year-old missing daughter?"

"Yeah." Charlie's voice was low and quiet.

"We got a tip from a pest control company. They heard a woman moaning inside. We got a warrant and found her."

Charlie swallowed hard to digest what the detective said, but it didn't add up. Charlie had to concede—Jase hooking up with a nineteen-year-old seemed probable, but torture and kidnapping? That seemed more like a setup. "I've known Jase a long time. He's not the type to hurt anyone, especially a woman."

The detective observed him, her eyes weary. Eyes that told him this wasn't the worst thing she'd seen. She exhaled. "I hope, for his sake, you're right." She stood next to the car, then leaned back down and stared pointedly at Charlie. "Sometimes it's the ones closest to us, we find out later, we didn't know at all. Mr. Erickson, my advice for you is to watch your back. You and your driver are free to go. But have your manager call our office if either of you plan to leave the city for any reason."

She slammed the door. Walking away, she rubbed the back of her neck and headed toward a group of officers who carried the equipment out. Officer Clarke opened Charlie's door and motioned for him to get out. When he stood, he was glad for the cool night air.

Not that he hadn't deserved it as a teenager, but he'd never sat in the back of a cop car.

Officer Clarke walked over to his squad car and pulled out a clear, zippered bag of items, including their phones, wallets and keys, and handed it to Charlie.

Charlie and Big Jimmy left amid a fury of flashbulbs outside the gated community. He'd dialed Kat and explained. She said she'd spin something in the papers, so the public would know he wasn't tied to the crime. Kat also conferenced in Charlie's entertainment attorney who helped them iron out all the details. She promised to call it into her media contacts first thing in the morning.

He apologized several times to Big Jimmy and shoved a generous tip in his hands. Big Jimmy laughed it off, claiming his teenage sons would get a kick out of the story. Then he dropped Charlie at his car in Leslie's driveway. Once there, Charlie scribbled a quick note and stuck it under her wiper blade. All he wanted was his own bed, but Christine was still there. Shit. On the bright side, the hotel would be quieter, plus the paparazzi didn't know he was there.

As he scrubbed off the day in the now familiar hotel shower, he couldn't shut down his mind. His best friend was accused of kidnapping, torture and if the woman died, he'd be tied to her murder.

They'd find the evidence to clear him. Jase always came out smelling like a rose. After his shower, Charlie cancelled his morning workout with his trainer, answered a few meaningless emails, then climbed into starched hotel sheets.

It was odd, but at that moment he thought of Leslie. What would she think of him once this hit the papers? And why did it matter so much what she thought of him? He hoped sleep would be easy but knew it wouldn't be.

Chapter Twelve

Leslie woke with a jolt. Only one nightmare, which, considering all things, was a good sign. But she'd slept through her alarm. Rubbing tired eyes, she glanced out the window. *Crap.* Sunlight filtering through cast shorter shadows than normal. No time for coffee or the paper.

Catapulted into her morning routine, for once she was grateful for her OCD. She'd already laid everything out the night before. She vowed not to think about Charlie while she brushed her teeth, dried her hair, or got dressed. It didn't work. Memories surfaced of how his mouth gaped when she wore the golden dress. Especially the way he said her name. She wanted to shut it all down the way she'd done all her life, but it kept creeping back in.

The note she found on her car read; "*Call you in a few days. I had a great time. I hope to see more of you, C.*"

She laid it gently in the front seat. He had nice handwriting. She read it a few more times at the red lights on the way to Nate's school. Nate must have said "Charlie" at least ten times before bed, so she could look forward to Nate talking about him for months. Even after this went south.

Leslie waved at Elvyn, or E as he liked to be called, as she entered PRP's parking complex. Elvyn was the all-knowing, always smiling, gate-guard. He'd been kind on her first day, admiring her Bronco and advising she not take anyone's crap. She liked his honesty and kindness. As her window slid down, she smiled and handed him her ID.

"Day three, little lady. How's it going?"

"Holding my own. Took your advice and grew a backbone. They're not happy about it, but they'll leave me alone."

"Glad to hear it," E said, as he scanned her card, slugged back a sip of coffee then punched quick buttons on his computer. She gawked in awe. The man was like watching a spinning carnival ride. "Hey, you read the paper?" He handed back her card.

"Not today, why?"

"Then you haven't heard the scuttlebutt?"

"Do tell." She glanced down for a second to place her card back in her wallet, then back up toward his face.

E looked up and down the drive to heighten the suspense. "Rumor has it a local young attorney has been charged with kidnapping and attempted murder, and our own Charlie Erickson was handcuffed at the scene of the crime."

"What?" Leslie yelped, then quieter, "That's not true. I know for a fact Mr. Erickson wasn't at the scene of any crime last night."

She stopped short as E held up the front page of the paper. A blurry, far-off picture of a man wearing the same white shirt and low-slung jeans. It was him, but how? The concise article didn't mention the attorney's name but hinted toward a more extensive review tomorrow. Of course, they homed in on the fact that Charlie was with him when the guy was arrested.

A honk of a horn behind her indicated she'd sat there too long. Waving at E, Leslie pulled away, then found a spot and parked. She dragged out her phone, and scrolled through to find Charlie and texted, *"You okay? Saw the paper."*

Something gnawed at the back of her mind as she stacked her belongings in her arms. Had he done something stupid after she dropped him off? Charlie hanging out with a criminal…didn't seem possible. The guy must've been released, or the grapevine would've been hot with the news by now.

Leslie slapped a hand over her mouth. She shook her head to stop from going into full-blown panic. If the cops asked where he'd been, he'd have given them a timeline. What if they came snooping around? *No need to panic until there's a need to panic,* her sister always said.

She sucked in a cleansing breath and locked the Bronco. The whistle of an incoming text caused her to stop in the middle of the lot to pull out her phone. She gave it her full attention.

"Tired but fine."

Leslie wrote back, *"Did I go on a date with a criminal?"*

It took him less than a minute to respond. *"It wasn't a date, remember? Not me. They wanted my friend."*

Mr. Miller, looking down his nose at her like she was a lowly employee, strutted onto the elevator before her. She half-wished the space had been full, so she could wait for the next one. No dice. They were all alone.

She stowed her phone and attempted early morning cordial. "Good morning, Mr. Miller. How are you?"

"Miss Carroll." He didn't answer her question. Dana was so much nicer than he'd ever be.

As the elevator doors closed, Mr. Miller pressed number four and cleared his throat. "Miss Carroll, it appears I have a career-making opportunity to offer you this morning. As you know, Dana is our most experienced costume designer, second only to me. But it seems she will be out of commission with a broken leg and cannot travel."

The elevator doors opened. Mr. Miller motioned for Leslie to exit the elevator first. She stopped just beyond the doors to wait for him to finish. Tension in her shoulders gripped all the way up her neck.

"As I was saying, Miss Carroll, I need someone who can act professionally. Someone who is a self-starter and can get the job done regardless of the conditions. Please understand, I don't make this offer lightly, nor have I *ever* handed this over to one so inexperienced, so if you were to say yes, I would need your complete focus on this job and nothing else."

Leslie nodded and waited. He hadn't yet told her what the opportunity was. She had to remind herself to lower her shoulders. Her stress lived there. With one finger, he pointed her to his glass office.

Tidy wasn't a strong enough word; it was immaculate. Nothing out of place, not so much as a pin. Awards and accolades sat on a shelving system flanking both sides of his desk. The rich, dark wood stood tall filled with pictures of Mr. Miller with the A-list actors he'd dressed.

It reminded her of an old country doctor's brag board of all the babies he'd brought into the world, except Mr. Miller's collage was perfectly organized. From any vantage point in the room, not one picture blocked another, as if they'd been placed by a designer. Mr. Miller put his bag on a tweed footstool, meant only for holding his bag. Then he hung his umbrella over a hook. When he sat behind his spotless mahogany desk, she sat in the empty chair in front of it. His long fingers folded together as he stared into Leslie's soul.

"Miss Carroll, if you agree, you'll go on location in Tennessee for our next film. You'll coordinate the wardrobe trailer, lead a staff, and ensure the costumes on set and all principal actors are tended to during the first few days of filming. This means long, unyielding hours, very little sleep, and little to no breaks. There is always something that needs to be done.

"You would need to arrive into Knoxville no later than Sunday, but I'd rather you get settled in on Saturday. Then you'll attend the riverboat gala kickoff party Sunday night in my stead and then dress the principal actors to shoot at five a.m. Monday morning. You'd arrive back here, ready for work again on Wednesday."

He didn't want her there, his mannerisms clarified it. Then again, why would he want someone so inexperienced? It was as if someone had pushed his hand and forced him to include her. And she might know who that someone was.

She straightened and answered, "I'd be honored. Thank you for putting your trust in me. I won't let you down."

Leslie stood, shoulders back and confident, as they shook on it. She retrieved her things and walked out of his office to her own cubicle. Mr. Miller dialed his phone, put it on speaker, then shut his door. She overheard him talking with a producer and making his travel arrangements for the coming weeks.

Leslie sat at her desk. Her legs quivered. A million thoughts zoomed through her mind like fireflies in June. She'd signed up for this. She knew the job included travel, but lots of movies were filmed in California on a sound stage, where she could *drive* to the location. Her unreasonable fear of falling out of the sky in a giant, tin torpedo surfaced. She had to slow her ragged breathing.

People traveled on commercial flights all the time, right? It was only the famous who flew on those tiny private planes and crashed to their death. What about care for Nate? And how would she get him back and forth to school? Aunt Reva could take care of him, but thanks to running over a dog five years ago, she didn't drive.

Coffee. Coffee would solve this. Leslie turned on her computer, grabbed her phone, then headed for the employee kitchen.

She passed Angela and Frank, who stood at the edge of their adjoining cubes, whispering about her, no doubt. Or Charlie. Either option pissed her off. They scattered like roaches back to their cubes when she got within a few feet of them. Chin high, she kept walking.

Rounding the corner into the small kitchen, she found Dana leaning against the laminate countertop. She stared at the coffee pot as it brewed. Her crutches were propped up behind her and her right leg was in a cast.

Dana's soft cry stopped Leslie in her tracks. She was taken aback by the colors in the large bruise on her face: black, blue, and deep purple in a perfect circle on her left eye. Leslie crept closer. Scanning her up and down, Leslie asked, "All of this from a shower?"

Dana startled and turned, her eyes weary and tear-stained, but she didn't miss a beat. "I'm a clumsy old woman. But I'm fine. Let's get coffee and go to my office. I want to prepare you for what to expect on location and how to deal with all the problems. We can plan today and gather everything you'll need tomorrow, okay?"

Leslie grabbed two coffee mugs and filled them, while Dana struggled to get her crutches under her arms then hobbled down the long hallway. She followed.

Moving papers from a chair, Leslie sat. They talked at length about the logistics of setting up a costume trailer. Dana gave her the inside scoop on the other assistants she'd supervise and schedule. She was relieved the assistant list didn't include Angela or Frank.

Pictures of Dana's grown son and daughter and two grandchildren littered her office. "You have a lovely family."

Dana craned her neck around and smiled. "That's kind of you. I have three kids. My eldest son and daughter are twins, both married and each has one child. It's amazing how much their kids look like each other. Then there's my youngest son in that picture over there." Her smile faded as she spoke.

Leslie had teared up, which didn't go unnoticed. The woman reached behind her then handed Leslie a small box of tissues. "You want to talk about it?"

I can't. God, she was exhausted. The first few days of work, keeping her guard up around Charlie, and the stress of finding caregivers for Nate while she was away, had all taken their toll. But in truth, Leslie was angry. Angry she'd never again share all her ups and downs with her twin. Not a day passed, especially raising Nate, when she didn't miss her sister.

And she had no one to blame but herself. "I'm sorry, Dana. I'm not a crier."

Dana cocked her head to the side. "Leslie, you know I'm not a gossip, dear, and anything you tell me will be in the strictest of confidences. What's bothering you?"

She considered what part of the truth she could tell. She liked Dana. She'd become a master at reading people from afar and she believed in her confidentiality.

Leslie took a deep breath and decided on telling mostly the truth. "I'm a twin, too. My sister died a few years ago. She was the only real family I had."

Dana let out a long sigh. "Dear, I'm so sorry to hear that. To lose your other half so early in life must have been horrible for you. How did she pass so young?"

"Cancer. Breast cancer," she clarified. *And a broken spirit.*

Dana got up and hobbled around her desk. She sat on the edge facing Leslie. "My husband died a few years ago. He was such a gentle soul. Retired from twenty-five decorated years in the service by the time we were forty-five. He stayed home and cared for our oldest son."

Dana looked down at her hands. "He's mentally disabled. Paranoid schizophrenia with a touch of oppositional defiant disorder…" She gazed out the window, then touched her eye. "My shiner here is due to one of his outbursts."

At the horrified look on Leslie's face, she rattled on, "Not on purpose. No. His anger was aimed at a sad lamp, which sailed across the living room at the same moment I walked in. Hit me in the eye and knocked me off balance." She looked down, "Hence the broken leg." Dana waved a hand in front of her face as if to erase it all. "Point being, I miss having my other half, the one I could share anything with. You feel the same, don't you?"

Leslie stood and hugged Dana tight. The moment she was positive she was alone battling demons, she found a comrade. She'd been so wrapped up in her own running and fears, she hadn't cracked open enough to notice another person's pain. Hadn't been close enough to even want to know someone else's troubles.

Her shoulders must've eased down an entire inch. Relief washed over her just from knowing someone understood. She hadn't belonged anywhere in so long, but roots were beginning to form. A new wave of tears surfaced. She picked up Dana's notebook and headed for the door.

Before she walked through Dana called out, "Leslie?"

"Yeah?"

"Please…don't tell anyone."

Leslie smiled. "Trust me, I'm a master at keeping secrets."

Chapter Thirteen

Charlie found sleep spotty at best. He'd struggled with nightmares about an evil member of the Torres family with a machete chasing him and Jase inside an abandoned house. When the dream man went after Leslie and Nate, Charlie sat upright in bed.

He'd answered Leslie's text and dozed back off. His first rehearsal wasn't until ten, so he tried for another hour of sleep, but then another nightmare hit. So vivid. When Leslie screamed inside the dream, it jolted him awake.

He ran thick, sleepy fingers through his hair. What must she think of him? The papers insinuated he was involved in the disappearance of the redheaded woman. Kat reported the woman was unconscious in ICU recovering from stab wounds and electrocution. Although Kat filed grievances with two local papers—demanding retractions for the lies about Charlie—she still made time to send him updates on the woman. She'd earned her keep this week.

He had to admit, living in a hotel during a scandal was handy. He imagined how the paparazzi must be camped out at his house. As far as he knew, Jase hadn't been released yet, but his entertainment attorney assured him a competent team of attorneys worked all night gathering information.

A knock on the door startled him. A groan escaped as he dragged his body out of bed, pulling on jeans and a crumpled T-shirt. He padded in bare feet to the door and unlocked the dead bolt. Damn, he must've been tired. He didn't even check the peephole. The door swung open, hitting him in the knee. A tall woman wearing a long, tan raincoat slammed the door behind her and launched herself at him.

Within seconds she had one hand in his hair and the other unbuttoning his jeans. Her familiar mouth found his. Her tongue searched, desperate for understanding. It took Charlie's unawake mind only a few seconds to realize he didn't want Christine touching him anymore. In his past, this interruption would have been welcome, but his heart wasn't in it. He grabbed her by the wrists and pushed her back, disconnecting their lips.

"Charlie," she gasped for air as any good actress would, "are you all right? The press is saying horrible things about you. I had to rush over."

"I'm fine," he said, releasing her wrists. He walked toward the living room of the suite and sat on one of the oversized chairs. He motioned for her to sit on the opposite couch.

Christine sat, but then bounced right back up, leveling a heated look at him. All traces of concern on her face were magically gone.

"I know what we can do to make all of this go away." She unfastened the buttons on her coat. A quick flash of skin. She was naked underneath, as usual. It's how she always made up with him. He jumped up and put his hands over hers.

"Stop, Christine, stop. That's not gonna happen." Her face registered confusion. "I'm fine. Jase is the one fighting for his freedom. I was with him last night when they took him in for questioning."

She looked as if someone slapped her. He'd never dismissed her before, especially when she was dolled up, naked, and in heels. Her face contorted like a disenchanted child. "Are you still angry over that thing with Phillipe?"

Charlie considered it, then shook his head. "I'm not angry. This isn't what I want anymore."

He walked into the kitchen portion of the suite and made coffee. Christine looked stunned, as if she would cry, but she was an actress, and she was good at crying on a moment's notice. She followed him into the kitchen with her arms crossed tight over her coat.

Her voice turned to a growl as she said, "Do you hear what you're saying? All the time we've invested in each other, to be over? Why?"

Charlie poured water into the Keurig and hit start. The gurgling sound was a welcome distraction while he gathered his thoughts. He didn't like hurting anyone, ever. And at the beginning of their relationship, she was kind and helped him hone his acting techniques. She wasn't as popular back then, and her ego wasn't as big, either. She was fun, before fame grabbed a hold of her and made her a conniving, snobby, entitled woman. She wasn't who he'd wanted for a while, but he hadn't fully understood that, until now.

"We grew apart a long time ago. What was left was toxic." Charlie lifted two white ceramic mugs from the cabinet and poured them both a steaming cup, adding cream to his and leaving hers black. His gaze drifted from the cups to her face. Real tears ran down her cheeks.

"You won't give me another chance? Look, I know…I took

you for granted. But I thought you'd always take me back. You look at me different, now. You hate me, don't you?"

He handed her a tissue box from the counter and picked up his coffee. "I don't hate you."

Christine wiped her eyes, changed her stance, then grabbed her mug from the counter. "I can make you happy. I want to take care of you." Her voice cracked as she took a sip.

"Chris, the kindest thing you could do for me right now is to give me my space. Move out so I don't have to live in a hotel anymore."

She sniffed, put her cup down, then nodded. She pulled a large phone out of the pocket of her coat and typed. Not looking up she added, "The press is camped out in front, so use the rear entrance. I'll have a crew of people over there to move my things out today."

They could be friends if this kinder side of Christine held out. But history taught him this gentler Chris would get eaten alive by the mean one any second. He hoped it didn't.

When she left, Charlie showered and changed. Kat and Big Jimmy met him in the lobby. They broke the news to him: the hotel was surrounded with photographers. Someone leaked his whereabouts and they found him. The vultures wanted information about Jase and the woman.

He knew nothing. Hell, his mind was so tired, his only goal was to make it to rehearsals on time. Big Jimmy opened the glass doors toward the waiting limo and pushed through the crowd like a bulldozer.

Charlie and Kat ducked and walked right behind him amid photographers yelling, "Charles! Charles Erickson! Look over here!"

Charlie jumped into the back of the long limo. When they were all buckled, Kat nodded toward the window. One of the back doors opened. Grunting and scooting in was the heavyset *Expose Weekly* host, Chip Burroughs.

Charlie squinted sideways at Chip, noticing the sweat gathered at the sides of his forehead and along his neck. He was cherry-faced, most likely from pushing his way through the crowd. Kat shot a reassuring smile to Charlie. He volleyed back a look that said he was less than pleased with her choice.

Big Jimmy pushed the gas slowly, allowing the throngs of photographers to move before he ran them over.

"Mr. Erickson," Chip Burroughs stated, using his 'on air' voice, "Kat was kind enough to grant me an exclusive interview."

Kat nodded toward Charlie. He glared back. They'd spoken about clearing his name, but not with this snake.

Charlie knew Chip all too well. The seasoned yet slimy reporter made up as much as he reported. Everything was sensationalized and reported to cast Chip and his network in a better light. Why would Kat trust him? Yes, he had a large reach. His show was in the number one spot, but all that wouldn't matter if he didn't report the truth. *Damnit, Kat.*

He crossed his arms. He wouldn't give the man anything he didn't already know. Tight-lipped, Charlie smiled. "All I can say is I had drinks with a friend, then dropped him off at home, where the police arrested him. I was with him the night they questioned him. That's all. I assure you, he'll be released today. He's innocent of all charges."

Chip scoffed. "Charlie, the woman was carried out unconscious. My source says he raped her, stabbed tiny holes in her like a voodoo doll, and had her hooked up to a damn electrical torture machine. She'll be lucky if she survives."

Crooked cops leaked bad information. His eyes narrowed but he managed to keep his voice even. "You should know better than most that ninety percent of what you hear, and what *you* report, isn't true."

Chip's lips hardened into a long line. "That's not *all* my inside source told me."

Kat sat up. "What else?"

The reporter's smug smile widened. He leaned back in the limo, patting the leather seats. "Nice ride. I guess you've enjoyed your fame—right, Charlie?"

"The point, Burroughs." Charlie said, gritting his teeth.

Chip sighed. "When the LAPD's IT guys swept Mr. Gilreath's computer, there was more than just underage porn on it."

Charlie stared. "I'm listening."

Mr. Burroughs sat up and lowered his voice as he said, "Complete and graphic, detailed plans to kill one Hollywood actor named Charles Erickson."

Charlie couldn't help it. He gut-laughed. Without missing a beat, he yelled out, "Bullshit. Total fabricated bullshit. What you idiots don't realize is we've been friends for life. Jason lived with my family throughout high school. We attended the same college, lived in a dorm together. He's closer to me than even Kat here. That's a good one, Burroughs, report that one."

The man shook his head in disbelief. "Charlie, I'm serious. Like volumes of ways to kill you. Even a time early on when he saved you from a tractor accident. Something about the throttle sticking and him wishing he had the balls to let you die."

That stopped Charlie in his tracks.

They'd been seventeen, about to leave for California, and his dad needed them to cut hay. The cutter on the tractor had gotten hung up, and Charlie climbed on the back to jimmy it loose while Jase drove. Jase gunned it, all in good fun, knocking Charlie to the ground and missing him with the blades by only a foot. Jase turned the tractor around and came toward him, but they both laughed it off. It was only a prank. Charlie's mind raced.

"Fabricated bullshit," he said again, but his voice was softer, unsure.

Big Jimmy pulled to a stop in front of the *Expose Weekly* studios. Chip sat open-mouthed, staring at Charlie. For once, Burroughs looked genuine. His eyes pleaded with Charlie to listen. He believed the crazy story, hook line and sinker.

"Charlie, look." He scooted forward on his seat. "On a personal level, watch your back. My source tells me this guy may not be who you think he is. Prelim reports indicate a split personality. And his evil side—doesn't like you at all."

Chip grunted and moved toward the door. Big Jimmy opened it, letting Mr. Burroughs out. He smiled at the people on the street as if he was running for mayor, before ducking inside the building.

Kat exhaled, then turned toward Charlie. Her voice sounding more feminine than he ever remembered, she said, "Charlie, I think you should heed Chip's advice. You know, I'm an observer of people. And it makes sense Jase would be jealous of you, your fame…your life."

When Charlie scoffed, she finished, "You can't see it because you're too close to him, but others can."

He ran his hands through his hair. This made zero sense. He and Jase had been inseparable for years. Jase had saved his ass more times than he could count. Wouldn't he have sensed it if his best friend hated him? He had to believe he knew Jase better than anyone. No, he wouldn't be swayed by the rumors.

Charlie sighed and shook his head. "Kat, no matter what they say he's done and no matter what their story—I don't buy it. He's like a brother."

He stretched out his legs. Grinning, he raised his arms above his head. "Let Chip report that horseshit—he's an idiot if he does." Kat lowered a serious look at him, and he continued, "You know he's gonna put his own spin on it, no matter what I tell him." For once, Kat didn't argue. He shot her his best Hollywood smile.

When it seemed Kat had dropped it, Charlie pulled out his phone. No messages from Leslie. Disappointment stabbed his chest.

Had they told her she was going on location yet? She'd probably be fighting mad if she found out he was behind that brilliant idea. He told himself he was helping further her career. But who was he kidding? Yes, he wanted her to succeed, but if he was honest, he selfishly wanted time alone with her.

He switched screens. No emails about Jase. With his pull, surely he was out on bail by now. He'd be damned if he believed all this plotting-to-murder-him bullshit was real.

Photographers and reporters swarmed the front entrance of PRP. Big Jimmy dropped Kat and Charlie off at the side entrance. They were buzzed into the building and headed for the elevators to get to the tenth-floor meeting rooms when Charlie spotted Mr. Miller. "Hello, sir, how are you today?"

Miller looked stunned, then like magic, his face took on an air of importance. Puffed up, he replied loud, so everyone around could hear, "Why Mr. Erickson, I am fabulous this morning, and you?"

Pompous ass. "I've seen better nights, but I'm well now, thanks. Wanna share an elevator?" Charlie knew full well his answer.

"Why yes, I'd be honored," Mr. Miller cooed.

When the elevator stopped on the fourth floor, Charlie couldn't help himself. He got out as Kat went up to the meeting to tell them he was on his way.

He tiptoed around the outside corridor of the offices. Most of the cubes were uninhabited. Rounding the last corner, he spotted Leslie's chestnut hair over the tops of the cubicles.

As he crept closer, he could see her dark eyes looked puffy. *Shit.* Had she been crying? His heart sank. Maybe the logistics of having a disabled son and traveling on location were too much.

He was a selfish idiot. Why hadn't he considered that before insisting she go? As he snuck up behind her with his hands in his pockets, his heart swelled. What control she had over him, yet she had no idea. He couldn't help but listen in on her phone conversation.

~ * ~

"I know, Aunt Reva, but there's nothing I can do. You could spend the weekend at my house. I'll have it stocked with food. I already spoke to Miss Kimberly. They have buses for kids like Nate. A retired bus driver sits with them too, so they're not afraid. He'll love riding on a bus." A pause then, "Well, he'll have to miss baseball. I'll call the director and tell her. I'll buy him a new toy for Tuesday to cushion the blow…What? Oh, my flight. It leaves at five Saturday morning, which gives me all of Saturday to organize myself and rest before Sunday night."

Leslie caught movement out of the corner of her eye. Assuming it was Mr. Miller, she hung up with her aunt. She jumped up, which sent her rolling chair sailing a foot behind her.

Charlie yelped. "Are you trying to wound me, Miss Carroll?"

She spun around and let out a frustrated sigh. Gathering her manifest book, a pen, and her cell, she shot back without looking at him, "Erickson, don't you have anything better to do?"

Charlie smiled. Before she could protest, he grabbed everything out of her hands. "Nope. Where are we going?"

"I'm going to the costume floor to check on progress." Leslie gritted her teeth and reached for her books, but Charlie swung them over her head and away from her arms.

"It bothers you when I come in here, doesn't it?" He leaned toward her. Close to her mouth. "You're worried about everyone's reaction. Or being the center of attention. Could it be, Miss Carroll, you're ashamed of having a famous boyfriend?"

Honestly, she could've spit fire. Stomping to the elevator, she lectured herself—ignore him and he'll go away. Jabbing the button, she crossed her arms and stared up at the numbers. Charlie sauntered up behind her. A low chuckle rumbled in his chest. The doors opened to an empty elevator. She rushed inside, pushed the buttons for the sixth floor and turned to lean against the back wall. She glared as he meandered in.

When the doors shut, she bounded toward Charlie taking him by surprise. She backed him into the corner next to the control panel, snatched her things out of his hands, then shoved one finger in his face.

"You listen to me." Her voice trembled, which pissed her off even more. "You are not my boyfriend. I have no boyfriend. Never have and never will. Stop showing up here and making me uncomfortable.

"Yes, it embarrasses me when everyone stares. You've bothered me *every single day* this week. The rumor mill is into overtime with you and me. And my only goal for my first week was to fly under the radar, which by the way, you've ruined."

She resituated the book slipping in her arms and continued, "I'm already on the shit list with Frank and Angela out to get me, and you're giving them more ammunition to hate me every day. I know you pushed for me to go on location for this film. Part of me is grateful. But then the other part is terrified you think there is something between us.

"Which. There. Is. Not. We will be going our separate ways from now on."

~ * ~

Charlie's face contorted with a pitiful attempt to hide his amusement. Her clenched fists under her book looked like she wanted to take a swing, and her voice cracked in anger. Her cheeks were bright pink with frustration. She was as close as she could get without touching him, which probably ticked her off even more.

He adored this strong-willed part of her, but amusement turned like a flash to anger of his own. She was breaking up with him before they'd even given it a chance. He leaned over and did something he'd never done before.

Charlie Erickson hit the stop button.

Chapter Fourteen

The elevator lurched to a halt, knocking Leslie off balance. Charlie's hand steadied her out of instinct, then drew back. His turn.

He stalked tall toward her, his throat tight. "You are the most infuriating woman I've ever known. So closed off. Why is dating a man such a big deal to you? Who's hurt you so badly, you can't even stand to be touched?"

Charlie didn't wait for an answer. He grabbed the manual and phone out of her hands and tossed them to the floor. She took instinctive steps backward, hands behind her splayed out in search of the wall. He stalked toward her until she was backed into the opposite corner. When her back hit the wall, her hands moved to his chest, holding him at arm's length. Her thin arms trembled, and it broke his heart. He bent toward her, while his hands held him up on the wall behind her. His mouth was inches from hers. Sweet lotion mixed with the smell of peppermint gum had his head spinning.

Transfixed on that beautiful mouth, he hesitated. He willed himself not to kiss her. The charge between them sucked him in. The old men's words from Nate's baseball game rang in his ears. If he kissed her now, she'd run. Her body quaked.

"I won't hurt you." His voice was a hoarse whisper. "I promise. But you have to let me in." He took a deep breath. "I'm willing to take it slow, but you can't keep pushing me away. I know there's light in you. You've got to decide whether you're brave enough to let it out. I won't bother you anymore. But I won't let you shut this down before we've given it a shot, okay?"

Her dark eyes widened. Ragged breaths came quick. When her lips opened slightly and her mouth moved toward his, it was like she was caught in a tractor beam. He froze. As if she were in a daze, her dark eyes were transfixed on his mouth. She glided toward him. When he could taste her breath, her trance broke. She jerked back and looked up, embarrassed.

When her eyes met his, he pinned her there, unwilling to look away until she answered. Finally, she blinked.

After a long breath, she nodded. He moved away, then bent over to pick up her things, handing them back without touching or words.

~ * ~

Leslie's skin felt electrified, but her mind was numb. Nobody had ever touched her like that. It stirred feelings inside she didn't even know existed. She stood, panting and shaking like a dog when Charlie passed back her manual and phone. Without a word, he touched the start button again.

One clammy hand gripped the rail to keep her steady as the elevator pitched back to life. Before she could process what happened, the elevator door opened on the sixth floor. She stumbled out, like in a dream, then turned to face him. She wished she could gather her wits enough to say something smart, but all she could do was stare at the beautiful, frustrated man as the elevator doors shut.

Leslie stood in front of the closed door. If only she could hold on to her scattered thoughts and stop her body from shaking. *What the hell was that?*

The scene replayed in her mind like an old movie stuck on repeat: stopping the elevator, yelling, his strong hands on either side of her. *Oh God.* She almost kissed him. A shudder wracked her body again.

After a minute of ping-ponging the events back and forth, she had a breakthrough. She'd wanted to kiss him. Really wanted to. That alone shocked the crap out of her. And when he whispered he wouldn't hurt her, she almost came undone. Nobody ever said that before. This was going to crash and burn.

Leslie's knees wobbled as she entered the room and flicked on the light. She was all alone in the massive workroom. The place was spooky—part perfect and part creepy, but she craved the quiet. She spotted an immense work surface like a long dining table in an old castle, capable of seating twenty people. She placed her book and phone on it and stood still, lost in in her own mind.

Squeezing her eyes shut, she forced her mind to name the emotion running rampant. Fear? Her issues with being touched didn't seem to stand a chance with Charlie around. Part of her wanted, even needed, to be held, but she couldn't fathom it. Images she'd suppressed since college would surface. She knew it. Even more disturbing was somewhere, deep inside, she knew she didn't deserve to be held.

She had to focus. Moments later, she forced herself to block it out. Time to work.

The task today was to inventory and pack up boxes of costumes based upon the director's notes and the scene sequence. She could do this; she had to focus. The infuriating Mr. Charlie Erickson would need to be blocked so she could concentrate on the book in front of her.

She sat and leafed through the notes of the movie. The plan was subject to change on a moment's notice, but it stated the later scenes would be shot first, giving the producers time to finalize the main female character.

A few of the earlier scenes seemed racy. Her stomach churned. She'd have to watch Charlie kiss another woman.

Which brought her back to the elevator and the heat. It'd traveled through her body like rum, warming as it went. He'd wanted to kiss her. Staring at her mouth, he'd held himself back, she could tell. It was ironic that she'd have been angry if he'd taken the kiss without making sure she wanted it, too.

But then, she'd almost kissed him.

Her stomach butterflied. The baffling part was she *did* want it. She was already in too deep. Could she tell him the truth? He'd run. She was sure of it. All men would.

Inexperience plagued her. Her sister would've known what to do, if only she was here. Leslie ran a hand through her hair and let out a long, exasperated breath. "Focus," she commanded.

Two hours and two exhausted interns later, she had all costumes marked with scene numbers, boxed, taped shut, and labeled for shipping. The interns transported the boxes on wheeled carts to the first-floor reception for pick up. They'd be sent to Tennessee and ready for the first scene on Monday. As she stretched, her stomach growled for lunch.

When she reached the elevator door, she changed trajectory and bypassed it. Stairs sounded better. She needed the exercise. *Right.* Plus getting on the elevator would only make her blush and give her the chance to run into a certain handsome actor who, she was sure, still lurked in the building somewhere.

She ran down the two flights of stairs, but when she opened the door to the fourth floor, she almost shut it back on instinct. A large male police officer towered over a petite, blonde woman sporting a badge. They blocked the hallway leading to her cube. They were speaking with Dana.

If she'd taken the elevator, she could've bypassed them. *Damn you, Erickson.* They hadn't noticed her. Yet. She contemplated shutting the door back and running. What if they discovered her identity? As if they could hear her thoughts, the blonde swung her head around, and the officer followed. They'd spotted Leslie.

The woman smiled like a cat playing with a trapped a mouse. "Thank you, Ms. Godwin, I believe we've found her."

Leslie took a deep breath, shut the door behind her then squared her shoulders. She strode toward the woman, who sized her up while pulling credentials out of her suit jacket.

"Miss Carroll?" the woman asked. Leslie nodded. "Miss Carroll, I'm Detective Michelle Majors. We have a few questions." The detective glanced around. "Is there somewhere we can talk privately?"

Leslie led the two down the hall, past a worried-looking Dana, past Frank's and Angela's stares, and into the small conference room next to Mr. Miller's office. Even the janitor appeared to watch them through the glass as Leslie pulled the blinds. With her back to the room she closed her eyes. *This isn't about you. They know nothing. Keep your answers short.*

When she opened them, she walked to the table and sat. The detective pulled out her phone and a small notebook then laid them on the table. Hands folded, she examined Leslie like a hawk, then hit the record button. "Miss Carroll—"

"Leslie, please call me Leslie." Her voice sounded too sweet, even to her own ears. *Get it together.* She hoped to win the detective over.

"Okay, Leslie," the detective said, then recited the Miranda Rights from memory. She didn't flinch once nor did she take her gaze off Leslie even for a second. She was all business. Leslie took a cleansing breath as the questioning began.

"Before we begin can you please state your name for the record?"

"Leslie Anne Carroll."

"Mr. Erickson indicated he was with you last night. Is that correct?"

"Yes."

"And your relationship with Charles Erickson...can you describe that for us?"

He's an annoying man who won't leave me alone and has managed to make me tremble every day since I met him. "Friends...we're friends."

The detective eyed her, then smiled tightly, as if waiting for Leslie to elaborate.

She clasped her hands together and waited. She would give this woman no speculative information.

The detective's eyebrows shot up. She nodded, then glanced back at her notes. "Miss Carroll, please give us a timeline of last night's events with Mr. Erickson."

Leslie ran through the night, leaving off the part where Charlie acted as if their time together was a date. She spun it to seem as if he attended The Challenger League as a favor. She recalled how he assisted in calling the game in the press box. But if he was asked the same question, he probably made it sound *way* more like a date.

Crap.

Hopefully this wouldn't make her lose credibility. It was perception, after all, that made each person see the same situation in a different light.

The detective listened to Leslie's timeline, which, judging by the checkmarks in her notes, appeared to be spot on with the times Charlie must've given. Detective Majors looked at the notes she brought. "Do you know Jason Gilreath?"

Calm, Leslie shook her head.

The detective pointed at the recorder.

"No."

"Has Charlie Erickson ever mentioned Jason Gilreath?"

"I only met Mr. Erickson Monday, so no, we haven't spoken but a handful of times."

The detective's stare narrowed. "Leslie, can you help me understand how you're twenty-five and our background check indicates you didn't get a social security number until you were nineteen? In fact, we show no records whatsoever until you turned nineteen. It's as if you didn't exist until then."

Leslie stood up and walked over to the credenza where a fresh pitcher of water and cups were sitting out. "That's an easy answer. Would you like some water?"

Detective Majors shook her head. She watched as Leslie poured herself a glass and took a quick sip, then walked back to her chair and sat.

"My parents," she began, smiling, "were California hippies. My mom home-schooled me and never took me to any 'quack' doctors growing up, so I guess it'd look like I didn't exist before eighteen."

"So you didn't work or go to school at all before the age of eighteen?"

"Not really. I worked for neighbors—babysitting, walking dogs, and light lawn care. Didn't need any money because my parents didn't buy 'stuff.' I told you…hippies."

Her practiced, easy-going smile caused the detective's shoulders to lower, but the woman's eyes said she wasn't completely sold.

The detective was petite like Leslie, but as blonde as Leslie was dark-haired. The woman looked as if she could hold her own, both physically and mentally. The smart ponytail at the base of her neck didn't move when she turned her head. Her eyes, blue like Charlie's, held a whole lot of cynicism in them.

Her eyebrows furrowed as if she sensed something was off but couldn't put her finger on it. This wasn't Leslie's first rodeo. She'd been questioned on several occasions. Knew exactly how to come across as truthful and genuine. But this detective wasn't buying it.

"So you didn't go to college after you finished your home-schooling?"

"No. I took a few years off to hike the California countryside then went into community college when I turned twenty. Took a lot of online courses. Pomona Pitzers; I'm a Sagehen," Leslie added, smiling.

Detective Majors nodded, then wrote notes. She turned off her phone, packed her things, and thanked Leslie for her time. They shook hands before the detective walked out with the other officer.

Leslie tidied up the conference room, pushing chairs under the table one at a time, slowly, to give her heart rate time to return to normal. That was too close. Chin high, she walked out amid stares and calmly headed toward her cubicle. She fired up her computer and googled "Jason Gilreath, Attorney."

When the image came up on her computer, it took all she had not to throw up in her trash can. The air around her face suddenly seemed hot and thick. She slapped one hand to her mouth as a reflex to hold in the scream. Tears stung. She pushed down the vomit creeping up her esophagus.

No. Omigod, no.

It was *him.* Him that took away everything from her and from Anne. The monster that woke her every night with flashbacks of a weekend she couldn't fully remember. Her eyes clamped shut. She'd never known his name.

Opening them again, she stared at the professional photo. Her fingers trembled on the keyboard. She'd have to be blind not to notice the resemblance in Nate.

Swiping at the corners of her eyes, she couldn't read fast enough. The article indicated Jason Gilreath had been charged with several counts of kidnapping, child pornography, and attempted murder. Not one bit of it came as a shock. Without a doubt, he drugged the woman and had done unspeakable things to her.

Her stomach roiled. She should help. Somehow, help. But she couldn't. It'd put Nate at risk.

Something else was eating away at her, too. She looked around. With only a few people at their cubes, nobody noticed her meltdown. Squeezing her eyes closed again, she shoved down the images. The ones she could remember. And pushed out the sadness.

She couldn't be with Charlie Erickson. Ever.

Of all people in the world, Charlie's best friend had to be Jason Gilreath. It didn't make sense. Charlie seemed normal. Annoying and frustrating, but normal. How could he be friends with a monster?

She stood. She'd forgotten to right the blinds in the conference room. Her legs wobbled. Inside the conference room, she paced to the window and stared down at traffic. Her arms wrapped protectively around her as her mind spit and sputtered.

Her past was colliding with her future. She had to stop it all before things got out of hand.

Chapter Fifteen

Charlie was out of sorts. Not only because of emotions that surfaced in the elevator, but last night's escapades made him tired and cranky. He'd slept through his normal ass-kicking with his trainer, which he needed, and had several missed calls on his cell from an unlisted number. Jase, no doubt.

He couldn't shake the ugly feeling of betrayal. Somewhere deep down, part of him believed his best friend was jealous. But jealous enough to want to kill him? Didn't add up.

During the day, he kept his mind solid while rehearsing, but it wandered when he took breaks. They'd gone over scenes for two straight hours. Kat read the part of the female lead since they still hadn't secured a leading lady.

Charlie stood by a window and stretched the stiff muscles in his legs. He'd need to run tonight. Perhaps he could talk Big Jimmy into running with him. Leslie's street was sidewalk lined. He could jog down her street, then stop in for a minute…

"No," he ordered himself. He gazed at the cars below, but only saw her face in his mind. She'd need space this morning. He was still shocked that she almost kissed him. But God, how he'd wanted her to. He realized quickly that she'd have to be the one to initiate. He was a southern gentleman after all. Even if his body didn't want to be. He'd see her on Saturday, but until then, he'd force himself to leave her alone.

~ * ~

Leslie picked up Nate and drove home. Her insides felt like twisted ropes tied in little knots. Worry was eating away at her.

She pushed it all down and made spaghetti while drafting a schedule for Nate's food for the days she'd be gone. Then she emailed his teachers and coordinated bus rides for school. After dinner they'd go to see Gramps, like they did every Wednesday.

Her dad was in a nursing facility on the outskirts of Palo Alto. One of the smaller and nicer nursing homes in the county. His memory had gotten so bad, he rarely recognized her. Then again, most days she didn't recognize herself either. With bags under her eyes and a lined face from her rough start into adulthood, she wouldn't pass for twenty-four on a bet. She trudged into his room holding Nate's hand.

As soon as they entered, Nate's gaze darted around the room. He tugged her hand then began his usual nervous flapping. This room made him uncomfortable. One wall held a TV that was never turned on, there was only one chair, and whenever he was forced to hug Gramps, he'd pull away. Her dad's mind began to slip when Nate was a baby, so they never bonded.

His nurse, Miss Cora, stomped into the room, with her purple scrubs and bright, white tennis shoes. "There's my boy. Nate, you come with Mama Cora. We'll go to the music room to listen to Miss Gregory play the piano." She glanced up at Leslie. "You all right, baby?"

Leslie shook her head and looked down. She didn't want the tears to fall. They'd make her weak again. Cora nodded understanding, grabbed hold of Nate, then led him out. He clapped his hands, happy to get to hear the piano.

Richard Carroll stirred as Leslie sat at the foot of his bed. She wiped her face. It'd only confuse him more to see her cry. He sat up, scratched his head and blinked a few times. Questions formed in his eyes. He looked from her face to his memory board next to his bed, and back. It would tell him she was Leslie and according to the board, she was his daughter. Most days he didn't catch the name change, but every once in a while his memory would zing back.

He scooted around in the bed, stretching to sit up higher, then looked down. Leslie looked away so he wouldn't be embarrassed. The nurses had once again taken off his pants. A trick they often employed to keep residents in their beds at night. Her father drew the covers up tight around his midsection and cleared his throat.

His face registered confusion and agitation, two of only a handful of emotions he could conjure lately. "Leslie?" Hesitation laced his normal authoritative voice.

Her head snapped up and their eyes met. She hoped her face wasn't blotchy. "Dad?"

He raised one old-as-hell-looking hand. "Now, don't get too excited, I see your picture here." He pointed to his board.

"Right" she agreed sadly.

"Why are you crying?" he asked.

She exhaled. "I miss you...and I miss her. I need someone to talk to."

His head swiveled as if anyone would be a better candidate than himself. He adjusted the covers again and pulled an imaginary fuzz ball off them. Once again, watching her. Then he squared his shoulders—something she'd seen him in his heyday when sentencing or encouraging a witness. "What's going on?"

"It's so complicated and screwed up, Dad. I wouldn't even know where to start." Leslie leaned forward and rested her head on her hands.

"Tell me and let me help."

She sat up automatically. He'd used his authoritative voice. People always took notice when he did. Especially in the courtroom. She knew he missed being there, where everything made sense and people listened to him. He'd been genuine and trustworthy too, respectable traits for a judge to have.

That period of his life it seemed he could remember with complete clarity, which, the doctors said was why he didn't recognize the woman before him now. He continuously looked for two red-headed little girls, not one dark-headed woman.

Leslie took a long breath. "Dad, I've met someone, but because of my past, I can't be with him. I'm afraid the world I've built will fall apart, and I'll break the promise I made to my sister."

Her father peeked over again at his memory board. But, there was no sister on it, only Leslie. His face contorted, perplexed, but he shook his head as if to shake the confusion away. "Does this man love you?"

Puzzled, Leslie's head cocked to one side. "What? No…I don't know…maybe."

When their eyes met again, for a second he seemed like he remembered her. She held her breath. He'd been so skilled at reading people before he lost his memory, but lately he wasn't skilled at much except being angry. Her gaze dropped to stare at the floor. Did Charlie love her? She wasn't sure having never been in a real relationship, but she knew one thing. She'd fallen for him. Hard.

"You wanna know what I think?" her father said firmly.

She glanced over.

"If this man loves you, no matter what happened in your past, he'll love you in the future, Anne, but you'll have to let him in and let him decide. You'll have to choose whether you are strong enough to take the chance of him rejecting you."

~ * ~

Leslie froze. He'd called her Anne. Did he remember something or was it an accident? He didn't even seem to catch it. Her phone buzzed. She glanced down. It was Charlie:

Promised myself I wouldn't text, but I had to. Sorry about the elevator. Ending this before we give it a shot seems unfair. I'd miss you. See you Saturday. –Charlie

~ * ~

Her father stared out the window probably already forgetting what he was saying. He turned, glanced at Leslie then peeked at his board again. He looked as if he wanted to ask her what was wrong, but he hesitated.

Instead he asked if she was hungry. She answered no, and they sat in silence for several minutes, listening to the comings and goings out in the hallway. Her mind spun in all directions.

"Where's Nate?" her dad asked, pointing to a picture of the boy on his board.

"He's with Miss Cora, Dad."

Nate came running in with Miss Cora hot on his heels, laughing. The boy stopped on a dime. Recognition mixed with anxiety crossed his face. He must've noticed the old cranky man was awake.

Leslie called to him, "Come here, Nate, say hi to Gramps."

Her father sat up and put on his best smile. "Come here, boy," he said to Nate.

Leslie stood, then took Nate by the hand pulled him toward the bed. The boy wouldn't look at him. Richard didn't understand why Nate was being disrespectful.

"Nate, look at me, please."

Nate strained to get away from him and from his mom, pulling in the other direction.

"Nate," Leslie said, gritting her teeth, "Gramps wants to say hi to you."

It took all she had to restrain him. The boy yanked even harder and whined. Leslie glanced at her dad, apologetically. Kissing him on the cheek, she grabbed her purse and was dragged toward the door.

"It's no use," Richard said. "I don't want to be around me either." She knew he was making a joke, but his eyes said he was only half kidding.

"Sorry, Dad. We'll be back next Wednesday, okay?"

"Leslie?" He pushed up to sit higher. "Remember, life isn't worth anything unless you have loved someone with your *whole* heart and been loved in return."

Leslie's mouth gaped open and for once she didn't mind at all that Nate was pulling one arm off. She stood frozen staring at her dad, while a smile tugged at her lips.

He'd quoted from a sign her mother had made. It'd hung in their nursery, over their crib when she and Anne were born.

Chapter Sixteen

Terrified.

The word didn't even scratch the surface of her emotions at 3:30 that Saturday morning. Most of California slept in peaceful darkness while Leslie snaked through long lines for LAX airport security.

She hoped her breakfast didn't make a reappearance. She'd read all about air travel online and knew what to expect; she had makeup and hair products in the appropriate size containers, worn comfortable slip-on shoes, and her laptop was tucked neatly in the top of her carryon. Her ID and passport matched perfectly. Nobody in airport security would suspect her identity was altered.

She stood like a felon in the security tube. Bare feet planted firmly on the footprints and her arms overhead as they instructed. It wasn't the first time she felt like a criminal. Her knees trembled. How much of her body could the guards see? Alarms had already sounded once when she'd forgotten to take off her watch. A female officer looked less than pleased to search her with a wand. *Rookie mistake.*

Gathering her belongings, she contemplated buying multiple tiny bottles of alcohol, if only for takeoff and landing. If she heeded late night Google's advice, these were the two scariest times for first-time fliers.

Walking toward her gate, she checked her phone for the hundredth time. No Charlie. Her heart and mind waged war with one another. Her heart wanted at least a shot, but her mind knew it wasn't possible. Her heart was currently in the lead. In a moment of weakness, she texted him last night, but he hadn't responded. It took twenty minutes to craft four words. *"Have a safe flight."*

Who was she kidding? Beside the fact his friend was a psychopath, she didn't have time to learn how to be a girlfriend. She had a career to worry about.

The flight crew boarded, then all passengers entered the jetway by zone. LAX was by no means deserted, but based upon the people waiting at the gate, this would be an empty flight.

Her muscles were tight as a banjo string as she rolled her small carry on toward the ticket counter. This was it. She breathed a sigh of relief as she rounded the corner onto the plane. An overly perky flight attendant, who must've drunk multiple shots of espresso, stood inside the door greeting passengers.

Once past, she stared down the long death tube. She pulled at her collar. The cabin was hot and dry, as if all the cool air had been pulled out and replaced with desert heat. Walking the plank along the narrow passage, her gaze fixed on the tiny reading lights illuminating yellow triangles in the semi-darkness, Leslie found her seat in a dim and empty section, all alone.

After shoving her carry on in the overhead bin, she was struggling to secure her seatbelt when the flight attendant strode down the aisle, making a beeline for her. The woman's face had changed from perky greeting to frustrated.

Oh, God. This was it. They knew.

"Miss Carroll?" the woman demanded.

"Yes?" Leslie's voice cracked.

"I need for you to come with me."

Leslie's legs wouldn't move. After a beat, she stood, straightened her cross-body purse and moved like molasses into the aisle to re-open the overhead bin. She grabbed out her carryon but her shaking hands lost control of it and it barreled toward the floor. She caught it awkwardly and lowered it.

Her mind raced. She'd be fired because she couldn't drive from California to Tennessee in two days. Or could she? Oh, right. No, she couldn't because she'd be in jail for using a false ID. God, what would happen to Nate? His identity would be compromised, too. Why did she take this stupid job? There had to be a way out of this.

The flight attendant marched to the mouth of first class and turned, waiting for Leslie to catch up. They'd stopped the inflow of passengers, so she could get off.

Security, she was sure, waited with handcuffs right inside the jet way. The flight attendant continued through the first-class cabin and off the plane. Leslie followed, wondering how far she'd get if she ran.

Inside the jetway stood two dark-suited men with security earpieces and stern looks. When she faced them, they sprang to action; one man grabbed her carryon and shot out the side door, down the metal stairs, and on to the tarmac, while the other took her elbow and escorted her down.

Maybe this was how they treated you when you faked an ID and got on a plane? If so, it was awfully cordial.

A few feet away sat an airport golf cart. They'd taken her luggage off the plane and it was tucked into the back seat. The first suited man waited at the wheel while the second helped her navigate the last few stairs, then placed her in the back seat and handed her ear protection.

The driver pushed the gas, jerking the golf cart to life. He sped around the sleeping commercial planes. Neither man said a word. Someone should be handcuffing her. Or at the least, reading her rights.

Her fear turned quickly to annoyance. "Wait…where are you taking me?" she yelled toward the front seat.

The man in the passenger seat turned and mouthed the words, "Private jet."

She wasn't being arrested; she was being hijacked. "I bought a ticket for that plane!" Leslie yelled, pointing toward it as it disappeared in the shadows of the early morning.

Ignoring her, the driver made several turns between parked planes. As they rounded the last one, a well-lit, luxury jetliner came into view. White ground lights pointed upward, illuminating the plane's shiny blue and tan stripes. The plane was immense, new, privately owned, and obviously expensive.

When the cart stopped, the two men sprang to action, carrying everything except Leslie's purse. Her carryon was handed to a man standing in the doorway of the plane wearing a tailored short black jacket and matching bowtie. He looked like a kind-eyed butler.

Leslie shuffled toward the red-carpeted stairs. This had to be a mistake. No way PRP would ask her to purchase a ticket only to have her removed to a private jet. As she climbed the stairs, a flurry of commotion caught her eye inside the lighted interior. Two flight attendants fluffed pillows, added blankets, and busied themselves making coffee.

The well-appointed interior smelled like new leather. From the walls to the carpet, the jet was clean, bright, and breathtaking. Plush, cream-colored chairs and couches anchored one side, while a long, sleek dining table stood on the other side. Each of the back corners held an expensive, muted flat-screened TV showing the morning news, flanked by a pillowed bench.

She took a few cautious steps inside. Her gaze darted from pilot to smiling co-pilot to butler-looking-man to two flight attendants. She shook their hands, cleared her throat, then directed her questions to the butler. "There's been a mistake. I'm supposed to be on a commercial flight. Do you—"

The echo of an angry voice rang out. Charlie's angry voice.

Her head snapped toward the back of the plane.

Legs spread slightly apart, chest out, and anger drawn tight on his face, he spoke through gritted teeth into his cell. His chest and arm muscles were taut and outlined by a crisp white button down and expensive, dark-gray dress pants. She couldn't tear her gaze away. Mid-sentence, his gaze locked on hers, and he stuttered. A quick smile of recognition crept across his face then he returned his attention to the conversation. Her breath caught in her chest.

Shut up, heart. She was angry.

Never taking his eyes off her, he growled one last time into the phone, "Sorry…Kat. You know what? I don't care what Jonathan says, I won't be answering his questions until I get a script that's viable. I'm not signing on to a hypothetical project. If he sends me the script, and the stats on timelines and pay, I'll speak to him. Until then, no. Hey listen, I gotta go, we're taking off. …Okay, text me when you get something. Thanks."

Leslie's eyes narrowed. She shot daggers through him with her stare. The air around her was stuffy and thick. The flight crew quickly dispersed to their stations leaving them alone.

She should've known. He had balls—of that she was sure. Before she could sling scores of angry insults tumbling through her mind, he spoke.

"Now, friend…" His expression pleaded as he stashed his phone and threw his hands in to the air, as if he was calming a spooked horse. He crept toward her. "Just wait… I have a perfectly sound explanation."

"Erickson," she said, teeth bared, "why did you have me taken off my plane?"

"Well…" he hesitated, "truth is, it'll take us about two hours instead of four to fly to Knoxville in this new beauty." He patted one of the oversized leather seats as he crept closer to her. "And because there's a time change, we'll lose a few hours. We've got a few errands to run when we land. Think of it this way, though, you've been upgraded."

He flashed his million-dollar smile and sat in a luxury chair as if it was perfectly normal to kidnap a person off a commercial flight. She ran both hands down her face. He didn't even think he'd done anything wrong. The click of the door latching behind her made her jump.

He held out a hand for her to take, which she stared at like it was a bomb. "We're about to taxi. Come sit."

The butler drifted up out of nowhere behind her. "Madam, I

hate to press you, but you must sit and fasten a seat belt. Shall I assist you?"

She ignored them both, then pointed a finger at Charlie. "I want off this plane. Right now. I want you to get me back on the flight I paid for."

Charlie ran a hand through his hair and pointed out the window. Her plane taxied to the head of the runway, fired up its engine, and began its run toward takeoff.

Leslie snarled. The butler cleared his throat behind her. There was no choice. She turned and smiled politely. "I'm sitting. Thank you."

She chose a short row of two seats next to the window, on the opposite side of the plane from Charlie. The plane rolled in reverse as Leslie buckled herself in. She didn't have time to think about the infuriating man; she needed to concentrate on breathing. Why didn't she buy alcohol?

She needed to stop the movie playing in her mind, where the plane couldn't take off and crashes at the end of the runway. She glanced around to make herself aware of the exits, acutely conscious of the ultra-handsome Hollywood star watching her the entire time.

Navy carpet, with a silver diamond pattern cut through it, looked as if nobody had ever walked on it. A string of tiny, white lights illuminated the walkway. Two massive, tan leather sleeping chairs sat behind her. On a small table next to her was a wine list and menu. She picked it up and thumbed through it after yanking on her seatbelt to ensure it was tight.

Placing the menu back down, she closed her eyes and forced her heartrate to slow.

The plane jerked into drive and pushed forward. Her body came to attention as if someone had inserted a rod in her back. Her phone buzzed. On instinct, she dug it out of her purse and glanced at it. A message from Charlie, sitting only a foot away.

At first, she slammed it face down on her lap. Not reading it. Damn him. Pulling her off her flight and panicking her like that. Who does that? She stared at the back of the phone until curiosity got the best of her. It wouldn't hurt to read one text before turning her phone off and ignoring him the rest of the flight.

Chin high, she read, *"It's 5am. How can you look so beautiful?"*

Heat spread across her cheeks. She clicked off her phone and stowed it back in her purse. Out the window, the darkness of early morning was pierced by flashing lights on the wings. With the interior lights dimmed, the reflection of Charlie walking toward her carrying his suit jacket made her heart flutter. She closed her eyes once again.

Heart one, mind zero.

The seat next to her moved. She opened her eyes and watched Charlie toss his sport jacket on the row in front of them and buckle himself in. He spoke as soon as he sat. "Look, I'm flying east, and you're flying east. You never know who you're gonna have to sit next to for a cramped five-hour commercial flight."

Charlie nudged her with his elbow as a smile played on his lips. Her very-recent favorite cologne filled the air. "This way, you get to sit next to someone you like instead of a random stranger."

Leslie turned and snapped, "What makes you think I *like* you?"

He chuckled, then stared deep into her eyes. Yeah, she liked him. God, how fast he could make her uncomfortable and giddy at the same time.

"What's not to like?" he teased. "Please don't be mad—I had good intentions."

The plane halted abruptly. The engine roared. Digging her nails into the arm rests, she willed her stomach to calm. Eyes closed. *Just breathe.*

Her seat jostled. She could feel him staring at her.

"Are you okay? Good God, you're pale. Are you sick… Wait, are you afraid to fly?" He didn't bother stifling the low chuckle humming in his chest. Her eyes flew open. She glared until he wiped off his stupid grin and cleared his throat. "Here," he held out his right hand, "give me your hand."

Her eyebrows pushed together as if he'd lost his mind. She didn't need his condescending attitude. She was determined to do this with no help from him, thank you. She tilted her head back and concentrated on breathing.

Charlie intertwined his right hand with her left. He disregarded the agitated look she shot him and closed his eyes, slanting his head back too. "Now, I want you to forget we're about to take off in a huge hunk of steel where one wrong move from the half-drunken pilots will land us in a pile of dust at the end of the runway."

She yanked her hand free and groaned.

"Kidding—I'm kidding…stop." He took her hand back and gripped it tighter. "Lean back," he instructed, before he brushed a dark strand out of her eyes. "Close your eyes." For once she did as he asked, but only because she was concentrating. Charlie rubbed the back of her hand with his thumb in a soothing rhythm. "Just listen to my voice."

Her heart pounded as if she were waiting to be shot out of a bungee jump ride. The massive engine roared to life. The noise doubled, and the plane thrust forward. Its force rammed all her organs toward her spine.

She didn't mind Charlie holding her hand. The plane lifted off the ground effortlessly, and her stomach dropped. She gripped his hand tighter.

"Hey," he said. She opened one eye. "We made it...we're in the air. Wanna see?"

Opening both eyes, she squinted at a flicker of the early morning sun rising on the left. Releasing Charlie's hand, she pushed up on the arm rest for a better view of the California landscape falling away. What an amazing sight. The plane climbed higher and higher. It pitched to the left as she leaned over Charlie to peer out the other windows. She caught herself from falling face first into his lap. What a klutz. Her face flushed hot.

A minute later, the plane leveled out, and the captain turned off the fasten seatbelt sign. The long-legged flight attendant scurried up. She seemed more interested in staring at Charlie than taking their order. To his credit, he didn't seem to notice.

Leslie ordered water while he ordered two mimosas. She slid him a look. "You must be thirsty to order two drinks."

"Nope, one for each of us, to celebrate."

"I don't drink mimosas."

"You want something else?" He turned as if to flag the flight attendant.

Leslie touched his arm. "No, I mean, I like them, I just don't...drink in public unless I can watch them make it." She winced as soon as it came out. Sounded pathetic even to her own ears.

He glanced over, eyes hooded as if he was figuring her out. "You worried someone will spike your drink?"

She raised her eyebrows, and he scratched his chin. "Hmm. How about this, when she brings 'em back, we switch. You get mine, and I'll get yours."

Truth was, it all came down to trust. Did she trust him? She locked on to his sincere face waiting for her reply. Finally, she nodded.

When the flight attendant returned, she placed a mimosa in front of each of them, along with Leslie's water. When she left, Charlie switched them.

He sipped his drink and smiled, nodding toward hers. She took a healthy sip and made a bitter face. His drink was too strong. Miss Legs obviously wanted him drunk.

She placed the mimosa back on her tray table, reminding

herself to sip, not gulp.

Charlie did the same with his. "How long have you had a fear of flying?"

She shrugged. "Forever, I guess. Never flown before today." She didn't look at him, knowing he'd have a smart-ass comment to say. But he didn't. She snuck a sideways glance. He looked out the windows ahead, an odd smile playing on his lips.

"What?" She sounded defensive.

"Nothing." He pointed to her drink, lifting his. "Let's celebrate your first flight."

She clinked glasses with him and took another sip. Charlie drank his and pulled out his phone.

"No matter what pompous title you hold, I don't believe texting is allowed while in flight."

His eyes danced, then he propped one leg on top of hers and gave her a smoldering look over the top of his phone. "I always get what I want, Miss Carroll. Haven't you figured that out by now?"

Shaking her head, she shoved his leg off. When he lowered his phone she shot back, "Not in my world. I *always* get my own way."

Charlie finished his text, shoved his phone back into his suit pocket, then stretched out his legs. After a second, he stretched his arms up and grinned. "So, you ready?"

"For what?" Her voice squeaked.

"A game…you a lefty or righty?" He jerked his chin toward her hands. She raised her right hand and shook it. Charlie nodded and held out his left hand toward her left hand to shake. She shot him a questioning look but turned toward him and shook his outstretched hand.

The butterflies must have enjoyed the mimosa, because they fluttered in her belly. And they were liking his touch. Or the mimosa. Or both.

"We're gonna play twenty questions," he announced with a devilishly beautiful grin. "Rules are you can only pass on one question the *entire* game—so use it wisely, and each time you ask a question you have to take a drink. If you let go of my hand or I let go of yours, we have to take a drink together."

She let go of his hand, "No. I don't…I don't like this game."

He shook his head and raised his drink. "Honestly, at this rate, Leslie, we'll never get to know each other, and we'll have to be carried off the plane." He grinned and took a swig. Lord, he was beautiful. Putting it down, he held out his left hand again.

Leslie exhaled, took a drink, then slammed it back on to the tray table. "Fine," she said curtly grabbing his hand. "Go."

Charlie smiled. "Good. Now, let's see…Oh, I got one. Are you parents alive, and if so, where do they live?"

'That's two questions," she pointed out.

"Fine," he conceded.

"Pass."

"Pass?" he said, smiling.

"Pass."

"You sure? My questions only get tougher from here. In fact, this one's a relatively tame one."

"Shit," she said under her breath. "Okay, so my mom died when we were little, leaving my dad to raise my sister and me. He lives in Palo Alto in a nursing home with Alzheimer's."

~ * ~

Charlie drank and placed his glass back down. He studied her. No wonder she seemed so alone. What would life be like without his mom? He closed his eyes and shuddered. He couldn't tell if the shudder came from the warmth of her hand or from her admission. When he opened his eyes, she nodded toward his drink.

He straightened and took his second.

Leslie's eyebrows furrowed as if she was conjuring up the most uncomfortable question to ask. "So why would you stay with someone mean and nasty like Christine, when you clearly didn't love her?" Satisfaction crossed her face. Looking smug, she sucked down her obligatory drink.

Charlie was stunned. Damn, she asked a tough, honest question straight out of the gate. He shifted in his seat; pressing his lips together, he looked her dead in the eyes. His answer would be precisely as honest. This was the opportunity he'd been waiting for.

"I thought I loved her…for a very long time. She was kind at first, but much more selfish and cunning toward the end. She used me when she wanted the attention, and when she didn't, she ignored me." He hated the pity written on Leslie's face as she listened. "I followed her around like a lost puppy until recently."

He took a swig of his drink. The warm effects spread through his body like lava. "Then, when I met you in the dressing room, you changed me. You didn't look at me like a movie star. It was like you saw the real me and not the famous actor everyone else does. I realized I'd been holding on to her for the wrong reasons."

Leslie's expression turned from pity to something else. Stunned? Or maybe she hadn't expected an honest answer. Mousy herself sat silent for a long moment staring into his eyes, until he scooted closer. Their eyes locked and their faces were close enough he noticed her breath hitch.

When he spoke his voice came out like a whisper. "I knew. When you called me a pompous windbag as you left the dressing room. Then again, when you walked toward me, full of confidence, and refused my lunch invitation. It wasn't that you turned me down. It was the way you didn't treat me like everyone else does. You put me in my place when I needed it."

His gaze locked on to his own hand, moving slowly toward her face. She followed his line of sight, then nodded. Light as he could, he cupped her cheek. Her skin was soft like a newborn calf. She trembled as her eyes closed. Out of fear, he pulled his hand back, but she caught it in hers and placed it back on her, leaning into the touch.

He had to get this out. She had to know how she affected him. He took a breath and continued, "You make me laugh and frustrate the shit out of me at the same time. You're one of the strongest and yet most fragile creatures I've ever met. I know I gotta go slow because of the sadness in your eyes. Someday, I hope you'll tell me. But until then, I want to spend as much time together as we can."

Charlie focused on her mouth. God, the urge to kiss her surfaced again. She smelled like soap and lotion and heaven. It took every ounce of focus not to kiss her deeply and run his fingers through her soft hair. He knew better. Touching her that way wouldn't just spook her, it'd drive her away. She'd then believe he was the big Hollywood player, bringing a girl to his jet to join the mile-high club.

He released her cheek then straightened up as her eyes flew open. "I think if we'd met in college, my life would be very different right now."

An internal battle raged across Leslie's face. She grabbed her mimosa as if the drink was water after being stranded three days in the desert. Her gaze never wavered from his as she slugged back the rest of it. He was proud of himself. He'd told her.

When she placed her glass back on the tray, she took in a deep breath, then exhaled. She pointed so he'd continue.

"All right then. Next…" He pondered for a moment. "How many boyfriends have you had?"

This was the question he expected her to pass on, but her mimosa was apparently beating down her cautious side. By the smug stare she shot him, he was sure she was well on her way to being spectacularly drunk.

"Zero," she said matter-of-factly.

Charlie almost spat his drink. "Zero?" he shook his head. "Not possible, right?"

~ * ~

Leslie laughed, which calmed her nerves. "Take two drinks, Erickson. This one counts for two."

He lifted an eyebrow and scrutinized her over the top of his glass. If she could make up something spectacular up on the fly, she'd love to spin an impressive story. The truth was startling enough, but she'd settle for her canned lie with a little truth mixed in.

"I had a rough start in life. Knew I wanted to be a mom early, so I made the decision, contacted a sperm bank, and God gave me Nate."

Charlie openly stared, but finally he spoke. "So, no boyfriends…ever?"

She stared at her hands and shook her head. Embarrassed heat raced up her neck. Yes, she was a twenty-four-year-old virgin…but *technically*—not. A screwed-up enigma that most men wouldn't want to touch with a ten-foot pole.

When she glanced back up, she expected laughter or at least shock in his eyes, but found something vastly different. A look of kindness mixed with wanting…almost hungry in his gaze. Her stomach clenched tight. Her hand twitched from the electricity and he released it. Together they groaned.

They'd both have to drink again.

Charlie took his, then pushed his glass toward her since hers was empty.

Miss Legs must've had radar. She flipped back the curtain. Casually tossing her hair, she asked if they needed anything.

"Yes, another round, and could you bring us something to eat, too?" Charlie didn't take his eyes off Leslie when he spoke.

"Of course, Mr. Erickson."

Her head spun. Or maybe it was the plane—she couldn't tell which. Thank God, Charlie ordered food.

"Next," he announced.

Leslie leveled a look at him, took his drink and swallowed slowly, giving her time to think. She wanted to learn everything: what he was like as a kid, was his family nice, and did he have any brothers or sisters—but somehow all those questions made her seem like a fan. She was sure she could get on one of a dozen fan websites and learn who he was on the outside. But she wanted to know things nobody else knew. She wanted the inside.

After a long minute of silence, she blurted out the first question that came to her fuzzy mind. "Tell me about Jason Gilreath."

Charlie stilled. His eyebrows shot up, then he shifted in his seat. "Jase and I have been friends since the seventh grade. When his father couldn't take care of him, he came to live with my family. We moved to California together, so I could pursue acting and he could go to law school. He's my oldest friend."

His tone sounded defensive. After taking another swig, his gaze shifted to stare out the window.

"But?" she prodded.

"But nothing. He's my friend, and he's been accused of some shit I don't believe he's capable of, that's all." Charlie bit his lip. "The thing is, and you can't tell anyone, but I heard that when they raided his house, they found plans to kill someone on his computer."

Leslie inhaled sharply and held it for a second. Her voice barely a whisper, "who?"

He looked at their joined hands. "Me."

When he glanced up, she must've looked horrified. He released her left hand and threw both hands up in surrender, then he added, "But Jase said it was all a set-up from a cartel family. He put away their only son last month for drug trafficking."

"And you believe him?"

"I don't know." Charlie shrugged. "I know the kid I grew up with didn't hate me. He pulled me out of a whole host of tough scrapes and defended my sister against bullies. He was part of my family."

Leslie stared at his drink. *My God.* How could he be so naïve? His friend was a monster. A monster she could never turn in. The scandal alone would've ruined her father's chances to gain the nomination for judge.

She was positive Charlie had zero idea what kind of man Jason was.

His words hung in the air. Miss Legs' counterpart strolled in with a tray of toast, eggs, fruit, and more mimosas. Before the flight attendant could set the food down, Leslie stood, looking for the restroom. She needed space. She spotted the sign at the rear of the plane.

A much longer walk to clear her head would've been nice, but this wasn't a cruise ship. Excusing herself, she walked down the aisle. Her legs were wobbly either from Charlie's admission, talking about Jason, or the mimosas. Her one focus—*don't stumble to the bathroom.*

Once in the bathroom she secured the door and leaned against the sink, staring at the woman in the mirror. Her face was flushed from the drinks and the proximity of Charlie.

What was she doing? She couldn't be crazy about someone like him. Someone *in the spotlight* and best buddies with the man who took her innocence away? And how could she tell him she lived a lie every day? Panic squeezed at her throat.

She needed to get herself and Nate as far away from Charlie Erickson and Jason Gilreath as possible.

But now that she knew what was on his computer, what if Jason came after Charlie? He wouldn't see Jason coming. He'd be blindsided by an attack because he believed his friend cared for him.

Some dream job. Let's see—so far, it landed her a first glimpse of attachment and heartbreak and plopped her right in the middle of her worst nightmare. She sat on the closed lid of the tiny toilet with her head in her hands.

Before the end of this trip, she had to convince Charlie to protect himself. She didn't want to worry about him after she disappeared. She'd have a hard enough time not thinking about him. And that shocked her.

Her heart must've somehow silently cracked open enough to let him in. *Shit.*

Stay focused. She needed to figure out a plan to start over in California on Wednesday. Maybe they'd move upstate. The idea alone thoroughly depressed her.

After a moment of feeling the bathroom spinning, she stood up, splashed water on her face, then dried it. She licked a finger and swiped it under each eye, fixing her smudged eyeliner. Charlie's words came rattling back into her head, *"I think if I'd met you in college, my life would be very different right now."*

Perhaps, if they met the first day of college, *before* the disaster, that would've been true. She was a different person then—fun, flirty, and carefree. Oh, but still with her smart-ass attitude he was drawn to. Maybe they'd have hit it off, but had they met after the first week, he'd have discovered what happened… what she did. And he would've run. Any smart man would've.

Leslie scooped cold water from the faucet and swished it around in her mouth. That mimosa was way too strong, and she blamed her unusually big-mouthed comments on it. After drying her hands, she took a breath and swung open the door, then yelped as she ran into Charlie's chest.

Concern etched his face as he stood watch on the other side. "You okay?"

She held a hand to her chest. "You scared me."

He watched her carefully. "Thought you were escaping by squeezing your tiny self through the toilet hatch."

She turned and headed back down the aisle, then called over her shoulder, "I'd push *you* out of the plane before I'd go."

Charlie chuckled, then passed her and took her seat closest to the window.

The scent from the warm food made her stomach grumble. Dang, was she hungry and tipsy.

He dug into the food and finished before she did. Hopefully, the food would stave off the headache that was coming.

Two fresh mimosas sat on the trays. He made a sign with two fingers indicating he'd already switched them and nodded. They finished their food, and she took a cautious sip, relieved to find this one had much less alcohol than the last one.

Maybe Miss Legs wasn't as hell bent on getting Charlie drunk, since he'd held another woman's hand the whole flight.

The other flight attendant took the plates and returned with two blankets, handing them to Charlie. Leslie looked from her to Charlie. He must have asked for these while she was in the restroom. He nodded at the flight attendant. Warning bells chimed in her head.

He handed her a blanket.

"Only an hour or so left. You'd better sleep—we've got a big day ahead of us." He lowered his seat, then his body, and closed his eyes.

Leslie tapped him. His eyes didn't even flutter, but the edges of his mouth turned up. She shoved him hard.

"What do you mean we? *I'm* going to my hotel to unpack. I've got to prepare for meetings and the dinner cruise tomorrow night." She might as well have been speaking to the dead.

"Nope," Charlie said, eyes still shut.

Leslie pushed hard on his arm, again. He opened one eye and grinned.

"Yes. I am," she declared. "I need the day to plan and put everything in order."

"You'll have plenty of time, trust me. We have a few stops to make before we head to the hotel," Charlie said before shutting his eyes again.

Leslie huffed and sat straight-backed for long minutes, staring forward until his rhythmic breathing, mixed with airliner noise, filled the silence. She turned to take in a good look as he slept. The upward curve of his lips and the hint of dimples made him seem peaceful and mischievous at the same time.

Conventionally handsome, his strong jaw and tanned skin made him look like the quintessential California boy. He had strong arms.

What if those arms were wrapped around her? Would the images return, or would her body melt into his?

Her gaze traveled to his defined chest. *Okay, stop.* What the hell? Her heart raced. She looked around. Nobody saw her ogle the man next to her, thank God. She fanned her face.

Pulling the lever, she laid her seat back, then slid down, careful not to jar him. Rolling to face him, she moved her body far away from his in the small space. Drawing the blanket up over her shoulders, she closed her eyes. Beside her, his cadenced breathing lulled her to sleep.

"There's more to life than getting into law school, Anne. And for once you should trust me and have a little fun, before you become a dried-up old hag, like Aunt Reva."

The tactic to shame her twin into going to their first college bar was working. Anne stomped around her sister, then shoved her legs into jeans.

"Swear to God, Linnie, if we get caught or something bad happens, I will never forgive you."

The scene in her mind shifted and changed. The musty stench of wet basement invaded her nose, followed by the smell of burning flesh. Hot, white electricity ran down one leg, burning as it raced to find an exit point. Her vision opened, clear only for a second. Long enough. A man stood at the foot of the bed. Surveying her.

A woman screamed. She bolted upright in her chair. Wide-eyed and heart pounding, she turned to find Charlie. He stared; panic lined his face.

"Honey, are you okay?" His voice was sleepy, unguarded, and southern.

"Yes." She slowed her breathing. "Who screamed? Is someone hurt?"

Her gaze darted around the aircraft. Nobody aboard except the flight attendants and butler man who stood at the rear of the cabin. All stared at her. *Oh, God, no.* "I screamed, didn't I?"

Charlie nodded, placing a glass of water in her hands. His arm raised like he wanted to rub her back, but at the last second changed trajectory. She focused on the seat in front of her. *Shake it off.* Memories had been flooding back for weeks, a little at a time, as if they were hinting at the future.

"I'm so sorry," she said. She took a taste of her water as tears pooled in her eyes.

~ * ~

Tremors rocked her body. God, he was shaking, too. She looked so frail. She took another drink before he took the sloshing water glass out of her hands. Everything inside him wanted to hold her and take this away, but he was afraid it'd hurt her more. When a tear made a run for it down her cheek, he could contain himself no longer.

In one fluid move, he lifted the small table separating the two seats and pulled Leslie next to him. A side hug. He convinced himself this was the type of hug you give to distant relatives and teachers when you graduate. She was bonier than he thought possible. He knew he wasn't supposed to touch her, but how do you console someone you care about who's hurting without touching them?

She squirmed at first, but then relaxed. "Erickson, I'm fine. It was only a bad dream. Really...I'm fine. Can you let me go, please?"

"No." He couldn't release her. Couldn't get the sadness out of his mind. Who had done things to her to make her nightmares that vivid? He shifted her closer. When she looked up at him with red watery eyes, his heart squeezed.

"Tell me," he pleaded.

She tilted her face toward his, begging. "It's nothing. I'm just..." She glanced down at her folded hands. A tortured struggle washed across her face. Did she trust him enough to tell him the truth?

"I've already told you," he said softly. "I won't hurt you, but you have to trust me."

Leslie sighed. "Old ghosts." She shrugged. "They haunt me in my dreams, nothing more."

This was only the tip of the iceberg, but at least she was finally letting him in. He gazed into her deep chocolate eyes and smiled. "Thank you."

The corners of her mouth turned up as she wiped under her eyes. Without thinking, he rested his chin on the top of her head and closed his eyes. Instead of stiffening up, her body relaxed even more into his. *Note to self. Top of the head is a safe spot.* He didn't want her to move away. He wanted to savor this moment.

She laid her head on his shoulder for a brief second, and he wished she'd wrap her arms around him and snuggle her face into his neck, but she didn't. Their quiet moment didn't last long. She wiped under her eyes again with the back of her hand then scooted over, back to her own seat.

~ * ~

The plane's descent was almost as bad as takeoff. Her embarrassing nightmare episode still hung in her mind. She grabbed her seat as the aircraft pitched hard to the left. Charlie grinned and offered a hand, which she took. Amazing. The tiny act of holding her hand, which was so foreign at first, now seemed natural.

A boom rang out from the floor, followed by a whine and cranking sound. Her eyes widened, then calmed. The wheels. Charlie was the epitome of cool. Head slanted back, eyes closed and goofy grin on.

She leaned back and followed suit. The plane touched down, jerking. Brakes squealed, and she squeezed both eyes shut. She was pretty sure she cut off the blood supply to poor Charlie's hand.

Charlie squeezed her hand then peeled his hand from hers. She opened one eye. He pulled on his jacket and sunglasses as the plane taxied toward the gate. "We're earlier than they expected. Hopefully, we'll get to the limo before the vultures with cameras get there."

"Charlie." She waited until he turned. "The hotel PRP paid for is right next to the airport. I don't need a car, I can walk."

He angled his head to one side and shook it. "I already told you. We have things to take care of, and then I'll drop you back off. Trust me, this once, okay?" He leaned toward her. "I promise."

She believed him. Her stomach wasn't tied in knots. And even though she wasn't in control, anxiety didn't overtake her. She trusted a man. Boy, that felt weird.

The doors to the plane opened. She gathered her belongings and strolled up the long walkway toward the airport. Following two large security officers, Charlie beamed beside her, his long legs slowing to match her shorter strides.

It was interesting to observe the faces of the travelers waiting for their flights. Only women appeared to notice Charlie, though most were playing on their phones or talking to one another. Except for a few cell phone snapshots, they passed through with little fuss. She was careful to look down as they walked side-by-side.

The end of the corridor connected to an escalator leading down to baggage claim and outside. Photographers with long-lensed cameras pushed each other on the sidewalk. They surrounded a blacked-out limo.

Leslie dug out her sunglasses, put them on then pushed strands of hair over her face. She couldn't be photographed with Charlie. If Jason saw, it might set him off enough to go through with his plans—whether Charlie believed it or not.

As they rode the escalator toward the glass doors, he cut his gaze toward her and smiled. He held out a hand, but she looked down at her full hands and shrugged. It was a good excuse, but even if they hadn't been full, she wouldn't have grabbed his hand. Not in public and not with cameras on her.

When she snuck a peek, that easy-going smile of his had

changed leaving a question in his eyes. When they reached the bottom, the photographers first followed Charlie, then like bees on honey, homed in on her.

An airport security guard took her by the elbow and led her through the gaggle of lenses, head still down. The noise level was shocking. Paparazzi yelled questions in her face: "Who is she? What's her name? Is she his mistress?"

Really? That one caused her head to snap up and glare. Only afterward did she realize they did it on purpose to get a better picture of her face.

Charlie's normal reserved, cool self, snapped. He shoved a few men out of the way, then pulled her away from the guard and toward the limo. Two men from the car sprang into action. One opened the door as Leslie and Charlie dove in, while the other grabbed their suitcases.

The two men struggled to get the bags in the trunk, but eventually slogged their way back into the car and navigated it through the photographers. She was hyperaware of the disappointment that rolled off Charlie. She could feel his body deflating. The thudding sound of lenses being shoved against the windows was the only noise.

He moved toward the open window separating the front from the back and spoke to the drivers, thanking them. His tone was clipped and tight. "Hey, Bill. How are ya?" He offered his hand to the older gentleman sitting in the front passenger seat.

"I'm well, Mr. Erickson. It's good to have you home, sir."

"Thank you." Charlie's voice sounded edgy.

He pushed the button to roll the window back up, then scooted next to her. He stared out his window, not angry, but he seemed perplexed. She pulled her sunglasses to hold her hair back, stole a quick glance his way, then touched his arm.

After a few beats, he turned toward her. His lips formed a thin line. "Did I lose you back there? Are we back to square one?" His arms were crossed, but his tone was forlorn not angry.

"What? No."

"Why not hold my hand? You didn't mind it on the plane. Why not now?" He paused, sadness filled his eyes, then he leaned toward her, clearly hurt. "Little strides with you, that's my goal. Don't send us backward—don't tell me now that we're out in the real world I can't...just don't push away."

His clear eyes bored into her soul. Her breath caught. The idea of his hands touching her made her blush. She was pulling away to protect him, wasn't she?

But if she was honest, this was also her defense mechanism, her protocol. Someone got too close, she pushed them away. That was the norm, and he'd already figured her out.

How could she tell him? He wouldn't possibly understand. She stared at the door panel as her mind spun. What was she so afraid of? Pain? She'd known her share of pain before, and more. Humiliation? Or worse?

The worst would be to fall for a man, then come clean about her life. Her lies. And watch that person leave. She'd never find that someone who'd love her unconditionally. Love her, no matter what she'd done.

"You wouldn't understand," Leslie grumbled, facing the window.

"You're right." He raised his voice as he said, "I wouldn't— because you won't let me in." Charlie turned again to peer out his window and added, "We have one stop to make, then you have about a thirty-minute ride to decide whether you trust me or not, because where we're going, there's no turning back."

Chapter Seventeen

Law school served Jase well today. How easy it was to convince his naïve boss of his innocence and to post his bail. But he had to concede his old life was over.

Even with the tough legal team his firm designated, the DA's office was inches away from indicting him, citing abduction and torture of the redheaded girl. They'd confiscated both his work computer and his home computer—his lifeline to the outside world—and his law firm had put him on administrative leave pending the outcome.

Worst of all, his best friend thought he was plotting to kill him.

Being locked out of his company didn't bother him half as much as what Charlie thought. Jase was released on bond to his ransacked home on house arrest. He sat in dirty sweats, watching mindless entertainment TV, while mixing his coffee with vodka.

They'd mentioned Charlie right before a commercial break, alluding to pictures of him with another woman, and insinuating he cheated on Christine. Jason knew better, though. That's what being friends with someone famous was all about.

He already knew Charlie and Christine broke up. Knew it before the papers and the fat *Entertainment Weekly* guy did. He'd done it to be with a woman with a kid. Dumb move, in his opinion.

The pretty blonde reporter sitting behind the desk turned her head and read dialogue from the monitor.

"On location for his next film, Charles Erickson was spotted with a woman who wasn't his leading lady. Is he cheating on Hollywood's sweetheart? Cameras caught the pair in Knoxville, Erickson's hometown. This comes on the heels of images of him handcuffed in connection with an attempted murder by his best friend, Attorney Jason Gilreath."

Jason squinted when cameras panned across the young woman's face. He dropped his alcohol-laden coffee on the expensive Persian rug, not moving a muscle to clean it up.

Air became thick and foggy around his face. Tears stung. It wasn't possible. Her hair was dark, but otherwise the same as when they met in the market. She looked thinner, but there was no mistaking those eyes.

His jaw dropped. Something inside him snapped, audible as if the room had creaked. Visions he blocked out rushed in. Naked women. All redheads. Prostitutes like his mom. He punished them like he always wanted to punish her for leaving. For choosing drugs and sex over him.

His arms shot up in the air. Rage raced up his chest and settled in his throat. He screamed at the TV.

Why? If she was alive, why hadn't she come to find him? She loved him. He had no doubt about that. Sure, he'd taken her like all the others, but then she molded to him. She'd spoken kindly and talked to him. She'd been the only person in the world who tried to redeem him.

Now, she must have been lured with the novelty of Charlie's fame. Sweat beaded on his forehead. He wanted to throw something heavy at the TV.

Maybe he hated Charlie Erickson after all. Not only was she alive, she was with *him*.

Jason pinched the bridge of his nose. The headache was coming again. This was all his mother's fault. Always had been. If she hadn't been such a useless piece of shit, hadn't been addicted to drugs and hadn't taken everything he and his dad had, maybe he wouldn't be in this predicament. Maybe he'd be like Charlie—happy, popular, and famous.

But Charlie had always been the lucky one. He had a damn Hallmark Channel family who loved him.

Jase stared at the TV as his thoughts nipped at the increasing ache in his head. The one thing, the only thing he wanted for himself, Charlie had taken.

He was the reason Jase's life was over.

He'd only played around with killing Charlie, but now...now he'd do it.

She'd see the light, once he was dead.

Chapter Eighteen

A ten-minute drive from the airport put them dead center of the University of Tennessee. The iconic Sunsphere, which separated downtown from campus, glinted, making her squint and pull her sunglasses off her head to cover her eyes.

College students with overstuffed backpacks spread out like ants traipsing up and down small mountains to get to class. She'd bet none of them got the freshman fifteen. Then again, she and her sister hadn't stayed in college long enough to gain those pounds, either.

Charlie hadn't looked her way, nor said a word. When the driver pulled up in front of the East Tennessee Children's Hospital, Charlie got out, walked around then opened her door. With a resigned look on his face, he held out a hand to help her out of the car. When she stood upright, he let go.

A stab of disappointment hit her chest. He didn't offer to hold her hand, and it was all her fault.

The driver handed Charlie a bulky bag from the trunk. She wrapped her arms protectively around herself and followed him inside.

One suited man and two prim, business-like women greeted them inside the door. They shook hands and exchanged introductions. The man was the Chief Administrator and the women were heads of HR. A young photographer was also introduced. One of the women volunteered to be their guide.

As they ambled down hallways painted with colorful blocks and childlike numbers, the nursing staff and parents whispered and gasped at the sight of Charlie. Most people didn't expect a movie star to stroll through a hospital.

Their guide announced that Charlie would be visiting rooms with sick kids today, beginning on the top floor. They walked off the elevator and into an expansive playroom filled with books, toys, and children in hospital gowns. Parents lined the walls as the patients all played in the center of the room. A few of the littles had masks and others had no hair.

Charlie breezed in, kneeling like he'd done with Nate. These kids seemed tiny and frail and their faces were aged. Leslie's heart tugged. Most were too young to know who he was, but the parents did. Opening the bulky bag, he produced toy after toy, hugging them and sitting on the floor to play as they crawled all over him.

She gaped in awe. She had to remind herself to close her mouth—twice.

Ten minutes before they had to move on to the next wing, with his sights trained on Leslie, Charlie whispered with a five-year-old girl. Her smile alone could light up a nation. She wore a bright pink scarf around her naked head. And her bluish-green eyes were the color of the sea.

She listened intently as he spoke into her ear, smiled, then made a beeline for Leslie. The girl grabbed Leslie's hand and pulled her to the middle of the room, then yanked her down to sit cross-legged amid a group of girls, who sat on the brightly colored rug next to Charlie.

Surrounded by Barbie doll boxes, Leslie began opening them. Pocket sized patients swarmed all around her, talking, sitting in her lap and playing with her hair. At their request, she braided Barbie's hair and opened packages of doll clothes. The pink-scarfed girl commandeered her lap and helped hand out clothes to the others. She talked non-stop.

Leslie's knee accidentally brushed Charlie's. Playfully, he caught eyes with her then looked down his nose at their touching knees. He reminded her of Mr. Miller and acted as if her touching him was scandalous. Leslie lifted her chin high and rammed his knee with hers again, smiling. Charlie grinned back. He tickled, gut-laughed, and used goofy voices as he played trucks with the boys. Parents snapped pictures right and left, but he didn't seem to care or even notice. He wasn't there for the fame. He was there for the kids.

When the guide told them it was almost time to move on, Charlie hugged and spoke with each child. Leslie's heart cracked open another inch or two inside that room.

Next, they were led down the hall and onto an elevator. Charlie's face had softened, but he still didn't reach for her hand. They stood side-by-side, arms so close they were almost touching, when Charlie playfully elbowed her.

"Stop smiling," he said, staring ahead and grinning widely, like her.

She shook her head, then commanded her lips to curve down, but they wouldn't. "Nope. This is too much fun."

Charlie nodded and nudged her a few more times. She nudged

back. Ridiculous. They were acting like two elementary school kids with a crush.

The elevator opened, and their guide took them down several more hallways. These were painted with geometric shapes in purple, green, and orange. Inspirational quotes were scattered every few feet.

They slowed as they came upon a massive room. Judging by the loud murmuring, broken only by the occasional laugh, she guessed it was a room full of teenagers. A man's voice quieted them, then announced why they were gathered. A hush came over the room. Charlie slowed his pace, took a breath, then he stepped in.

The noise was deafening. The teen girls' high-pitched screams made Leslie want to turn around and go back to the smaller kids. She hung back with the guide while Charlie spoke to the crowd of sick teenagers.

Out of his bag, he pulled three new, not-yet-available-to-the-public gaming systems with four controllers each and a stack of games. He handed them to a crowd of lanky boys at the back of the room. They cheered, then rushed toward a long wall where a giant TV was mounted next to the windows.

Charlie stared at the girls and smiled—all Hollywood charm. He asked if they wanted to do pictures, after seeing over fifty phones pointing toward him. The girls squealed and selfies with Charlie were snapped all over the room. Group pictures took forever as each one wanted it on her phone.

At one point he caught Leslie's eye and mouthed the word "Help." Grinning, she shook her head.

When they finished with the teenagers, they traveled down another set of hallways toward a new area of the hospital being built. The hospital administrator met them next to a doorway covered in heavy plastic.

Leslie and Charlie were given hard hats. They toured the new wing and were introduced to several crusty-looking board members, who softened immediately when Charlie cut up with them. A copper bench with an engraved sign above it was covered in clear plastic. It read: The Erickson Wing, donated by Charles Erickson in honor of his parents Tom and Pat and especially his big sister, Frances.

The hospital photographer wanted to get a picture of Charlie with the head of HR and the board members shaking hands in front of the sign. Leslie stood behind the camera perched on a tripod. She smiled as the photographer positioned them perfectly so the sign, the bench, and the people posing could be captured in the photo. That was until Charlie messed it all up by moving out of the picture and holding his hand out for Leslie.

"She needs to be in this one, too," he announced, as he waited for her to take his hand.

She shook her head. "Charlie, they need this picture to be you and them," Leslie pleaded.

He stood his ground, stock still and extending his hand. He pinned her with his eyes. It was her decision. Did she trust him? Fear held her back. Then again, fear had held her back since that awful weekend in college.

Leslie set her jaw, smiled at him then took his hand. The grin he volleyed back at her could've lit up a town. Charlie loosely wrapped his left arm around her. The photographer didn't seem to mind that he had to rearrange everyone. He squeezed Leslie even closer to Charlie to get a better view of the plaque. She melted into his side. It almost felt normal. Except, a warning shudder ran down her spine.

As the picture snapped, Charlie shook hands with the head of the hospital. Everyone smiled, except Leslie. She hadn't thought this all the way through. The picture would not only be in the local paper, but since it was Charlie, it'd be spread worldwide.

Her stomach churned. She'd exposed them both to danger without realizing it. And it was all her fault since she hadn't told him yet. This was what happened when she thought with her heart instead of her brain. God, this was bad.

~ * ~

Twenty minutes later, their car turned from the interstate onto a two-lane back road, flanked on both sides by farms and trees.

Leslie cracked the window for much-needed air to focus. A crisp spring breeze cooled her forehead. Not a cloud above them disturbed the pale blue skies that blanketed lush green mountains on either side of the road. The size of the houses ranged from stately manors, to old farmhouses, to worn shacks and trailers. Farms, mostly cattle, horses, and corn, littered the roadside as the mountains spread out. Fields of green grass went on forever.

She glanced over at Charlie. Would he still want her if he knew the truth? She scolded herself for yet another mistake she was about to make. She leaned over and grabbed his hand, intertwining their fingers and whispered, "I'm in." His eyes widened as the corners of his mouth crept up. She raised her index finger. "But…I need to go slow."

Charlie nodded, then drew her hand close to his mouth and waited. When she nodded, he kissed her hand.

As they rounded a hard curve in the road, a long, white, wooden fence on the right side of the road came into view. The driver turned on his blinker, as Charlie squeezed her hand.

"Just one warning," he deadpanned, "they're huggers."

They who? The car whined, trudging up the long driveway bordered by white fencing. Two beautiful horses munched on grass next to the driveway. At the top of the hill stood a grand, white two-story house with a wrap-around porch. White icicle Christmas lights hung lazily from the gutters. The driveway curved around to the back of the house.

Bill tilted his head back toward Charlie. "Do they know you're coming this time, sir?"

Charlie beamed. "Dad does."

She dropped his hand. Panic rose in her throat. *His parents?* Her gaze darted from the house to the fields. She opened her purse, pulled out lip gloss, then applied it with a shaky hand. She straightened her shirt and picked a few stray fuzzballs off her pants.

Meeting his parents? They barely knew each other. Why would he bring her here?

Just as the car stopped, Charlie touched her hand. "You look perfect. They're gonna love you. One warning, my sister is—"

"Charwie!"

Leslie turned. A heavy-set woman squealed with delight. She wore pink My Little Pony pajama bottoms and a green T-shirt that read "My dog is smarter than your honor student." When she saw Charlie, she lumbered around the side of the house and picked up what looked like a brightly colored bazooka filled with water.

Charlie whispered theatrically, "Whatever you do, do *not* get out of the car." Charlie let out a whoop and darted out the door with his hands in the air. "Sissy, you wouldn't hit an unarmed man, would ya?"

The woman giggled and turned her body at the perfect angle so Leslie could get a good look. Her wide, toothy grin lit up her entire face and made her already petite eyes appear even smaller. Her gait when she ran was awkward, and she giggled loud with every step. Sandy blonde hair like Charlie's bounced in a ponytail atop her head. Her deep green eyes were a stark contrast to Charlie's blue ones and yet the exact same shape.

Sissy peered inside the car and smiled another magnetic grin, which Leslie returned. Then she stalked around the car toward Charlie as the driver got out and unloaded the bags.

The girl watched Charlie, her gun at the ready. He ducked down, then ran and snatched the water bazooka out of her hands and sprinted toward the house. Sissy squealed again, laughing and chasing him toward a garage attached to the house by a portico.

Leslie stepped out of the car, stretched then walked to the edge of the driveway. The fresh air was intoxicating as she sucked in a deep breath. This felt nothing like the thick air of California. Chilly wind from the top of the rolling hill cut through her sweater. She hugged herself and surveyed the landscape.

The view was so clear, she swore she could see for miles in all directions. Tree-lined ridges flanked lush, green fields, separated only by a stream or occasional valley. It was a breathtaking view that overtook her mind. She'd pitch a tent right there to wake up to that every morning.

"Beautiful, isn't it?"

Leslie spun. A stunning woman with a worn face and Charlie's clear, blue eyes had crept next to her. Leslie'd been so enamored with the view, she hadn't noticed. The woman's expression was regal yet kind and inviting.

Leslie nodded, then gazed back out at the mountains. "Yes, ma'am. I'd sit out here all day, if I could."

The woman put her hand out. "I'm Pat. Pat Erickson, Charlie's mom. Please call me Pat or Mom. Actually, I answer to just about anything."

"Leslie. Leslie Carroll. Charlie's…friend." Leslie shook Pat's hand.

Pat smiled. "Good to meet you, Leslie." Then she leaned close and whispered, "You're the first 'friend' he's ever brought home."

Leslie blushed.

Behind them, a clicking sound made them turn together. Charlie, with his water gun tucked under his arm, had his phone out snapping a photo of them. When he got caught, he grinned wide, then shoved the phone in his pocket just in time. Sissy squealed and ran toward him with the water hose.

"Mom! Make her stop!" Charlie yelled.

Pat wrapped her arm around Leslie. "Sissy, don't pick on your baby brother. He's fragile, and he's brought a girl home."

Sissy stopped mid-run, dropped the water hose, then marched over to where Pat and Leslie stood. When she got close enough, she came to a halt, put her hands on her hips and said angrily, "Who are you?"

Leslie took a step back. "I-I'm Leslie. I'm your brother's friend. It's nice to meet you," she stammered.

Sissy's face exploded and in one fell swoop, she picked Leslie up, hugged her and said, "Welcome to the family!"

Charlie had to ask Sissy three times to put Leslie down, stating she wasn't a toy.

Pat hooked elbows with Leslie and led her toward the house. Calling back over her shoulder, she said, "Charles Thomas, bring in the bags while I show our guest to her room."

His grin told her he'd known his mom would insist they stay.

Leslie caught his eye and shook her head. She couldn't stay with strangers! What would her boss think? What about her hotel reservation?

Lord—to sleep in the same house as Charlie. The man who looked and smelled decidedly male and awoke feelings she'd never had. *Thank you but no.* That would be a disaster. She'd have to find a way to decline without offending anyone.

He shrugged as if to say, 'good luck,' then ran back to the car, thanking Bill and the other driver and sending them on their way.

Leslie took a deep breath, then said, "Mrs. Erickson, thank you for the invitation, but I should stay at the hotel my company provided for me."

"Well, dear, let's assume you stay for the afternoon. I'm sure Charlie will take you back whenever you like. Or first thing tomorrow." Her eyes twinkled.

Great. New plan. Stay for a few hours, get to know his family, thank them, then call an Uber.

They entered the house through a squeaky, screened backdoor that led into a remodeled farmhouse kitchen. A man, presumably Mr. Erickson, sauntered in wearing red-plaid pajama pants, house shoes, and a worn-out T-shirt. He held his newspaper at eye level.

He didn't notice Leslie as he flopped into a worn chair at the kitchen table. His reading glasses slid down on his nose, but he didn't seem to care. He was way too engrossed in the paper. He was shorter than his wife, but not by much. Charlie got his strong jaw and dimples from the man, but unlike Charlie, he was dark-skinned and dark-headed with flecks of gray in his hair.

Pat glanced over at Leslie then pointed toward Mr. Erickson. Leslie shook her head and shrugged. *What did she want?*

Pat mouthed, 'coffee cup,' then nodded toward the coffee pot and winked. Leslie padded over and picked up Mr. Erickson's coffee cup, then walked to the pot, and filled it with steaming black coffee. She set the cup in front of him and waited.

He folded his paper without looking up and grabbed the cup. "Thanks, honey."

Leslie answered, "You're welcome."

He froze mid-sip, then slowly tipped his head up toward the

voice and laughed. "Well, hello there." He lowered his cup then stood to shake her hand. He searched Pat's face for an answer with eyebrows up as if to say, 'who is this' but Pat only shrugged. She seemed to delight in her husband's current state of confusion.

"Uh, I'm Tom and you must be…"

Charlie swept into the back of the room and grabbed his dad from behind, around the shoulders lifting him off the floor before Tom finished his sentence. "Don't even think about it, old man."

"Charlie!" his dad exclaimed, turning around and hugging his son. "So good to have you home, son."

Tom embraced Charlie, tight. An odd tingle of jealousy ran down her spine. He had a close family who loved him. He glanced over. A look of understanding crossed his face.

He bounded over and stood next to her. "Dad, this is Leslie. Leslie, this is my dad."

Tom Erickson walked toward Leslie with his hand out, but when he reached her outstretched hand, he tugged her out of Charlie's grip and hugged her.

"Nice to meet you, Leslie." He fist-bumped Charlie behind her.

Tom then held her at arm's length to examine her. Her face flushed hot. She'd never been hugged this much in her life.

"Dang, boy, she's pretty!" Tom announced. "Skinny little thing, though—Charlie, don't you feed her?"

A whole new wave of heat raced up her neck.

Pat moved toward Leslie and held out her hand, which she was grateful for and took. Pat walked between Tom and Charlie drawing Leslie along behind her.

His mom said to the men, "Boys, lunch will be ready in thirty minutes. Go play checkers while I show Leslie to her room."

Scuffling broke out between Charlie and Tom as they laughed and shoved each other out the back door.

Once she rounded the corner heading up the stairs, Pat released Leslie's hand. Pictures of Charlie and Sissy at every age lined the stairwell. Most were of them together, posing, playing dress up, and riding horses.

"Part of the reason Sissy is so advanced, despite having Downs, is because of Charlie. Even at a young age, he was able to take information that was difficult for Sissy and break it down into pieces she could understand. She was the one who convinced him to go to Hollywood and make a living as an actor. You have any brothers or sisters, dear?"

"I have a twin sister," Leslie said, touching a picture of Charlie in high school absentmindedly. Then she corrected herself. *"Had* a twin sister."

Pat put a hand on Leslie's shoulder. "I'm sorry, dear. When did she die?"

"When we were nineteen." Her voice was no more than a whisper.

His mom watched her for a beat, then changed the subject. "Come on up. I'll show you to the guestroom."

The guestroom was bigger and nicer than Leslie's bedroom at home. Calming pale-gray walls with white trim were inviting. Yellow accent pillows brought a pop of color to the king-sized bed. Handmade, thick, navy satin curtains framed a huge window seat with an oversized cushion.

Books lined the built-in shelves on either side of the window. Leslie's suitcase and carry-on were stowed in a corner of the room. Just beyond a walk-in closet was a Jack-and-Jill bathroom which led to another bedroom.

Pat walked through the bathroom and shut and locked the opposite door from the inside. From the quick glimpse, the room looked like a boy's bedroom. Charlie's bedroom. Now Leslie *knew* she wouldn't be staying. No way she could sleep or, nightmare in her case, with him sleeping a few feet away.

Pat left Leslie to unwind for a few minutes.

She sat on the edge of the bed and kicked off her shoes, then grabbed her phone and texted Aunt Reva to check on Nate.

Reva reported Nate had eaten all his breakfast, which made Leslie relax. The boy had a bad habit of refusing to eat when anything in his schedule changed. But she told him about the trip several times, hoping he'd have no issues. The cars Charlie brought him the night of his baseball game were now his constant companions.

After ending the call with her aunt, Leslie looked around the room. Okay, so she'd eat lunch with his family, have some conversation, be gracious and grateful, then excuse herself and call an Uber. She could do this.

Leslie scooted onto the bed and rested her back against the headboard. Between getting only a few hours of sleep the night before, mimosas and nightmares on the plane and the full morning, she was worn out. She lifted her phone and began checking emails from PRP. When she read the same sentence through drowsy eyes three times, she gave in. A ten minute siesta wouldn't hurt. Leslie recited the same mantra she used at home. *No bad dreams, no bad dreams,* then drifted off to sleep.

~ * ~

Charlie and his dad argued playfully over imaginary, non-regulated moves. His mom brought mason jars full of sweet tea out to the porch. Smitten, his dad thanked her and smiled broadly. He loved that his parents still adored one another. He longed for a relationship like theirs.

As usual, his mom, hands on hips, got right to the point. "Charles Thomas. Why haven't you returned our calls? We've been worried sick about you and about Jase. Why didn't you tell us you were coming home? And why didn't you warn us you were bringing someone with you? Did you know the woman they found inside Jase's house? How is he?"

Charlie swallowed his tea and set it aside. "Jase is back home under house arrest. His firm is working to clear his name. I'm sure they'll find out who's framing him."

He moved a checker and shot a smug look at his dad. "Leslie works for the production company of the film we're shooting this week. She's a costume designer."

His mom laid a hand on his shoulder. He looked up. "I'm sorry I didn't call, but you always said, you'd rather me be home than anywhere else, right?" He fluttered his lashes.

She shook her head and smiled.

"Mama's boy," Tom said under his breath.

"Pansy," Charlie retorted.

His mom took a deep breath and continued, "So...she was a twin?" she asked, eyebrows up.

Charlie stopped smiling as he searched her face and took in her meaning. He stared at the table then back at his mom. "Was?"

Pat nodded.

"I think I'll go check on her," he said patting his mom on the arm.

~ * ~

Charlie bounded up the stairs, two at a time. He tapped on the guestroom door before opening it. She was curled up in a ball, asleep. He crept back out into the hallway and took a blanket off his bed, then snuck back in and covered her. She stirred a little but didn't wake.

Kneeling next to the bed, he gently moved a strand of dark hair off her face. Her skin was so pale. She had no idea how beautiful she was. He stroked her cheek with the back of his knuckles.

Why hadn't she told him she was a twin? Even worse, she told his mom and not him. They'd met less than an hour ago. Who was he kidding? He'd only met her a week ago.

"Why won't you talk to me?" he whispered, not expecting an answer.

Her eyes flew open, then darted around in panic as if she was trying to remember where she was. A few seconds of alarm, then she locked on his face and exhaled. "Your family is great," she mumbled, groggily. "And now I understand why you have a hard time not touching people."

Charlie nodded and snickered. Her eyes held his for a moment, then she looked away.

~ * ~

No nightmares, thank God. She looked into Charlie's eyes. They held regret mixed with pity.

She knew this was coming as soon as she opened her big mouth and told his mom. Shock had flashed across Pat's eyes. These were the little details Leslie rarely shared with anyone, on purpose and no matter what. Why in hell had she told Pat?

Leslie searched Charlie's eyes, then shifted to his strong jaw. A face the whole world knew well. When she first saw him, all she noticed was his movie star persona. Now, he was just Charlie. A normal, handsome, kind guy who acted like a goof around his family.

At some point, she'd need to tell him the truth about Jason. He needed to know, to protect himself. Could she do it? He'd never look at her the same. It seemed her life was all about sacrifice.

She cleared her throat and began, "My twin sister died right after Nate was born. She battled for several months with unchecked and undiagnosed stage four breast cancer. We're identical—well, we *were*. When we were small, our dad couldn't tell us apart if we dressed alike, which we did pretty often just to frustrate him."

Charlie smiled—a goofy grin, yet sympathetic.

"What?"

"Thank you," he said, his voice cracking.

"For what?"

"Sharing something with me—that's real."

Just then, Pat called everyone to lunch, loud as if she was calling in the herd from the field. Leslie startled and stilled, but Charlie only stood and stretched like this was normal. It was a little after one, and even though her body was on California time, she was hungry.

After lunch, Mr. Erickson volunteered to do the dishes. She attempted to help, but he wouldn't hear of it. He handed her a jar of tea, turned her, and gently nudged her toward the back porch swing that overlooked the basketball court where Sissy and Charlie were horsing around.

"Young lady," Charlie's dad said, sounding stern as he walked toward her carrying his own jar of tea.

"Yes sir?" She stopped swinging to listen.

"You didn't eat much." A twinkle of humor gleamed in his eye as he watched her. Then he sat next to her on the swing. Mr. Erickson let out a sigh. "My son...can be intense, I know, but he's a good man with a kind heart. Don't hurt him, and he'll be yours."

Leslie sat stunned, unable to breathe deep. Why was he telling her this? This was the surest way to get her to run. Her heart swelled and yet felt foreign. Hope grew in her chest, but then her brain reminded her of the truth. This relationship wasn't possible. She willed her heart to slow.

After a long silence, his dad spoke again. "Leslie, I shouldn't have butted in. I apologize. Charlie's never brought a girl home, so I assumed... I didn't mean to overstep my bounds. Forgive me?"

She turned and shot him a kind smile. "Of course, Mr. Erickson, no harm done."

"Call me Tom?"

"Sure." She nodded.

Charlie strode up and made a beeline for Leslie. No shirt, he glistened with sweat, his face flushed and gloriously sexy. Something about the way he looked at her made it hard to breathe. Placing his hands on the seat of the swing, he leaned into her as if he was about to kiss her.

She froze, head tilted as far back as possible, staring as if he'd lost his mind. Using the distraction, he grabbed Leslie's tea out of her hand and gulped it.

"Sorry," he offered, shooting her a half-apologetic look.

"Help yourself," she replied sarcastically.

Charlie grinned, walking backward and shaking her tea at her. He winked at his dad when he challenged her. "Think you can take it from me, then be my guest."

Leslie leaned forward, gripping the swing and getting her feet under her.

"Is that a challenge, *Mr.* Erickson?"

His Hollywood *Sexiest-Man-Alive* smile came out in full force.

Shit. She didn't exactly have on running shoes, but the old spunky her never backed down from a challenge.

The instant Leslie darted toward him, he let out a high-pitched squeal, turned and leapt over the banister and steps without touching one. She scampered down them two at a time and rounded the corner after him. Charlie's dad's laughter echoed on the wind.

"Give me back my tea!" She yelled at the beautiful, shirtless man running in front of her.

Jogging past the basketball court and onto the sloping grass, Charlie yelled back, "You said to 'help myself' so I did. Honestly, Leslie, you say one thing and mean another."

She groaned, then dug in closing the gap between them. Thank God, just beyond a small patch of trees Charlie got winded and slowed his jog to a walk. When she caught up to him, he held her tea high over her head and walked backward, grinning like he'd won. After a few minutes of looking like one of those yappy little jumping dogs, she crossed her arms in defeat and walked past him.

It was then she noticed a looming red barn, she hadn't been able to see from the driveway. The closer she got the more in awe she was of this place.

Out of the corner of her eye, she saw that Charlie had sidled up to her and stopped. He watched her and beamed with pride. She rolled her eyes at him then snagged her tea back. After a sip, and with her chin high, she gaped at the landscape. The sun cast short shadows over the expansive, yet neatly trimmed red barn. She'd never seen anything so beautiful.

Charlie hadn't even turned his head to look at the barn. His eyes were on her. And he stood close to her, inside her bubble. Only this time, it didn't bother her at all. In fact, she'd have been completely comfortable with her hands on his bare chest. Or maybe on his face. No, wait…in his hair.

Stop. What was she thinking? Whatever it was, it made heat crawl up her neck and land on her face.

"Hey, *ginger,* let's get you out of the sun, you're turning pink." He smiled down and touched her on the nose.

No way she could look at him or his drop-dead gorgeous smile.

Chapter Nineteen

After salvaging a dusty, slow CPU from his basement, Jase combed the internet. He clicked the buy button and waited. He'd found the exact shirt and jeans she wore the night they met. He was glad he'd taken the time to memorize the tags in her clothes. It was something he routinely did back in college. Couldn't remember why. But now he was too set in his ways to perform such menial tasks.

A drag off his joint, and he was invincible.

"There you are." He blew smoke at the screen as he scanned the electrical parts website and waited for a page to load.

When it did, he squinted, then found the voltage meter he'd been looking for. He'd use a higher current this time. To train her, like Pavlov's dog. He'd have her salivating and coming every time he rang a bell or in this case, every time he fired up the machine.

He leaned back in his chair, aroused, as he hit the buy button once more. Everything would ship overnight to the remote property in Tennessee. He was pleased he had the foresight to set up accounts and property in a different name.

He still had her shoes hidden in a locked box under one floorboard. It also held pictures of most of the girls he'd taken since her, too. He already ordered the cord he wanted, hair color and makeup that would make her look exactly as she had before. His plan was taking shape. For the first time in years, the familiar pull of anticipation ran through him.

Jase looked around the room: vodka bottles, roaches, trash, and half-eaten food everywhere. Shit, he didn't care. He wouldn't be living in this hellhole anymore. He'd need to make one more call before his flight to get her back.

Chapter Twenty

The barn was newer than the house and majestic in size. If she hadn't been so embarrassed by her thoughts, she'd have been awestruck.

Lazy rolling fields flowed away from the barn. Whoever built it had placed it in the perfect middle of the property. A honeysuckle sweetness floated on the cool breeze that kicked up.

Once she finally had the courage to look him in the eye, Charlie raised his eyebrows then strolled through the barn's massive arched doors. Doors big enough a semi-truck could fit through them. Off to the left, the only other outbuilding was a quaint chicken coop.

Curiosity made her follow. When she rounded the corner, she found him waiting for her reaction, again beaming with pride. The inside was immaculate and grand. The two-story, eight-stall masterpiece housed the most beautiful horses she'd ever seen.

She strolled toward a sweet-eyed brown mare on the right. All the horses had nameplates on their stalls. This was Lady, and next to her were Pumpkin, Max, Fiona, and four more she couldn't read.

That trademark horse scent, for Leslie, brought back memories of her sister. The hay looked fresh, but somehow soft, as if you could lie down on it and nap. Antique oil lamps, tacks, saddles, and rope decorated the walls. Benches sat between a few stalls in the wide hallway. The second story had a loft where she spotted a TV and a couch.

Charlie fingered a saddle as he spoke. "Built this for my parents five years ago. The land rolls perfectly for horses, but there was no barn. They dreamed this up, drew plans, and I had it built. The loft was for me. So I'd come home and relax between movies." He ran a hand through his hair. "I don't get out here as much as I'd like, though."

His whole face glowed. This was obviously home. He glanced over and caught her watching him.

She cleared her throat. "How many acres do you have here?"

"Ninety-two," he said as he walked over to a horse named Max and rubbed his nose. "They bought extra in case Sissy or I wanted to build a house. I have thirty or so picked out to build my own horse farm later, or a summer house for when I settle down. Do you ride?"

"A little."

"Come on."

He held out his hand, and for once, she didn't hesitate. She took it and walked with him to prepare two horses.

Bent over, Charlie explained the parts of the bridle and the history of the saddle, while strapping them onto his horse. Without looking up, he said he'd help her mount her horse when he was finished. After cinching his saddle, he stood to move toward her, and stopped. Leslie was mounted, feet in stirrups and stroked Lady.

Charlie shook his head. "And you let me drone on about the equipment?"

Leslie laughed. "Why, Mr. Erickson, you say one thing, but mean another. You ready to ride or you want to give me a thirty-minute dissertation on the history of the horse?"

His eyes narrowed as a smirk crept up his lips. "Okay, smart girl. Just a tip—try not to get lost." He nodded toward the door. "Hypothermia is a real threat in these mountains. Nighttime temps in the spring drop to around thirty. So as your official tour guide, you'd be wise not to piss me off, or I might accidentally lose you—on purpose."

She shot him her best smile. "We won't be gone that long. Some of us *work* for a living and need to get to our hotel. So get moving, old man. Lady and I are ready."

He narrowed his gaze, with his lips upturned. Girding up the last few straps on his horse, Max, he whispered something in the horse's ear before climbing on.

Leslie patted Lady. She'd noticed early on the ridges in the horses teeth and the way they jetted outward. She was an older horse, but still strong and silky. She'd kept one eye on Leslie from the first moment she walked into the barn.

Filled with wonderment over the endless open fields, Leslie made a kiss noise and Lady walked out into the sunshine. Leslie turned in the saddle toward the house and squinted. The top of the roof was barely visible. When she turned back, the expansive fields in front of her took her breath away. Visibility was endless. Everything was painted in Crayola Kelly Green. The smell of an earlier rain mixed with cool leaves made the smog in California seem like breathing paint-chip dust.

There was nothing like this in any of the cities where she'd lived.

Charlie and Max strode up beside them. Charlie leaned over and handed her a pair of sunglasses. She took them, gratefully, and placed them on her face. Charlie stared a beat too long, then cleared his throat, made a sound and he and Max took off.

Leslie squeezed her legs together and made a kiss sound. Lady walked, then sped to a trot, on to a gallop, and finally to a full run, chasing Charlie and Max.

Leslie grinned wide. She hadn't been on a horse in years. It felt good. Really good. And brave. Charlie and Max were stopped just before a small patch of trees, waiting. Charlie's face at first looked concerned, but quickly turned to amusement as they came closer.

~ * ~

She could handle herself on a horse. And she wasn't afraid to go full speed—well, at least on a horse. He smoothed Max down as he waited for them to catch up.

He stared as she rode toward him. Something punched him in the gut. He liked having her here. With his family, in his house. She fit in here. Even if she didn't think so. When did that happen?

Riding up, pink cheeked and windblown hair, she couldn't have looked sexier. She flipped him off when he smiled, which made him laugh. Charlie turned and coaxed Max to a walk. Leslie followed with Lady.

When they reached the tree line, they got off the horses to walk. Going through the dense forest instead of around would shave thirty minutes off the time it took to get where he wanted. She was so calm and at ease around horses. "When did you start riding?" he asked.

"When we were about four, I think. My sister and I competed. I always wanted to wear a cowgirl hat and be a barrel racer, but my sister wanted to run dressage—jumping fences and wearing stupid costumes. She, of course, got her way. She was older, and the whole horse thing had been her idea."

"A cowgirl, eh?"

She smiled, then stuck out her chin. "I think I'd look good in a Roper hat."

Charlie bit his lip and nodded. "You would."

She glanced down at her hands, then back up. Her expression was grateful yet embarrassed.

He nodded toward a small lake at the north edge of the woods. They headed for it. After letting the horses drink, they tied them to a nearby oak tree. He produced a small plaid blanket from his saddlebag and tucked it under his arm as they ambled toward the water. It shocked him when she grabbed his hand.

Sitting shoulder to shoulder on the bank, they talked. The calm water sparkled and lit up her face. Out here, she seemed more at ease. Younger even. He learned a little more about her childhood, but not too much. She told him exactly what he assumed he could discover in public records.

Her mother had died when they were babies, and her father raised them all alone. He'd entered a nursing home a few years ago, when he began getting lost inside his own house. Leslie's tone told Charlie she carried guilt about it.

But she grew somber and quiet after talking about her sister's cancer. She'd taken care of her. Even held her hand and kissed her as she passed out of this world. He thought of Sissy. How shortsighted doctors said she'd never go to school, never live past twenty and never talk. She showed them.

Leslie said she carried a picture of her and her sister lying side-by-side in the NICU at Pomona General, holding hands. They'd come into this world only four minutes apart. And it was the only time they'd ever let one another go. When the tears in her eyes threatened to spill, she stood, picked up a small rock, and skipped it into the lake.

Charlie couldn't get enough of her. She was good at everything she touched. She could ride and argue, she loved the outdoors, and she could skip rocks even better than he could. But none of those reasons were why he was falling in love with her. It was the glimpses of light and the wonder in her eyes that made him dream of a horse farm and a family again.

His need to be near her caused his legs to move before his brain registered. He positioned himself next to her and stared out at the water.

The low growl of thunder off in the distance gave him pause. Storms rolled in super quick in the valley. Charlie ran over and untied the horses, while she scooped up the blanket. By the sound of the thunder, they didn't have much time.

She looked at the sunny sky above them, then back at Charlie as though he lost his mind. Lady neighed, picking up her hooves one at a time, dancing and tossing her head. Leslie handed him the blanket, then calmed her by speaking softly.

He was already on Max and trotting away when he stopped and turned. "You better hurry—you're gonna get soaked!"

~ * ~

Leslie laughed, hoisting herself into the saddle and taking her time. "What's wrong, pretty boy—can't get your hair wet?"

"Suit yourself," he said, turning Max toward the barn and

taking off like a shot.

She patted Lady. "We'll be fine."

The downpour overtook her and Lady not even halfway back to the barn. She was wet down to her underwear. The rain came so fast, it was as if someone turned a fire hose on her. And so thick, she had to slow the mare. When they rounded the last corner, and darted under the cover of the barn, Charlie and his dad were waiting for them, both dry.

Tom took Lady by the reins, so Leslie could climb down. She couldn't look him in the eye. Charlie came out of nowhere and grabbed her around the waist and guided her onto the ground.

"Not a word, Erickson."

"I wouldn't dream of it." He stifled a smile.

"Damn weather here," Tom told the horse as he led Lady back to her stall to dry her off.

"Your dad thinks I'm an idiot," she stated matter-of-factly.

"You're a California girl—you can't help it."

He wrapped a blanket around her shoulders. She shivered. The rain had brought with it a cold snap. A puff of smoke sauntered from her breath.

"You can change here," Charlie said as he led the way toward the loft.

As she reached the top, he squatted in front of a credenza and opened a few drawers. He pulled out navy sweats and black socks. By the way he turned them over in his hands, he didn't recognize them. He raised them to her, and she nodded gratefully.

Next, he held up a new pack of white briefs and raised one eyebrow. Blushing, she shook her head, scooped up the sweat suit and headed for the tiny bathroom.

Her teeth wouldn't stop chattering. She was cold to the bone. After locking the door, she caught a glimpse of herself in the mirror. *Oh, God.*

Makeup ran down in perfect semicircles underneath her eyes, and her hair hung in strings, like someone placed a dark used mop on her head. Perfect. With a click, she turned on the heater in the ceiling. She stripped her wet clothes off and spread them across the shower curtain rod near the heater.

A shudder ran through her—as much from the cold as the vulnerability. Quickly, as if she'd get caught, she used the blanket to dry her body, then pulled on the navy sweats and stared at her chest in the mirror. Nothing poked out, but only because she stood under the warmth of the heater.

Sleeves and pant legs rolled up, she took a last look. Her only saving grace was that navy was a good color for her pale skin. She fixed her face, finger combed her hair, before she helped herself to a spot of toothpaste.

Arms crossed so she didn't headlight, she came out of the bathroom and found Charlie sitting on the edge of a brown leather sofa, punching buttons on one of three remotes. Engrossed, he didn't look up when she walked out of the bathroom. Good.

She sat next to him, picked up one remote and inspected it. The batteries were in backward. She fixed it and turned on the TV in one quick movement. Charlie cut his eyes toward her with one cocked eyebrow. Leslie shrugged, grinning.

They sat back in unison. She hadn't gauged the space well and ended up too close. Their shoulders and thighs touched. Lord. She'd about sat on top of him. The heat radiating from him was inhuman. And for once, even though it was accidental, she invaded his bubble instead of the other way around. He glanced over and nodded as if to say, 'good job.'

Controlling the remote, Charlie seemed careful not to stop on the entertainment news stations. Probably didn't want to know what the world thought of him right now. That's why he had Kat. It was her job to worry about things like that.

The rhythmic drumming of rain hitting the barn roof combined with the hum of the heater and the warmth of Charlie's body had Leslie fighting to stay awake. He stilled when she rested her head on his shoulder and closed her eyes.

But like someone stuck her with a cattle prod, she bolted upright. She couldn't nap there. Her nightmares would slip out again. She needed to go to her hotel room. Needed to get organized. Charlie did too.

"What's wrong?" Charlie sat up straight when she did.

Leslie hesitated. The last thing she wanted was to offend him or his parents. She couldn't remember the last time anyone had been so nice. But there was no way she could stay.

Before she could answer, he rose from the couch. "You hungry? I'm gonna run up to the house and grab a snack and a few beers. Then we can watch whatever you want, 'kay?"

"Charlie," she exhaled, and reached for his hand. "This is great. Really. Your family is great. But I need to get to the hotel before it gets too late."

His face fell. Returning to his seat, he kept hold of her hand and took a long breath. "Wait. Listen, I promise you'll be fine. I'll even sleep out here, if it makes you more comfortable. Just please...stay.

From tomorrow night on, after the Riverboat Gala, we'll be working thirteen-hour days, napping for short spurts, and stuffing food in our mouths between scenes. That's how this part of filming is done. I want to spend time with you this afternoon before we have to get back to reality."

She looked at her slim, pale hand in his. It fit perfectly. She sighed. It did sound better to relax at his parents' house than sit in a stuffy hotel room. Leslie nodded. "Maybe. Can I give you a maybe?"

Charlie squeezed her hand. "Mom is making her famous lasagna tonight. You don't want to miss that."

He kissed her on the top of the head and jumped up, giving her no room to argue, then turned and bounded down the stairs. As he jogged through the barn, he grabbed a raincoat hanging on a peg and, pulling it on, he disappeared around the corner.

Leslie sat back, numbly flipping channels. As soon as the commercial was over, the female host of an entertainment gossip show stood on stage. A stock photo of Charlie smiling hung behind her. Leslie sat up and turned up the volume.

"On location for his next film, Charles Erickson was spotted with a woman who wasn't his leading lady. Is he cheating on Hollywood's sweetheart? Cameras caught the pair in Knoxville, Erickson's hometown. This comes on the heels of images of him handcuffed in connection with an alleged attempted murder by his best friend, Attorney Jason Gilreath."

The video feed was quick, not even five seconds, but any idiot would know it was her. Charlie's phone, face up on the trunk, buzzed. It showed three missed calls: one from Christine, one from an unknown number, and one from Jason Gilreath.

Leslie's became ragged as a shudder racked her body. She'd been so enamored by this place, she'd temporarily forgotten she couldn't be in this fairytale romance with this very famous man. Not when his best friend was her monster. That was exactly the reason she couldn't stay here, because of *him*. How would Charlie react if he knew the truth about Jason and about what she'd done?

Failing at holding it all in, she laid her head in her hands. The show continued to talk about Jason and the charges pending against him.

Everything she'd worked so hard to conceal and protect was out there in the open, exposed. If Jason had a brain, he'd know she was with Charlie. He'd come after them both. She got up from the couch to check on her clothes, but before she could get there, Charlie's phone buzzed again. The icon popped up indicating an incoming email from

Jason.

Curiosity got the best of her. She opened the app and read message. "Dickhead, since you aren't answering my calls, I've resorted to email. Be advised—the girl you're with isn't who you think she is. I'd like to meet. We need to discuss the case. I'm innocent of all charges, including whatever shit they told you they found on my computer. All lies. Call me. Jase."

"What are you doing?" Sissy's high-pitched, accusatory voice echoed in the barn.

Leslie slapped a hand to her chest and spun around. She bobbled and almost dropped Charlie's phone, but held it behind her back. Sissy stood at the top of the stairs, wearing a bright yellow raincoat and frog-covered rain boots. Her hands were placed firmly on her full hips, with the same overprotective angry look spread across her face, like it was when they first met.

"Sissy," Leslie said, out of breath, "you startled me. I'm watching TV. What are you doing up here?"

Sissy appeared to forget about Charlie's phone and smiled. "We're watching baseball at the house. Daddy wants me to drag you up there."

Leslie snickered at the girl's honesty. "Charlie's in the kitchen getting snacks. Why don't you go ask him?"

Sissy nodded, stomped over, squeezed Leslie, then bounded down the stairs. "Okay, bye!" She smiled before lumbering toward the opening in the barn.

Thinking fast, Leslie hit delete and returned the phone to its place. Her hand still clutching her chest, she jogged into the bathroom. Bra and underwear were still wet. She pushed them closer to the heater. Charlie's heavy footsteps on the stairs caused a moment of panic.

She sure hoped she'd backed out of the app on his phone.

He rounded the corner and put a tray of food on the trunk next to the remotes and his phone. He glanced up at Leslie, and their eyes locked. His gaze was intense. It told her he thought she was the most beautiful creature in the world. She'd seen a mirror. He must've done shots on the walk back.

His face took on a look of something else. Something much hotter. He shook his head then grabbed the remote, staring at the entertainment station for a split second before changing it back to football. "Snacks are here," he announced.

Leslie crossed in front of him and sat on the far end of the couch.

Charlie shot her a funny look. "What's wrong?" he asked.

"Nothing."

"Why aren't you sitting over here?"

"'Cause I'm sitting here."

"Bring your scrawny butt over here." He patted the couch next to him.

When Charlie opened the bag of chips and Leslie didn't move, he picked everything up and scooted it toward her end of the couch. When he sat, unlike her, he made sure they had space between them. He shoved a chip into his mouth and grinned straight ahead. Then he popped open a beer and tilted one toward her. She nodded, took it, then said, "*Expose Weekly* just ran a piece about Jason Gilreath."

Charlie fussed with the cheese and crackers, while his face contorted. Brief, but she caught it. He paused, she guessed, to consider his reply. "The more I think about it, the more I know he's innocent. It doesn't make any sense. He could've killed me a hundred times over growing up, but he never laid a hand on me."

"That was before you were famous."

"So?"

"Don't you think he's a hair jealous of your fame?"

Charlie scratched his head. "Maybe, but to consider killing his best friend? What would that solve? He's a lot of things, but a murderer—I just don't see it. He's harmless."

Leslie turned, placed her beer on the coffee table and gasped. "Harmless? He's unstable!" She stood and raised her voice. "Charlie, you can't be that naïve. This man is dangerous, don't you see? It's one thing to unintentionally harm someone, but to fantasize and plot it out on a computer? That's premeditated. And psychotic. Have you told your family about that part?"

She hadn't meant to flip out or yell, but it was her duty—no matter what happened to her—to protect him. His long-standing friendship blinded him. He couldn't see what was right in front of his nose.

Charlie leaned back, crossed his ankle over the opposite knee, and hung his arms on the back of the couch, grinning. "You worried about me?"

"Answer me."

"No." He shook his head, never breaking eye contact. "Why would I burden them?"

Leslie rolled her eyes. "He's been released from jail."

Charlie stared off and pondered that for a moment. "I'll tell them when I'm ready."

She cocked her head to the side. When he finally looked up,

she raised one eyebrow and smiled devilishly. "You'll tell them now, or I won't stay."

Checkmate.

Chapter Twenty-One

Charlie was right. His mother's lasagna beat any Leslie had ever had. Sissy entertained them with a round of stand-up comedy including verbally abusing her brother. Leslie's stomach muscles ached from laughter. This was the finest evening she'd had in a long time.

She and Charlie tag-teamed dishes. When the last plate was washed, she nudged him and slanted her head toward his parents. He smiled, goofy and oblivious. She elbowed him this time, hard. But he still grinned at her. He wasn't getting the hint.

"Tell them," she mouthed slow.

He wiped his wet hands on a dish towel, his gaze never leaving hers. Bending, he kissed her on the head. "Yes, ma'am," he whispered, sending shivers down her spine.

He strolled out of the kitchen and into the dining room. He asked his parents and Sissy to come to the den and sit. Leslie stood on tiptoes as she put away a plate and craned her neck to see.

He sat opposite them on the ottoman and spoke in a low voice. His family didn't move a muscle.

After several minutes, his mom jumped up as if something bit her. "Jason Gilreath!" She uttered his name as if it were a curse word. "I knew something was off with that boy." Pat flitted around securing all the windows, fluttering about like a lost bumble bee. "...raised him like he was my own after his cracked-out mama left him like trash."

She trotted into the kitchen and grabbed Leslie around the shoulders. Leslie stilled as the woman hugged her from behind. "Thank God, you had the good sense to make Charlie tell us." Pat released her and darted through the rest of the kitchen, checking windows and doors.

As Leslie turned, Charlie leaned against the door frame. An odd smile crossed his face. His eyes locked on to her as his mom scurried out of the room.

He sauntered over, and without so much as a word he stopped inches away from her. She could feel the heat rolling off his skin through his shirt. His hands were clasped behind his back as he leaned toward her.

"Thank you for making me tell them."

Leslie looked into his eyes. What if Jason hurt him? Tears stung. She'd miss him. She hadn't let herself dive into how much he already meant to her.

A sob that defied logic bubbled up in her throat. That's when her heart commandeered her mind. She wrapped her arms around his waist and buried her face in his chest. Charlie didn't move an inch. His heart thumped strong and fast under her cheek. She squeezed her eyes shut but no flashbacks came.

Being the southern gentleman he was, he never offered to move his arms around her. After a few beats, she let go, then stepped back, looking up at him. She raised one hand to cup his cheek. Her chest stung with breathing that felt like she'd just run a 5k. The tears that pooled were about to release.

The pity in Charlie's eyes, almost undid her. He began to speak but she put a finger to his lips, gave him a pained smile, and pulled away. She scurried from the kitchen, darted up the stairs then into the guest room.

Once there, she locked the door and rested against the wood. *Stop. You can't change the past or alter the future. It is what it is.*

Leslie paced the floor for a few minutes willing her heart and mind to slow. She took a few steadying breaths then wiped her eyes. She'd done what she could to warn them all. His family was on alert and so was he. If Jason came after him, he'd at least been warned. She considered leaving Charlie a note explaining her past. But that seemed like the chicken way out. And he deserved more than that. She couldn't dive into that now. Later.

For now, Leslie grabbed her phone, redirecting her thoughts to her responsibilities. Time to call and check on Nate. Sitting on the edge of the bed, with one foot on the floor and the other underneath her, she dialed. Aunt Reva answered on the first ring.

"Hi, honey." Her aunt's voice sounded exhausted. "Nate's doin' all right. He keeps asking where you are, and I hate to tell you this, but he started wheezing this morning."

Leslie bent over, pinched the bridge of her nose and closed her eyes. "Oh, no. Did you use the nebulizer?"

"I did tonight," Reva replied. "He finished right before a woman came to the door."

Leslie snapped upright. Hackles up. Nobody came to her house. Ever. "What woman?"

Reva took a breath. "Detective Michelle something. I wrote it down. Hold on."

As Reva scuffled around for the note, dread sank into Leslie's belly. Detective Majors might know more about her identity than she let on.

After she hung up, Leslie pulled out her laptop, fired it up, and emailed both Mr. Miller and Dana. She explained the normal rapid progression of Nate's past illnesses. Apologizing profusely for the timing, she alerted them she might have to fly out the following day. An ER visit with a child with autism wasn't something her Aunt Reva could handle.

Dana wrote back within a minute. Her eye was healing nicely, and she was scheduled to fly into Tennessee late Monday night, crutches and all.

~ * ~

Having Leslie in his house, but unable to touch her, was maddening. But, she'd hugged him. The willpower it took not to allow his arms to move around and cradle her made him feel superhuman. Afterward, he felt he could conquer the world. But it also unlocked a yearning. What would it feel like to hold her once? She was becoming his addiction, his drug.

Occupying his hands and mind downstairs was no easy feat. Mainly because he knew she was up there and everything inside of him just wanted to be near her. Even if they just sat in silence. He'd be fine for several minutes with his mind occupied, but then her footsteps would creak above him. Charlie tried sitting in his room and flipping through old yearbooks, but that brought on a melancholy mood. Most of the pictures were of him and Jase.

When the tinkle of her shower floated into his room, his mind wandered to her body. Visions of her rubbing his soap on her body, drove him mad. He bounded back down the stairs, needing air before he drove himself crazy.

Sissy was reading a book and listening to her iPod. His dad was cleaning one of his guns, as only a southern man understands when his world is shaken. His mom stood in the kitchen, arms wrapped around herself, staring out the window.

"Mom? You okay?" Charlie placed a hand on her shoulder.

"Oh, Charlie, yes, I'm fine…just worried. Will they put extra security on the shoot this week?"

"There's already a lot of security on set." He draped an arm around her. "It'll all work out. Dad won't let anything happen here, and I can take care of myself. I promise." He smiled at his mom.

Her face changed from worry to admiration. "I always knew

you'd succeed at whatever you wanted to become."

"Oh yeah, how?"

"When you were a toddler, no matter what you did, you put your whole self into doing it." His mom bent over to grab a speck of dirt off the floor. When she rose back up, she smiled.

"What?" he eyed her.

"You love her, don't ya, son?" His mother always had a way of getting to the point.

He shrugged. "Yeah," he admitted, suddenly self-conscious. "But it's early, and there's so much I don't know about her. She's guarded. It's gonna take time to get her to trust me."

Pat smiled. "I predict we'll see her again."

"If we're lucky." He kissed her cheek. "I'm gonna go for a quick walk around the barn," he said, unlocking the back door. He grabbed one of his dad's hoodies off the peg.

Pat looked alarmed. "I don't think that's a good idea, son."

"I'll be fine, Mom. A quick walk to clear my head."

~ * ~

Leslie checked the door between the bathroom and Charlie's room for the fourteenth time after wrapping the towel around herself. A hot shower was mandatory to focus her thoughts.

She had to tell him the truth, but her heart was too involved. He needed to know what she'd been through. To prepare himself for whatever Jason had planned. Her gut lurched. She'd never told a soul but her father. Even then, Anne had done most of the talking. Guilt had quieted her.

Charlie wouldn't want her after she came clean. Nobody would. But he'd be safer. And that was the important thing. There was no way this would end well for her heart. Then again, sacrifice was her life.

Dressed in slick baby blue pajama bottoms, white footie socks, and a white T-shirt, she brushed out her wet hair and rubbed lotion on her face. She could do this.

What if he didn't believe her? Or worse, what if he looked at her with different eyes. She couldn't take that. She gathered her things and laid out an outfit she could throw on, just in case.

She shuffled down the stairs. Hesitating, she looked again at the pictures. She'd grown today: from her first plane ride to hand holding, to meeting his family, to hugging a man. A man she was attracted to, which was the biggest leap of all.

When she reached the bottom of the stairs, a boom shook the house. She froze mid-step. In slow motion, her world stopped as

Charlie's father darted out the backdoor with a rifle. His mom screamed, and Sissy jumped up from her chair and ran past Leslie toward her bedroom, terrified.

Leslie ran toward the open door on instinct. She and Pat arrived simultaneously and rushed through to the outside.

As Leslie sprinted the worn path leading from the house to the barn, her worst nightmare flashed in her mind. Jase had found them and killed Charlie. She knew it. The only man she'd truly ever let into her life. And in an instant, he was gone.

Charlie's dad bellowed out a noise as if he'd run into a wall. Her lungs burned as she pumped her arms and sprinted ahead of Pat. As Leslie topped the hill to the barn, she saw two male figures standing toe to toe in the barn's floodlight. Her heart nearly raced out of her chest.

What if Jase recognized her? She didn't care. She had to find Charlie. She darted down the other side of the hill directly toward the two men.

Chapter Twenty-Two

"Damn it, Charlie!" his father yelled. "You scared the shit out of us!"

"Sorry, Dad, I wasn't gonna let that raccoon eat Mom's chickens. I grabbed the shotgun from the barn and aimed the damn gun in the air, for crying out loud. Sissy would have bawled for days if I'd shot that stupid raccoon."

Color seeped back into his father's face. Leslie and his mom barreled toward them. Leslie's face was pale, like she might be sick. She stopped short while his mother jogged until she reached her husband and son. She grabbed the two and hugged them tight.

Charlie looked over at Leslie while his mom held him. Her face was splotched. Her wet hair hung down in strands, and her socks were soaked brownish green from running in wet grass. She slumped over with her hands on her knees. He released his parents and walked over to her, hesitant and keeping a small distance, as if she were an injured wild animal.

When her head jerked up to meet his, he smiled and mouthed, "I'm sorry."

"It's okay," she whispered, her voice hoarse and laced with unshed tears.

Charlie shuffled closer. She straightened and reached for his hand. He ignored the hand, scooped her off the ground, and held her in his arms. This time, she didn't stiffen or complain. She melted into him, holding her arms around his neck tight, her feet dangling in the air. She leaned back to face him and muttered the one word that would change him, forever.

"Please."

Charlie's eyes widened. It took one look to know. "You sure?" he whispered.

Anticipation ran through him like lightning. Desire for her was more than he could bear. Every muscle in his body stood at attention all at once. Never had he been this attracted to a woman. Slowly, he placed her back on the ground and moved his hands from her waist, past her shoulders, up her neck and into her hair without ever breaking contact.

She didn't pull away, and he'd be damned if he'd stop until he was connected to her.

As if in a dream, faraway whispers of his parents walking around the far side of the barn floated to his ears.

Charlie's breathing slowed. He hesitated, taking in every inch of her face: her full pink lips, head tilted back, exposed taut muscles in her neck and her eyelids gently closed. He dipped his head closer and kissed her. Lightly at first. She tasted sweet and minty.

When low moans escaped her throat, he deepened the kiss. Taking his time. Exploring. At first, her kisses were guarded and stiff. Then, like the release of a gate, she flipped, wrapping her arms around his neck and fisting her fingers in his hair. Kissing him with her entire self. Her tight body leaned into his, arousing nerve endings in every muscle.

When a quake flooded through her, her body went limp.

He had to stop.

Pulling back, he held her. His gaze took in every inch of her face as she fought to regain composure. She swayed. If he were to let go, she'd fall. They both panted.

He waited for her eyes to focus. When they did, he smiled.

When she returned it, he felt like the luckiest man alive.

~ * ~

Leslie's head spun like a tilt-o-whirl. Her racing heart and jerky breaths were plain embarrassing. She never imagined she would've welcomed his hands on her. She placed two fingers to her lips where the pressure of his lingered. The longing for his mouth back on hers was frightening. She was as giddy as a young girl being kissed for the first time.

The visions. They didn't flood back. That alone shocked the crap out of her. She expected them to pour down over her like a cold waterfall. When they didn't, she let go. And when she opened her eyes, the most beautiful sandy haired, blued-eyed man she ever laid eyes on smiled ear to ear. At her.

Since that fateful first week of college, she'd been a prisoner locked in a glass box she couldn't shatter. Someone else had to do it. And if she was being honest, she hadn't been ready to come out. Until now.

Charlie had broken it into a thousand pieces and stomped on them. She couldn't wipe off her smile with a jackhammer. Brain be damned—her heart won this war.

In one swift move, he turned, crouched then hoisted her onto his back. She wrapped her arms and legs around him, then squeezed his shoulders to thank him. Her stocking feet were soaked, and her toes were numb from the cold.

Heat from his kiss and the muscular back touching her chest caused her to sigh louder than she meant to. He stilled and slightly turned his head as if to say, 'stop that.' She affected him. She nuzzled her face into the side of his neck, and he squeezed her legs into him. A throaty moan vibrated through his back, sending a zinging warmth to places inside her she didn't know even existed.

When the light from the back porch hit their faces, she heard him say 'uh oh' under his breath. Through the back-door window, she could see his mom frantically dumping out a drawer and searching through the contents as if whatever she looked for would save someone's life.

"Young lady, you open this door right now!" Charlie's dad yelled. Then louder, he yelled down the stairs, "Find that key yet?"

"No," Pat yelled back.

Charlie put Leslie down and sighed as they trotted up the steps and entered the house. "Sissy hides when she gets scared. I'll get her. Would you make coffee for my parents? They'll need it when they come back down."

Leslie nodded and gathered what she'd need to make a pot.

~ * ~

Charlie made his way toward her room. He pushed past his parents in the hallway and knocked.

"Go away," Sissy called out.

"Sis, I need to come in. Open up or I'll get a hanger and come in anyway," Charlie said.

"I'm not coming out."

Her muffled voice told him she was under her bed. He jogged down the hallway to Leslie's room. A shampoo smell from her recent shower lingered. He hesitated only a second, then grabbed a wire hanger and straightened out the hook. He hurried back to Sissy's room, put the straight end into the hole in the doorknob, turned it then popped open the door. His parents leveled a look at one another. Sissy's purple socks stuck out from beneath the bed. Charlie snaked on his belly to lie beside her.

"What'cha doing, puddin'?" he said in his worst southern accent.

Sissy smiled despite herself, then her face changed quick, regaining her anger. "Why, Charlie? Why does your friend want to kill you?"

She always understood more than he figured she would. "I don't know, sis. Maybe he's jealous or maybe he's just messed up. I don't know..."

"I don't want you dead," Sissy said very matter-of-factly. "Will you kill him if he tries to kill you, Charlie?"

He stared. Probably not. He wasn't sure he had it in him to kill anyone. Sissy edged out from under the bed, sweaty and covered in dust bunnies. They both stood, and she hugged him as he picked fuzz out of her hair.

"Don't die," she said, then walked past him to her bathroom.

His dad stood in the doorway gazing at his children, his eyes misty and his face solemn. "Boy?" His father's tone had a warning to it.

Charlie turned around. "Sir?"

"If it's between him and you, son, you don't hesitate. Shoot first. Ask questions later. You hear me?"

"Yes, sir."

Chapter Twenty-Three

Single-minded and persistent, Jason used the credit cards he opened in his cracked-out whore-of-a-mother's name in college. He had to hire a pilot. He'd be back in Tennessee around daybreak. The drug lines, electrical stems, and bindings were all packed. They need to be tested and re-secured enough to hold her. What a rush to place her naked body in compromising poses and record everything.

What if Charlie touched Anne naked? Had his way with her? Jason shuddered.

Or worse, what if she was now brainwashed to believe she was in love with him, like everyone else in the world? He'd need to kill Charlie in front of her. She had to know there was no future with him. Jason stood and paced.

Running fingers through his dark hair, he looked around the room. As his plan took shape his mood lightened considerably. He'd need to cash in big favors, but he'd have Anne again, in a matter of hours.

He'd double chain her this time. She'd never be able to leave him. Ever.

Chapter Twenty-Four

"Don't take this wrong, but you can't touch me today."

Charlie sat back in the car he reserved to take them to the hotel. The driver had put on soft music for their early Sunday morning drive. He narrowed his eyes playfully as she continued.

"Look, I don't want to give anyone at PRP any reason to believe we're together. They don't need to know. Let's go about our meetings as if we're friends…and," she held up both hands, "before you get angry, it's not that I'm not proud to tell the world we're together, but I can't risk blowing this. I need this job." Leslie looked out the window for a moment, then added, "I need to prove to myself I can do it."

Desire to touch her would always be there. She was the most beautiful creature he'd ever encountered. He could pretend to be friends for a few days; what would that hurt?

"Okay," he conceded, then took one of her raised hands and pulled it to his lips. "But…prepare yourself." He grinned.

Like a mirror, she grinned back, but narrowed her eyes. "For what?" She eyed him as she scooted back against the seat.

"After refraining from touching you all day, I'm going to be in desperate need tonight. You may have to randomly hug me…a lot."

Leslie smiled and glanced down. "I think I can manage that."

~ * ~

The Metropolitan Hotel was built by a New York billionaire and his wife, who found their Zen in the Smoky Mountains near Knoxville. They were less than impressed with the local Motel 6 and built a five-star next to the small airport.

It looked as if someone had dropped a Vegas show in the middle of an empty field.

Its shiny grand foyer was three stories high with a diamond chandelier at the center that sparkled reds and yellows down onto a glossy marble floor. Luxurious fabrics and Italian paintings hung from the windows and walls, and the staff treated even the production crew as royalty.

Scattered around the foyer were stately white columns as wide as the redwoods in California. The mahogany front desk shone like a new bar that'd never seen a drop of whiskey.

The driver followed Leslie's request and delivered her first, then drove around before dropping off Charlie. Four guards stood like statutes, surveying each person as they entered the grand lobby. Two were stationed at the main doors while two checked IDs and room keys as guests entered the elevators.

Good. PRP wasn't taking any chances.

Leslie checked in and found her hotel suite—an enormous two-bedroom condo complete with a tricked-out living room and full gourmet kitchen. Before even dropping her bags, she called the front desk to tell them they'd made a mistake. The concierge informed her she was in the correct room.

Unpacking, she hung her blue silk dress to knock out wrinkles from being in her suitcase. Silver, strappy heels she'd found at a second-hand store sparkled below the dress. The rest of her outfits she arranged in the closet with matching shoes beneath. Yes, it was OCD, but it gave her a sense of control.

Two back-to-back planning meetings were scheduled first thing, then she'd call to check on Nate. After that, she'd scour pages of notes and drawings conveying which costumes should appear in each scene.

She'd commit them to memory for the first days of shooting until Mr. Miller and Dana arrived. In her room, she held a short meeting with two female production assistants. Thank God they were younger than her, with even less experience. That gave her a boost of confidence.

Between meetings, Leslie scurried through the lobby, keeping close to the outside windows for better cell reception to call home.

As she marched past the front desk, a polite but heated discussion between two female managers in matching navy suits and a tall, irate woman caught her attention.

"What do you mean, someone else has my suite?"

Leslie ducked behind a column. She'd know that temper tantrum anywhere.

The woman raged on. "The mistake needs to be corrected. Now. I need a suite in this hotel. It should have been reserved in my name. I want whoever has it to be removed and my things put in the suite across from Charlie Erickson."

She should've known they'd cast the witch opposite Charlie. And he probably had no idea. Charlie must have upgraded Leslie to the suite near his without knowing who they'd hired.

A shiver raced down her spine. As far as she'd come this weekend, she wasn't ready for anything physical. Part of her was angry for his meddling in her business once again, but another part was elated. He wanted her close.

A third manager, tall and thin, with pale gray hair and a confident stance, slid into the discussion. He redirected the other two to help other guests, cleared his throat, then leaned over the counter. "Ms. Langford, the guest in that suite requested it several days prior to your phone call this morning. You were told, by me, the only hotel room left was a one-bedroom suite, and you accepted. I do apologize if you feel the smaller suite isn't up to your standards. We'll gladly refund your deposit and arrange transportation to whichever hotel you'd prefer."

His tone was formal and tight and tired of her temper tantrum. He pulled out a form and typed something into his computer

Christine's tone and demeanor switched from super angry to ultra-sweet. "Mr. Morgan, I *need* one of the suites, top floor, two bedrooms—not a one-bedroom, tiny, efficiency. We often have creative meetings in my suite to go over lines, and Charlie and I need private time away from the rest of the crew. Couldn't we make an exception, just this once? I'll even pay for the other guest's stay if they'll consider moving. Can't we ask them?"

Leslie's heart dropped. If the manager said yes, she'd be asked to move, and Christine would know it was her. She held her breath, waiting for his reply.

Mr. Morgan seemed unmoved by her performance. "Miss Langford, Mr. Erickson has a suite with a living area, and if it's bigger than yours, have your creative meetings in his suite instead."

The woman let out a growl of frustration that echoed, then situated her Prada higher into the crook of her elbow, raised her nose before she shoved her designer sunglasses back on her face. She spun and stomped toward the elevators. Two bellhops scurried behind her, toting her bags.

When the elevator doors closed, Leslie exhaled, rolling out her shoulders. Then her stomach lurched. *She* had to dress the evil woman. Perfect.

She and Charlie needed to be discreet. No doubt Christine could make her life hell. She was more important to PRP right now than a newbie costume assistant. Although punching the woman's lights out when her mouth got out of hand would be satisfying, Leslie shook her head and headed back to her meetings.

The production crew had been invited to a catered luncheon

inside the grand ballroom. Rumor had it the chef had been flown in by the owner.

Leslie and her two assistants stopped inside the ballroom door. Black-suited waiters fluttered about, filling water goblets on tables anchored by tall centerpieces made up of hundreds of white and silver sparkling flowers. It looked more like a wedding reception than a production crew luncheon. She and her assistants were sorely underdressed.

Several crew members lined up on both sides of the table for the buffet. Her stomach growled on cue. Two secondary actors filed into line in front of her, gossiping about Hollywood socialites.

Her two costume assistants drooled, mouths open. Grabbing a plate, she rolled her eyes. Fame wasn't real. Real people became famous. She knew the difference now.

One of her assistants gasped. Leslie didn't even flinch when Charlie grabbed a dish on the other side of the buffet and began filling his plate.

She tried to focus on the scents of prime rib and grilled shrimp, mixed with spicy rice and pans of fresh steamed vegetables, instead of the handsome man across from her. But every few feet, she could feel his stare.

"Good morning, Miss Carroll." Charlie stated without a hint of his southern drawl. The Hollywood man was back.

She glanced up and replied just as formally, "Mr. Erickson, Good morning to you, sir."

As they moved down the food line, an extra roll landed on Leslie's plate while her head was turned to speak behind her. Turning back, she narrowed her eyes playfully but Charlie had already moved down the line speaking with another actor.

Leslie hung back, taking her time with the green beans. She needed to let space fall between them. Just in time, too, as an impeccably dressed Christine waltzed into the room with her entourage. A short-haired, snobby-looking assistant and her steroid-using bodyguard flanked her.

At the look of murder on Charlie's face, Leslie knew—Charlie hadn't been told Christine was made the lead. His knuckles where white, gripping his plate. His teeth clamped tight like they were encased in concrete.

Christine wore a sleeveless salmon-colored silk pants suit. The thin material didn't hide the fact that she wore only a tiny thong underneath. Obviously, she hoped to attract everyone's attention, most especially Charlie's.

He and Leslie turned away from the spectacle and the food line in unison, toward the drink table.

Leslie fumbled a little, trying to grab her drink and move away as fast as she could. Watching Christine enter the room, she felt a surge of insecurity. Why would he want a *mousy* and afraid-to-be-touched girl, when he had a supermodel who wore see-through clothes like Christine?

Still seething, and without warning, Charlie put his plate down and rearranged Leslie's to make it easier. He shot her a tight but friendly smile when he handed back her tea.

She mouthed 'thank you'—grateful the considerate man she'd spent the past day with was still underneath the famous persona.

As they parted ways, he made a beeline for one of the producers, standing off to the side. The look of determination meant he was about to give him a piece of his mind regarding their casting choice.

Her two assistants waved her over. As she sat to eat, Christine headed straight for Charlie.

"Charlie, honey," she trilled aloud, grabbing his arm. "Darling, did you make that plate for me?"

He leveled a look at her. "You hate onions, and this one is full of them."

She smiled at the little people, then shot a look to her assistant who ran over and made her a plate. Christine held Charlie's arm as they moved toward the head table.

Leslie scowled as she took her first bite.

As lunch wound down, Phil Jones, the executive producer, stood and tapped his glass. The room grew silent. "We start at four a.m. tomorrow, but first, a reminder—the limos will load at three-thirty sharp, outside the lobby. Make sure you're ready and not still applying your makeup—Charlie."

Charlie nodded as the crowd laughed.

Phil resumed, "We're being treated tonight to a sunset cruise on the *Tennessee Riverboat*. We'll get to dance to live music, eat a hearty southern dinner, and enjoy drinks to kick off our first week of filming." The crowd clapped and cheered. "Security," he added, pausing to allow the crowd to quiet down, "has been increased tonight, so don't forget your ticket. It's the only way to get onto the boat—no exceptions."

Security. Danger was still out there. She'd been so tied up in meeting his family and not driving herself crazy, she'd temporarily pushed it to the back of her mind. But now, it was front and center. Her monster knew exactly where she was, but her fear now wasn't for herself, but for Charlie.

At least she knew what she was up against. She stole a quick glance at his handsome, chiseled features, and her heart beat a little faster. She still needed to tell him. Today. She'd corner him on the *Riverboat* and come clean.

Mr. Jones made a joke about the film. As the crowd laughed, the fire alarm blasted loud and shrill.

Everyone startled. A few even let out a scream. Four uniformed security guards snaked through tables to stand behind Charlie and Christine. The alarm didn't stop.

Leslie looked around at concerned faces and landed on Charlie's. His eyes were intense. He pointed to her and motioned for her to come to him. She shook her head. There was no viable reason why a costume assistant needed to be next to a principal actor.

One of three managers stood in the doorway and yelled over the top of the alarm. Management hadn't seen smoke or fire, but since the alarm was pulled, everyone needed to evacuate. They apologized and requested that the guests exit in a slow and calm fashion. Everyone was instructed to stand outside until the fire department could sweep the hotel.

As everyone stood, Leslie lost sight of Charlie. Panic swept through her. A diversion. This was Jason's work, meant to get them outside where he could pick Charlie off. She knew it. She had to keep him safe, but somehow not alert everyone.

Leslie hatched out a split-second plan, grabbed her two assistants then headed for the outer rim of the room. She wanted eyes on Charlie. She yelled over the alarm mixed with the murmur of the crowd, pulling them with her against the flow of bodies heading for the door. "Ladies, it's our job to ensure the principal actors get out. We're gonna hang back. The head table will be the last out."

Her stomach flipped as memories of gunfire the night before, flooded back. And the kiss. *Focus.* She shook her head, dislodging those mental images.

Up on her tiptoes, she craned her neck, but couldn't find his sandy blond hair anywhere. People were pushing and shoving as they herded past them, through the door.

"I don't see them," one girl screeched, looking a little panicked.

"Shouldn't we go outside?" the other girl whined.

Leslie turned on them. "You are an employee of PRP and as such, Mr. Miller would insist we make damn sure everyone gets out of this building, especially our principal actors. Keep a lookout and let me know when you find Mr. Erickson and Miss Langford."

It worked. The girls both hoisted up on tiptoes like prairie dogs.

"Miss Carroll," one girl yelled over the noise, "Miss Langford is walking out the front doors with her bodyguard, but I don't see Mr. Erickson."

Two lighting guys, who'd eaten lunch with them, grabbed all three women and pushed them toward the exit. Leslie protested but the calm and orderly exit had turned to loud chaos. They couldn't hear her.

She spun and darted back through the sea of humans as if she was swimming the wrong way up a strong river. She had to see him and calm the fear growing inside her. She should've told him already. What if Jason took him? Charlie wouldn't know the truth, and he'd be blindsided.

Clutching a column, standing on her toes, she took one more look around the emptying ballroom. Still no Charlie. Knots tightened in her stomach. A familiar, warm hand wrapped around her waist, pulling her back into the flow of people. One look at Charlie's relieved face, and her entire body relaxed.

He pulled her next to him, guiding her with his hand on her back as they made their way out into the lobby. She smiled up at him, relieved he was safe. The crowd thinned.

He looked straight ahead but spoke to her. "I've been warned." He cut his gaze down and continued, "Nobody on the crew is to find out Christine and I have broken up until the end of shooting this film." Anger rolled off him as he let go of her back. Six firemen passed by in a hurry.

"I'm sure we know who suggested that," she shot back. Leslie shoved her hands in her pockets as she walked toward the glass doors. It was time. She had to prepare him. He needed to know everything to be able to defend himself. "Hey."

He glanced down, then opened the glass door as she walked through. "Yeah?"

"I need to tell you something…" They walked straight into a wall of people packed together under the portico outside. Cold spring rain drizzled. Nobody wanted to get wet.

There was no way she could explain what Jason did, with everyone standing so close and listening.

Charlie's eyes narrowed. "What's wrong?"

He could already read her so well. Worry lined his face.

"Nothing, really. But I need to…"

The alarm stopped, and the crew cheered. People laughed and

joked like they'd been released from class early. Nobody paid attention to them.

Charlie's eyes never left her face, trying to read it. "Whatever it is, you can tell me."

She took a deep breath, then let it out. "I..."

"There you are," Christine interrupted.

She stepped between Leslie and Charlie, facing him. Then she turned and looked from Charlie's face to Leslie's. She spun toward Leslie and stared her down.

Graceful and smooth, Leslie stepped back. Her smile was tight but polite. Then she turned to follow the crowd who were filing back into the lobby.

Christine sidestepped until she blocked Leslie's path. Hands on her hips, she looked like an angry lion, ready to pounce.

Chapter Twenty-Five

Charlie wanted to snatch Christine baldheaded. Fury rose in his chest at the way she looked down at Leslie, then trapped her.

To her credit, Leslie stood tall, crossing her arms and impassively staring right back at Christine. She surprised Charlie with her confidence and candor.

"Miss Langford, how are you?" Leslie spoke formally, sidestepping the actress, but Christine mirrored her move and stood in the way.

"I'm doing well," Christine drawled, brow furrowed. "And you are?"

"Leslie. Leslie Carroll. I'm the costume designer who'll be assisting you for the next few days. Mrs. Godwin or Mr. Miller will take my place on Wednesday."

Christine narrowed her rounded eyes, but never lost her smile. "I believe we've met before…" It sounded like a question, and she waited for an answer.

"Not formally, no, but I measured Mr. Erickson last week, when you two had a *discussion* in the dressing room."

"That's it!" Christine said brightly. "I never forget a face."

"Well, if you'll excuse me." Leslie nodded to Christine and then turned to him. "Mr. Erickson, thank you again for making sure I got out of the building safely."

Humor danced in her eyes, but he could tell she was spitting mad.

She scooted past Christine.

He watched Leslie walk away with one eyebrow cocked as a smile tugged at his lips. Christine stared at Leslie too, then glared at Charlie as if he called her a bad name.

~ * ~

Leslie's ears were hot, and curse words spun around in her mind as she bypassed the elevator. She needed the stairs. Damn manipulative bitch. That was the best one. She refused to be intimidated by that woman. As she entered her room, her cell dinged. It was Charlie.

Very professional. Mr. M would be proud. Want to hang before this stupid boat thing?

Leslie smiled. Yes, yes, she wanted to hang and most certainly wanted to hug him and feel his strong arms wrapped around her and breathe him in. Oh. And kiss. A lot. But she couldn't.

She still needed to tell him the truth, but she desperately needed a nap. She'd been awake most of the night, terrified someone would hear her nightmare. She typed a quick response. *Nope. I have more important things to do.*

His reply came back quickly. *Surely not.*

Yep. Gonna take a nap.

I'll be right over.

She sucked in a sharp breath, then ran over and checked the lock.

Two dings of her phone came back immediately. *I bet you checked the door...lol.*

Wanna meet in the hallway at three-twenty?

She exhaled and wrote back. *Deal.*

A real cat nap, a long shower, and an hour later, Leslie was ready for the big night. For once in her life, her makeup looked flawless. She'd taken extra time with her eyes. She'd lined them with hints of greenish blue to bring out the whiskey in the brown.

Her dark hair she'd swooped up, with a few tendrils hanging down here and there to complement the neckline on the pale blue satin dress she'd made. It was sleeveless, floor length, and fit like a glove.

Her aunt lent her a silver wrap that matched the new-to-her shoes. She stood tall and felt regal, like a movie star. Thanks to the shoes, she'd be staring at Charlie's chin instead of his chest. If they were allowed to dance.

A new record. She was ready to go with at least thirty minutes to spare when her door thudded faintly three times, like a small child's fist knocking from the hallway.

She strolled to the door. Maybe Charlie finished early too. Instinctively, she checked the peephole first. His door, straight across the hall, was closed. Movement in the right corner of the lens caught her eye.

A familiar figure came into view. She wore sparkling Dolce heels, a fluffy cream-colored bath towel, and—thanks to her situating said towel—nothing else. Christine stood at the mouth of Charlie's door and held up a key card, inspecting it.

Leslie's stomach knotted, and she held her breath. What the

hell was she up to now? And how did she get a key card to Charlie's room?

She couldn't rip her gaze away. Christine's hair, twisted in an elegant French knot, bobbed as she bent to mess with the lock. As if someone blew a silent whistle, she rose up, pulled her shoulders back as she lifted her chin.

In one swift movement, she turned the handle, pushed it open, then slipped into the room, catlike. It was as if she'd been a secret thief for years. Once inside, she dropped her towel and the card at the threshold.

Leslie's body overtook her mind. Her fingers shook racing to unlock her door. She flung it open and strode four long strides to Charlie's door, which still hung open. She wasn't prepared for what she saw. A naked Christine, wearing only heels, sprawled across a wet Charlie on the couch. Upon closer inspection, he wore only a low-slung towel.

This naked meeting wasn't planned by him. She knew that. But this kind of thing had obviously happened before. Leslie's mind reeled. Christine's hands pulled at Charlie's towel as her mouth found his.

Before Leslie could move, a small cry escaped her throat. In the seconds it took for Christine to throw herself at Charlie, he'd gone from head tilted back and looking asleep, to fully alert. She'd never be able to give him that. Never be able to be that uninhibited. Maybe he needed that kind of physical attention. Leslie stumbled backward, her hand covering her mouth. When she turned to run toward her room, Christine's shrill laugh, mixed with angry words from Charlie, echoed through the hallway, and his door slammed.

Leslie grabbed her silver clutch, room key, and ticket, sitting by her door, then ran toward the elevators.

By the time the elevator reached the bottom floor, she had choked back every tear. She'd been so stupid. She had no one to blame but herself. She'd allowed someone to get too close, and she paid the price. *It wouldn't have worked anyway; she was about to tell him the truth.* Her mind congratulated itself, then consoled her heart.

Pressing her hand to her chest, she pushed down the stab of hurt.

Why wouldn't he want Christine? She had a flawless body. And obviously no reservations using it, unlike her. Leslie shook her head. But he didn't want Christine, he said so himself.

But he's a man. A man with physical needs Leslie can't satisfy. Self-pity and anger raced each other through her mind. She'd never be able to compete with Christine's spontaneity or her candid nakedness.

Leslie's hands trembled as she marched off the elevator in perfect time to line up for the first limo. The lighting guys and her two assistants waited for her to catch up.

She walked toward the open limo door, shoulders back and tall. Self-preservation would win out over self-pity. She never had much use for pity. She looked better than she ever had, and she'd be damned if anyone, especially that ho Christine Langford, would ruin this night.

She clicked her phone to vibrate and tossed it into her bag. The girls admired her dress while the lighting guys had to pick their chins up off the floor. That lightened her spirits. As the five situated themselves in the limo, her phone buzzed.

At first, she ignored the constant noises coming from her purse. The darker headed lighting guy, who sat too close and smelled like an entire bottle of cheap cologne, finally asked, "Aren't you curious who's blowing you up?"

"Nope," she lied.

"Ah, gotcha. Ex-boyfriend, I assume?" God love him. He was attempting charm.

She nodded then shrugged, turning her attention to the girl's conversation. Quickly, she opened her purse and clicked her phone to "do not disturb."

The limo ride to the waterfront was only a few minutes. When they pulled up and stopped, all five gawked at the massive riverboat.

A red-carpeted gangplank stretched out toward the gleaming white vessel. A man, dressed in a black tuxedo, opened the limo door then reached in to assist Leslie as she stood. She walked the red carpet toward the boat, open mouthed, amid photographers snapping pictures. She didn't even care. She was stunned by the enormous, sleek two-story ship.

Handing over her ticket, she boarded. The captain made a comment about the beautiful women boarding as he shook her hand.

She gave the captain a polite smile, then moved her attention to the interior.

Late afternoon sun glinted through windows and bounced off the floral arrangements perched on the tables. Reds and yellows splashed the white walls. Ladder backed chairs enveloped white linen tables that bordered the outer rim of the room.

An old-world bar with two smiling, young bartenders stood toward the front of the boat. The back of the ship was secured by an expansive two-story outdoor deck with tables and chairs. Twinkle lights and hanging lanterns dangled all around the outside of the boat. It would look romantic once the sun went down. Great.

As the film crew arrived all dressed to the nines, Leslie grew more nervous. Charlie would pull up any minute, furious she'd left him. Squaring her shoulders, she no longer cared. *He'd realize soon enough that she wasn't the girl for him anyway.*

She imagined what naked-ho Christine Langford would wear. Leslie'd need a drink if she was to watch Christine flaunting herself all night.

Leslie walked upstairs followed by her two production assistants. Belly up to the bar, she ordered a glass of sweet pinot from a female bartender.

The bartender's fingers were tattooed with an intricate Indian design, much like the henna tattoos of the newly married. She popped open a fresh bottle and poured. Unopened bottles were always the best. It made her rule of keeping her drink in sight much easier.

Handing over the glass, the bartender complimented her on her dress. Leslie smiled and hoped nobody in the industry asked her the designer.

She meant to sip the wine, but after two gulps she took a breath, then downed the rest. The bartender looked equally impressed and entertained, then refilled the glass without a word. This wouldn't be so hard. A few more drinks of liquid courage and she'd be able to tell that beautiful, muscular, blue-eyed man to hit the road.

Warm breezes pushed through the open doors leading from the bar to the back deck. Leslie strolled toward the aft, then leaned against the rail and gazed down at the throngs of people walking toward the vessel.

After inhaling the first wine, she sipped the second, pretending she didn't care who came aboard. Nerves fluttered in her belly each time a new car pulled up, and crew members poured out. All the limos looked similar except the last one. It was longer and sleeker.

She knew it was them.

When the attendant opened the back door, the lump in her throat threatened to close her airway.

Charlie stood, his blond waves flipping in the breeze. His heather gray suit fit him perfectly and his white tailored shirt made his beautiful tan skin glow. He looked the part of the hot Hollywood actor. The photographers ate him up. And yet, she glared. Raw anger and betrayal both flashed in her mind.

Charlie's gaze searched the ship and then the people ahead of him. When the paparazzi yelled his name and snapped pictures, he shoved sunglasses on and smiled. But she knew him well enough. His face was tight with a mixture of anger and worry. He was looking for her.

~ * ~

When Charlie spotted her on the top deck, he stopped to stare, forgetting the paparazzi and everyone in the world. Relief washed over him. She was safe. The silky blue dress clung to her curves and rippled in the wind. The sun at her back made her look angelic. She'd looked beautiful the week before in the costume, but this ... this was stunning—and maddening.

Charlie glanced ahead. One of the executive producers and the director also spotted her. They stared too. He studied her face. She looked angry.

Wait—he was the one who should be angry. Leslie glared as she finished the drink in her hand. He turned back toward the limo, obligated to help Christine. He was sure it was in his damn contract somewhere. She stood as tall as Charlie, looking radiantly evil in a gold dress with a plunging neckline. The paparazzi photographed them rapid fire as they strolled down the red carpet.

Charlie glanced up as Leslie turned away. Part of him was grateful she didn't see. If the shoe were on the other foot, he'd be damned if he could stand still while she touched someone else, even if it was platonic. It was too far to gauge her mood, but he was sure it wasn't good. Charlie dropped Christine's hand, picked up the pace, greeted the captain and crew, then took the stairs two at a time.

~ * ~

Leslie's stomach churned. She strolled back to the bar and asked for another glass of wine. *This would be the last one.*

She sensed Charlie at the top of the stairs before she noticed him. He stood, staring a few feet away. Anger rolled off him as he eyed her. His arms were crossed over his chest.

If she hadn't been so angry, she'd have told him he looked beautiful—thanks to the wine. She thanked the bartender then turned her head toward him.

"You didn't wait for me," he spoke low as he stalked toward her.

"Nope," she agreed flatly.

She lifted the glass to her lips, never taking her gaze off him. When she didn't speak again, he walked around her, brushing her back with his warm hand before ordering a beer. When the bartender handed over his drink, the smile Charlie shot the woman was polite and tight.

Leslie shuddered. His damn touch caused a warm sensation to spread throughout her body. She shook it off and looked around. The upper cabin was filling, and a few crew members stared. She didn't care.

Charlie took a long draw on his beer. Angry eyes locked on hers. He moved closer. She staggered back a few inches, torn between his anger and hers. He was too close. And she couldn't concentrate on *her* anger with him that close.

Turning, she walked to a high bar table that butted up against the windows overlooking the water. She set her glass down and swayed. Note to self: *gulping might not have been the best idea.* She held on to the seat and pulled at one of the straps on her silver heels.

Charlie followed, positioning his beer next to her wine. He leaned over; his mouth close enough to hers that his breath tickled her cheek. "I called you about a hundred times. Why did you leave me?"

His voice sounded more hurt than angry. Leslie's jaw tightened as tears threatened to pool.

"Why would I stay?" she asked, fuming.

He leaned back, confusion lining his face. He grabbed his beer bottle and pointed it toward her, raising his voice slightly. "Because you promised to meet me in the hall."

Leslie picked up her glass and took a sip. "That was before."

"Before what?" he annunciated each syllable.

More guests filed into the bar, ordering drinks, appetizers, and sitting at tables all around them.

Leslie took a long breath. Anger filled her entire body, which shook. She wasn't tipsy enough to forget they were in the public eye.

She leveled a look and lowered her voice. "Before I watched you and a naked Christine go at it on your couch."

She raised her glass. Her stupid voice betrayed her and caught on the end of the sentence. It was as if saying the words out loud made them true—and so painful.

His face fell like he'd been hit with a truck.

Leslie didn't want to hear what came next...the lies *or* the truth. Either way, it was too raw. She'd never felt this angry or jealous before, and damn it, it hurt. She placed a hand on her chest to push the pain away.

Christine was a snake of a woman. A snake who pegged her as mousy in the first five minutes of meeting her. And, damnit she was right. But nevertheless, a snake who wanted Charlie for herself and knew how to get his attention. If she was being honest though, it wasn't exactly Charlie's fault. It was Leslie's fear of intimacy and fear of not being enough that fueled her insecurity.

She raised her glass and gulped her wine again, hoping it would quench the lump forming in her throat. At this rate, she'd be fairly plastered in no time. Dinner might have to be skipped altogether.

Damn wine. Damn emotions, too. If this was caring about someone, she wanted no part of it. Screw it, she'd disappear out of his life as soon as they got back to California anyway.

As the boat swayed, she held the table. She needed to sit, but her heart told her to run.

Charlie took a swig of his beer and pulled out his phone.

When he gave no explanation, she shook her head, defeated. The lump in her throat, now scratchy and dry, gained ground. Tears threatened to fall.

In one not-so-swift move, she took her wine glass and headed toward the stairs. She wouldn't look back. And damnit, her tears better not fall until she was out of his sight. She'd stick to the opposite side of the boat. The last thing she wanted was to see the happy couple in action.

Charlie thumped his phone down on the table and leapt up, catching her right before the stairs. He snatched her around the waist and lifted her off the ground, then carried her squawking and complaining back toward the table. The bartender and most of the room looked on as if he'd lost his mind. By the look on his face, he couldn't have cared less.

He sat on one stool and pulled her to stand in front of him. One arm wrapped around her, the other picked up his phone then held it to his ear.

"Come upstairs," he commanded through gritted teeth.

Leslie pushed against his chest and glared. How dare he pick her up like a child? She was a grown woman in heels and makeup and…

A few seconds later, as if on cue, Christine strolled up the stairs. "Well, look what we have here." She glared from Leslie to Charlie and back. Smug and smiling, she ignored the rest of the guests.

The bar turned silent as everyone stared at the three of them. Charlie wrapped his arm tighter around Leslie. "Cut the shit. Tell her why you were in my suite."

"Hmm." A smile played on her lips. "I don't know, honey, is this a trick question?"

Charlie released Leslie and stomped toward Christine. By the murderous look on his face, he wasn't playing.

The ship lurched slightly as it backed away from the dock. Leslie staggered, then sat.

Christine's face lit up as Charlie came toward her. It was as if this was a game and provoking him turned her on.

"Tell her the truth or so help me God, I'll cut my losses, walk off this film and pay Kat extra to smear your name all over town."

Leslie's wine-soaked mind perked up. *The truth?*

"She knows why I was there, Charlie," Christine said batting her eyelashes.

Quick as a cat, he sidestepped around her and walked toward Phil, who stopped on the stairs to talk shop with the director.

Christine followed his stare and changed her tune. "All right, all right. Keep your pants on—shit. A kind janitor in the hallway let me *borrow* his master key card. The water in my shower had a smell to it." She wrinkled her nose. "So I needed to use yours." The witch stared at Leslie but spoke to Charlie. "Anyway, it's not like you haven't seen and touched absolutely *everything* I have."

"Then what happened?" His jaw muscles tightened.

"Well, I walked in…and you were sitting on the couch in a towel. I thought it might have been an invitation—you know, for old times' sake." She shrugged.

He glared. "You threw yourself on me for the second time this week. And what did I tell you?"

She looked from Charlie to Leslie. "What do you mean?"

"Tell her."

Christine looked like she'd chewed dirt. "I don't remember exactly what you said, Charlie, but it was some BS about not wanting me and being in love with the mousy seamstress."

Leslie's breath caught.

Christine strutted around Charlie and beelined for Leslie. "So, *you* have my suite? Well, I'll tell you what, costume girl, I guarantee when Mr. Miller gets here, you *will* be giving me the bigger room."

"You can have it," Leslie said, without missing a beat, then she pointed at Charlie. "But you can't have him."

He beamed at Leslie then walked around Christine. Gently pulling Leslie off the stool, he took her place on the seat, then pulled her back in front of him. His arms shook as he wrapped them around her. She glanced up at his beautiful face. When he locked eyes on Christine, some of his anger returned.

He lifted his beer. "No worries, Chris, she can sleep in my room." His raised voice made sure everyone at the bar heard him.

Leslie's face turned immediately hot.

Christine stared at him for a beat, her eyes narrowed. Then she glanced around at all the onlookers. Apparently, he'd never talked to her that way in public.

"Now, why don't you go downstairs and convince the 'little

people' how great you are?" Charlie added, "Oh, and Chris...mess with either one of us again, and I'll tell anybody who'll listen *exactly* what kind of person you are. Got me?"

He slugged back a long draw. Christine glared as if she was plotting Leslie's death, then turned and huffed down the long staircase, past Phil, leaving them alone.

After a moment, the murmur of the crowd cranked back up to loud. Leslie slid from Charlie's grasp. and wobbled toward the bar. She needed water. And a moment alone. Emotions foreign to her raged to the surface.

She should have been elated. He'd done nothing wrong. But she'd been so quick to assume he wanted that kind of woman, the sexually adventurous kind—and she'd been so eager to believe he couldn't want someone like her. Ashamed, she stared at her fingers wrapped around the glass of water. He'd said he loved her. In front of all those people.

That made telling him the truth one thousand times harder.

Charlie followed her to the bar, finished his beer, then ordered his second. After thanking the bartender, he held out his hand.

Glancing up from her glass, she shook her head. "Walk with me?" she offered instead.

He frowned and motioned for her to lead the way. She walked toward the deserted back balcony. The vessel turned away from the large dock and moved down the river. *Focus and walk straight.* She gripped the rail every couple of feet, to steady herself.

They stood a foot apart, leaning over the side of the boat, facing out. Estate-sized homes passed on both sides of the boat as it picked up speed down the Tennessee River. The sun was setting, and lanterns were being lit behind them.

Charlie's anger seemed to dissipate the moment Christine walked away. He played with a curled tendril of hair hanging down Leslie's neck as it tossed and flipped from the wind. He was breathtaking. He'd appeared to have forgiven her the second he found out Christine had planned for Leslie to see her jump him. Leslie needed to clear her head in the breeze. The multiple glasses of wine were messing with her resolve. She'd enjoy tonight and pretend she wasn't about to disappear again. These would be the memories that would sustain her when she left him. But she knew it was time.

She'd make sure he knew the truth by the end of the night.

She cleared her throat and glanced up to find his eyes locked on hers. "I owe you an apology." She stated it more to the wind than to him. He stopped playing with her hair.

"I didn't even ask…I assumed the worst." She gazed out at the water. "I'd love to blame it on being new to all this relationship stuff, but I think it goes deeper than that." She exhaled, then added, "I'm sorry."

Charlie moved in, closing the gap she made between them. He reached for her hand. Holding it up to his lips, he kissed it. "I had to hem my pants," he said out of the blue.

"What?"

"I went downstairs, and the concierge found a guy to hem my pants. They were way too long." He looked down at his shoes. "I was waiting for him to bring them back, which is why I didn't even look up when my door opened."

"Why didn't you bring them to me?" Leslie asked, jerking her hand back and absentmindedly pulling on his pant leg, checking if it was done correctly. It wasn't. "I would've done a better job."

Charlie swatted her hand playfully from his pants. "I wanted you to feel like my girlfriend tonight and not a seamstress. I wanted you to have time to work on your own dress and hair and makeup and not be rushed or worried about someone else's outfit."

Tears welled again, and she pushed them down. He put his hands on her waist and pulled her closer to him.

She tensed up at first, then melted. "You're supposed to pretend to be with Christine."

"I think that's pretty much shot to hell now, don't ya think? Besides, let 'em fire me."

The PA system turned on with a shrill noise, then Phil's voice boomed throughout the boat. "Ladies and gentlemen, dinner is served."

They turned and followed the crowd, amid stares, downstairs to a packed dining room. The clinking of plates and the low drum of conversation filled the air. Just before the bottom, Charlie elbowed her, winked and whispered, "Keep your phone handy."

She leveled a look at him, then sidestepped around the maze of tables toward one at the back marked for costume. Charlie picked a seat at the head table several chairs down from Christine. Phil and a few other executives sat between them. As the salad was served, piano music floated in the air. Leslie's phone in her lap buzzed.

It was Charlie. *Got an idea.*

Leslie smiled, took a bite then typed back, *I'll alert the media.*

Funny. Pretend we're sitting together.

She shot back a smiley face and a heart.

Her phone buzzed again. *You look stunning*

She looked up from her phone. When their eyes met, Charlie

nodded to confirm.

She glanced around. Nobody noticed or cared they were texting. She typed, *Thanks* then sipped water as the waiters buzzed around delivering the main course.

When hers was placed in front of her, she swallowed a few mouthfuls. It was delicious. Then she surveyed the room. People were eating and chattering, laughing comfortably. Yet, a tingling crept up her spine. She felt eyes raking her up and down. Someone tracked her. She could feel it.

Swallowing her last bite, she dabbed her napkin at the corners of her mouth and looked around. She glanced up to find Phil with a strange look on his face. He grinned and raised his glass. She nodded back, took a sip, then her phone vibrated.

Truth or dare?

She typed quick, *Nope. You first. Truth or dare, Erickson?*

Then she placed her phone down on the table and shook off the uneasiness. She glanced up to see his reaction.

Charlie looked down. The edges of his lips lifted. He typed something back then turned his attention to someone's joke at his table. *Dare, Miss Carroll. Always dare.*

She wrote back, *Find the shyest wallflower here and ask her for the first dance.*

While he read, his eyebrows rose. Before she could finish the next forkful, he stood and walked directly toward her.

No! I didn't mean myself! Charlie grinned, reading her panic perfectly and at the last second, passed her and chose a quirky but shy makeup artist sitting at a table behind her. Whew.

The young woman stood, hesitant. Her short brown hair was pulled back with a shiny silver clip, and her plain black dress and low heels were set off by a long silver necklace. She looked embarrassed yet elated that someone had noticed her.

He twirled her to the live band's jazz music. Others followed. Leslie was proud of him—he was such a good sport.

She excused herself from the table and headed for the restroom. Before she left, she made damn sure Christine was occupied. No bathroom brawls were needed on this luxury liner.

When Leslie returned to her table, the lighting guys and her assistants were dancing, which left her alone. As she scooped a giant forkful of crusted tilapia into her mouth, someone slinked into the chair next to her, placing a hand on her shoulder.

She coughed and choked then stared wide eyed at Phil. Apologizing, he handed her a water. She swallowed hard and continued to cough. Finally, she caught her breath and laughed.

"I'm so sorry. Are you all right?" Phil looked concerned.

"Better now. What a great night. Thank you for inviting me."

Phil had an easy-going smile despite his high stress job. "I'm glad the studio was wise enough to send you on location for this film."

"Thank you. I'm grateful to Mr. Miller for having faith in me."

Phil drew near to whisper, "To be honest, I had a hand in bringing you here with us."

Leslie leaned back. She'd had enough wine to ask direct questions. "Why would you do that?"

"Chemistry, of course."

Leslie cocked her head to the side. "What chemistry?" Her voice was harsher than she meant it to be. *Please God, say this man wasn't coming on to her.* He'd seemed so nice.

"Between you and Charlie."

She looked anywhere but in his eyes. Warmth rose up her neck to her ears

Phil smiled. "Look, it's part of my job to seek that kind of heat between actors. I love finding it. It's what good film is all about. The studio overruled me with Christine. But man, the crackle we all noticed in the room between the two of you…wish I could bottle and sell it. You should consider acting."

He took a long swig of his drink, then stood and held out a hand. "Dance with an old man?"

She placed her phone under her napkin on the table and stood, regaining her smile. "Of course. I'd love to."

Across the dance floor, Charlie swung the shy makeup artist around, but kept one eye on Phil.

Phil guided Leslie to the dance floor and boogied as if he'd been a professional dancer in a former life. He spun, turned and dipped her. She was blown away. She'd never seen anyone his age able to swing dance like that. When the song ended, the tempo slowed.

Charlie positioned himself next to them. Phil's face erupted in an *I-knew-it* smile.

"Would you like to trade?" Charlie's eyebrows rose, blue eyes sparkling in the candlelight.

"Of course," Phil said, winking at Charlie and chatting with the makeup artist as they danced away.

He pulled Leslie in, staring deep into her eyes. Her face warmed from the heat in his gaze, like she stood too close to a fire.

She focused out the window, rather than meet that look again. It did things to her.

The sun was almost gone, casting long, orange shadows on the estates as they passed. He pulled her in even closer, crushing her to him. She laid her head in the crook between his neck and shoulder. That was where he smelled best, right there. She closed her eyes.

Never in a million years did she imagine she could be this calm with someone holding her. Even a week ago, she would've fought like a cornered cat. She only danced with Nate and her father—on his good days.

She concentrated, memorizing every second of this, knowing it'd be over soon. The music stopped and the band took a break. Phil announced speeches would be next and everyone needed to take their seats. Charlie held her hand as long as possible as they parted ways, making her giggle before heading back to their tables. When Leslie returned and pulled her phone from under the napkin, a note fell into her lap. She turned it over.

"If you want Charlie to live, meet me upstairs. Alone."

Her chest tightened. This wasn't possible. How could he have slipped past security? She trembled. Leslie took a deep breath and a gulp of wine. With a shaky hand, she grabbed her phone and waited for laughter in the first speech before ducking out of the room.

As she topped the stairs, a thin man with dark hair, dressed in a black waiter's coat sat at the bar. No drink in front of him and no bartender in sight. They were all alone. Leslie's whole body quaked. A shot of anger coursed through her. All the things he'd done to her and her sister and he sat there, like a regular human at a bar. Of course, at a bar was where it all started.

"He's not right for you." The slimy voice from her nightmares was low and hoarse.

"What do you want?" Hers sounded too high pitched, as if it'd come from someone else.

Jason's head turned slowly to face her. His eyes. *Dear God.* She wanted desperately to look away, block it out, but Nate...Nate had his exact eyes. Her stomach churned.

"All I ever wanted," he stood but didn't move an inch toward her, "was you."

Hungry eyes raked her up and down. Her jaw tight and trembling, she clenched her fists. She'd kill him this time. He was smaller in person than she remembered in her nightmares. And he didn't resemble the stock attorney photo the entertainment channel had been plastering on TV. Dark and hollow shadows hung under his eyes. His pasty, yellowed skin looked as if he hadn't seen the sun in years.

"Tell you what...come quietly and he won't die. Make me

chase you—he dies."

"We're gonna swim to shore?" she gestured toward the window.

Jason's mouth twitched as a flash of anger lit his face. "I'll find you." He enunciated each syllable. "Tell anyone, and not only will I kill Charlie, I'll go after Sissy, too."

Leslie gasped. He took one last look, mouthed the word "tomorrow" and walked behind the bar. He slithered through a door and closed it without a sound.

Her hands trembled. She fought the urge to scream. Sweat gathered at her temples, and it took a full minute for her brain to register what came next. Her dreams had been preparing her. Reliving the torture so she'd be better equipped when this day came.

A quiet cry escaped her throat. Sissy. She'd grown up with Jason. She might get confused and trust him. If he sweet-talked her, he could lure her away from Charlie's parents. One thing she knew for sure—she'd walk through hell again to save Sissy and all the people she'd grown so fond of over the last few days. Especially Charlie.

Laughter from the bottom of the stairs wafted up, pulling her out of her trance. She started back down, holding the railing for support.

She hesitated on the next to the last step. Phil said she should be an actress. This was trial-by-fire acting. She sucked in and blew out a deep breath before entering the dining cabin again.

Speeches were over and most everyone milled around the room, talking.

She scanned for Charlie. He stood on the opposite side of the room. When she found him, he'd already found her. One eyebrow cocked in question; he inclined his head to ask if she was okay. She shot him her best reassuring smile. She should win an Academy Award.

The boat slowly returned toward the dock. Charlie made his way around the room until he found Leslie and pulled her aside.

"You all right?" He pulled her wrap off the back of her chair and placed it on her shoulders.

"I'm okay, just a little too much wine. I'll catch a car back to the hotel. You can stay, if you want." Her voice sounded high and optimistic.

Charlie wasn't buying it. He shook his head and leaned down. "I saw you. I saw the look you had when you came back downstairs."

Phil snuck up, interrupted in perfect time and slapped Charlie on the back, slurring his words slightly. "You ready for tomorrow, chief?"

Charlie leveled a look at Leslie that said they weren't finished, then turned to Phil. "Of course."

"How about you two kids ride with me back to the hotel?"

Charlie shook his hand, gratitude filling his eyes. "We'd love to."

Phil offered his arm to Leslie, and she took it, walking toward the red carpet and the waiting paparazzi. She hoped he couldn't feel her trembling.

She couldn't shake the knowledge that Jason was aboard, following her every move.

When the limo stopped in front of the hotel, she rubbed her eyes, then picked up her high heels she'd kicked off and hooked them on her pinky. She scooted out of the limo.

She and Charlie bid Phil goodnight as they exited the elevator on the top floor. Charlie leaned against her door frame as she fumbled in her tiny purse for her key card.

"Les?" Something in his voice stopped her search. She glanced up.

"Something happened on that boat." His voice was a whisper.

When her eyes betrayed her trust and filled with tears, he pulled her in, crushing her to his chest. She couldn't tell him, he'd die. But if she did, maybe he'd be better prepared. Better able to defend himself. Even warn his parents, and Sissy.

"Truth or dare, Miss Carroll?" he whispered.

"Truth." She spoke into his chest.

His phone rang before he could say another word. He looked down at the unknown number as Leslie turned the knob to her suite.

"Hello... Detective Majors, I'm fine." He glanced up at Leslie, and she motioned for him to follow her inside. Instinctively, Leslie locked the deadbolt behind him as Charlie listened. His face lined with worry, then red with anger. "So he's here?"

She robotically made coffee. A menial task mixed with caffeine, that's what she needed.

Talking low, Charlie paced in the living room. When he hung up with Detective Majors, he dialed another number. Over the gurgling coffee pot, he spoke into his phone, "Dad?"

Good. He was warning his parents. She hoped they'd leave right now. Minutes later, when he joined her in the kitchen, he grabbed a mug of coffee and sipped it, but kept his distance.

The silence grew until he finally spoke. "You saw Jase tonight."

She'd choose honesty as far as she could. "Yes."

"What did he say?" His voice quaked with anger.

Tears pooled once again. "I can't say."

He placed his cup on the counter and moved slowly toward her. She welcomed his touch, but feared she'd lose the battle with her emotions. Strong arms wrapped around her again. Then he pulled her back and held her chin, eyes leveled, he whispered, "You have to trust me."

Leslie swallowed over the hard lump in her throat. A few tears escaped as she whispered, "He said if I come quietly, he won't kill you or Sissy."

Charlie's jaw clenched tight. He growled low in his throat. "He will never touch either of you." He held her for another moment, then whipped his phone out, dialing a number as he walked back to the living room. Leslie carried both coffees and sat them on the table.

"Phil, it's Charlie."

Within ten minutes, he had effectively convinced Leslie to stay in his suite. He promised to sleep on the pull-out couch with her in his bed, so he'd know she was safe. Phil had two security guards placed outside his door. Leslie gathered clothes she'd need for the next day, as if it were a normal workday on set.

It looked odd, her handmade dress hanging among his tailored suits and designer jeans. That must be how she looked standing next to him. Even worse, the whole room smelled like him.

If circumstances hadn't been so dire, this would have been a maddening room to sleep in. As it stood, her only concern was stopping the nightmares that would come.

Charlie knocked at the door. Already tucked into bed, she rolled on her side. "Come in."

He entered then walked to the side of the bed and knelt, grinning. "Sleep. You'll get a whopping four hours." He grinned and pushed back a strand of her hair. "They're gonna catch him. I promise, you'll be safe on set tomorrow. Phil's team will make sure of it."

Leslie touched his arm. "Not worried about me, I'm worried about you and Sissy."

"Dad took Mom and Sissy to my grandmother's as soon as I called him. If I know him, he packed every single gun in the house. They'll be fine."

She exhaled. Charlie stood, leaned down and kissed her head, then shut the door with her in his bed.

Three less people to save. She needed to celebrate the small things. She'd sleep in Charlie's bed and she was learning how to trust a man.

Now, if she could figure out a way to tell him about her past without losing him—she'd be happy.

Chapter Twenty-Six

The staging area was an old, dilapidated factory anchored by ten acres of rolling grasslands. At the opposite end of the ten acres was a large turn-of-the-century farmhouse. Both buildings had been quickly rehabbed, but the factory still smelled like rotting oil. The principal actors' trailers were lined up like a Christmas parade on one side of the factory.

Security was heightened at every door. Phil had ordered the limos again to take everyone to the staging area. Charlie had winked at her as he climbed into his.

The flurry of activity at five-fifteen in the morning was staggering. By five-thirty, all the principle actors were in their trailers doing makeup and hair. Leslie and her small crew delivered costumes for the day based on the scene schedule. Each time the door opened or closed, she jumped. She was on edge and her second cup of coffee wasn't helping.

Her heart sank as she noticed a change. Since they secured a female lead, they were leading off with section #87—one of the three primary love scenes between the main characters.

This was his job. It wasn't as if he did it because he had feelings for the witch. Leslie's stomach rolled, but she'd have to put it out of her mind and do her job.

She was given another ten workers to help dress the extras in the warehouse. Her two girls were running from trailer to trailer. The schedule indicated they'd be night shooting from two a.m. to five a.m. the next day. When were they supposed to sleep?

She asked one of the male assistants to run Charlie's costume to him on purpose. Her female assistants were falling all over each other to get that job. She'd delivered two costumes to secondary actors, then carried the golden dress to Christine's trailer.

Leslie knocked on her door, but nobody answered. She knocked again, louder.

"Costumes!" she bellowed. The door swung open, and Christine stood wrapped in a baby blue silk robe, her hair and makeup were done, flawless as usual.

Christine spoke quiet and menacing as if she was the spider speaking to the fly. "Well, hello, Miss Carroll, nice to see you again. Been a busy girl this weekend, haven't you?"

Leslie'd been prepared for this. She gave her a tight smile then walked up the metal stairs into the trailer. *Stay professional.* The sound of the door slamming closed behind her, made her jump.

She placed the box on the couch and pulled the gown out. When she turned, Christine towered over her. For once she stood her ground and didn't back up. "Since you haven't been properly fitted for the dress, I'll need to pin it in places."

When Christine stood, glaring and didn't move, Leslie added, "Would you change into it so I can spot alter it?"

Without a word, Christine dropped her robe to the floor. She smiled, apparently delighted in the embarrassment on Leslie's face. She looked like a Victoria's Secret Angel, in a pricey bra and panty set with thigh-highs and high heels.

Chin high, Leslie stared her down. Christine glared back. Then she snatched the dress out of Leslie's hand.

"This," Christine motioned to her body, "is what Charlie's accustomed to having, *mousy.*"

Leslie twisted her head up. Anger filled her. Professional attitude flew out the window. "I guess he got bored and needed a change of scenery."

Christine's nostrils flared. "I've had him on *every* surface of his house. Imagine that while you make him pancakes, homely housewife."

Turning her back on the woman, Leslie grabbed her costume bag. Then she turned back, arms folded and waited.

Finally, Christine slipped her long legs into the dress. Leslie fantasized about making her look like a fool. But that would only reflect badly on her and the costume department. She could accidentally stick her with pins, though. That might be fun.

Just as Christine pulled the dress over her shoulders, her trailer door swung wide open, and Phil entered out of breath. "Christine!" he yelled, wide eyed.

"Phil—good God, I'm dressing!" Christine turned so Leslie could zip the dress. Phil's entrance startled her enough, she zipped hastily, and snagged a small piece of Christine's skin in the zipper. Oops.

"Ouch, you twit!" Christine growled.

He continued, looking around Christine at Leslie. "It's Charlie…he's gone."

Earth crumbled away beneath Leslie's feet. Forgetting herself, she pushed past Christine. Right into Phil's bubble. "What do you mean gone?" she demanded.

"The guard outside Charlie's trailer was beaten unconscious. They've taken him by ambulance. There's no sign of Charlie. A van tore out of here through security, injuring two guards in the process." He paced. "Knocked down a whole section of fencing we'd put up."

Leslie screwed her eyes shut. No. Not him. Her. He was supposed to take her. She'd known it all morning. This couldn't be happening.

Her phone rang. With trembling hands, she dug through her costume bag and grabbed it. Please God, let that be him.

It was an unknown number. "Hello?" her voice shook as she answered.

"Miss Carroll, it's Detective Majors. We need to talk."

She excused herself and wandered outside. "Do you know where he is?" Tears skewed her vision.

"No. Not yet. We tracked Mr. Gilreath to Tennessee yesterday, but he gave us the slip. He's in partnership with a felon out on parole who helped him fly under the radar. My team is working with local law enforcement to uncover how these two men are connected. We hope it'll give us a lead. Airports within a two-hundred-mile radius are on lockdown for any unauthorized departures, so they won't be able to fly back to California, if that's where they're taking him. At this point there isn't much to go on, which is why I'm calling you."

Detective Majors took a deep breath. "Listen, my gut tells me you weren't completely honest with me, last time we spoke. If you want to help Charlie stay alive, I need for you to tell me *everything* about Jason Gilreath and, Leslie, I mean *everything*."

Her knees shook wildly. She crouched on the sidewalk. Two detectives entered Charlie's trailer, while two others were posted outside. Tears streamed down her face.

"Okay," she stammered, "I'll do it."

Chapter Twenty-Seven

Leslie found a small, empty room inside the factory. Four gray block walls stood with one long fluorescent light that hung from the discolored ceiling. It flickered every few minutes, and the room smelled like old car parts. She pulled the heavy door most of the way closed behind her and sat on the edge of a metal chair she found facing the opposite wall.

She took in a long breath after stating her name and agreeing to be recorded.

Detective Majors began with the toughest question of all: "What is your relationship with Charles Erickson?"

Her worried mind fizzled and her hands shook. The truth, the detective needed the truth.

Without thinking she whispered, "I am in love with him."

The detective cleared her throat then asked, "How did you meet Jason?"

Leslie's heart pounded. She'd never talked about it. The pain of the ordeal she shared with her sister was not something they ever spoke about. Her mind blocked a good portion out.

"My twin sister Anne and I went to a bar the first weekend we were away at Cal State. Anne was…" Leslie rolled her shoulders and scooted back in the chair. "Anne was studious. I had to beg her to go. We were barely eighteen. I'd heard if you paid a certain bouncer, you could get a stamp to get in during Beer Bust—where you pay one price for a mug of beer and refills were free."

"Which campus?"

"San Bernardino."

Fingers clicking on a keyboard rattled through the phone.

"There's no record of you going there."

"There wouldn't be. My name wasn't Leslie."

Detective Majors exhaled. "What's your real name?"

"Linnie Marie Carroll."

More clicking. "Continue," the detective demanded.

"We ordered beers. Felt grown up. Then we sat with a group of kids near the band. My sister was the introvert, but she flirted with this guy who followed us from the bar to the table. When the band took a break, I went to the bathroom. When I got back, Anne's face was pale. I rushed to her; she was dizzy. She looked terrified. I—"

Detective Majors interrupted, "Someone poisoned her drink?"

Leslie closed her eyes, remembering. "I've gone over it a thousand times. Whatever it was, it was put in our drinks at the bar." She swiped at tears with the back of her hand and continued, "Anne's eyes wouldn't focus, and her words were garbled. The boy she'd been talking to offered to help me get her home, so…" Leslie scooted forward on the edge of the chair to slow her breathing.

"Go on," the detective prodded.

Her voice cracked as she said, "I didn't have a choice. I couldn't carry her out the front door. Police were heavy on the strip. Our father…he couldn't take another hit. He was up for re-election against an opposing judge who hated him. The man was dying to uncover a skeleton in our dad's closet. We'd have ruined him." She took a long breath. "He'd warned us. Warned us before we left, not to get into trouble. But I didn't listen.

"We carried her out the back door and laid her in the back seat of the boy's car. When I sat in the front, my vision blurred. The air was stuffy and hot and the doors…he'd locked the doors."

Leslie's breathing came in ragged fits now, but she couldn't stop. "I can still smell the pleather interior of the car mixed with liquor."

"What happened next?"

"He drove…the opposite direction of our dorm. I argued with him, but then…then my words didn't make any sense. Anne was passed out in the backseat. I remember the streetlights flying by and then nothing."

"When did you wake up?"

She covered her eyes, holding in sobs she could feel building. "Two days later."

"What happened during that time?"

She hesitated. Every fiber of her being didn't want to say it. Saying it out loud made it true. Most days she pretended it was only a nightmare. Fresh, hot tears pooled in her eyes.

"We were both…abused." She exhaled and let them fall.

The line went quiet for a moment. No doubt, Detective Majors waited for Leslie to stop blubbering and catch her breath.

Detective Majors took a breath, then spoke. "Look, I know it's hard, and I'm sorry you've got to relive it, but I need an exact account of the abuse. I need to find a pattern in his behavior. What did Mr. Gilreath do to you and to your sister?"

Her body quaked so much the chair squeaked She didn't want to say the words. She and Anne both believed that if they said them aloud, it would make it true.

"I...don't remember but a few things that first night. But by the looks of the room...I woke on blood-stained sheets. Over the next few days I was savagely raped over and over. Drugged, or punched in the face. Violated...in every way imaginable. He chained me to the bed. I remember the thick rope he'd pull to suspend me. Leather cuffs wrapped around my ankles and wrists with wires leading to a big square machine. He'd dress me, then zap hot electricity into me to get me to perform. He'd make me undress myself and touch him. He took lots of pictures and videos with a huge camera on a tripod."

She squeezed both eyes closed. Her spotty memories phased in and out of her mind like a skipping video. "None of the photos or evidence would've survived the fire, though."

"Fire?"

"Yeah," she said, taking a deep breath.

Detective Majors switched gears. "Tell me about the house. Where was it?"

"Off North Park. An old abandoned campus house. The homeless used the upstairs when it rained. But the basement was locked off. It was one long hallway with several rooms. Mine and Anne's both had bare, stained mattresses sitting on rusty metal bedframes."

"Leslie, hang on," Detective Majors cut in, speaking quickly and harshly to someone else. "I want a sweep of all residential and commercial properties sold to Jason Gilreath in the last ten years. Get back with me ASAP. Sorry Leslie, continue."

Leslie shook her head. Memories, like a wall of snapshots, flooded her mind. She had to keep going. "Once the drugs wore off, I made sense of my surroundings. I heard a faint cry. My sister's. Sounded like she was in the next room. I tore my skin pulling my wrists from the cuffs and escaped the bed. I froze and listened. Except for her, there was no noise.

"I opened my door and crept down the hall, then tapped on the wall three times. It'd been our signal between our bedrooms as children. Anne whispered my name. I opened the door. She was bound and naked like I'd been.

"As I freed Anne, above us footsteps made the ceiling creak. We froze. She was in a lot worse physical shape than me; blood was everywhere. I thought I could fight him off. Everything changed when we heard voices and more footsteps. There were at least three people, and one was a woman."

The warehouse door behind Leslie creaked. She spun to find Christine propped against the wall, hanging on every word. She wore faded jeans and a designer shirt, and a look of shock plastered on her face.

Leslie covered the phone. "Can I help you?" she spat.

"I-I need to talk to you, when you're done. Please." Her tone was oddly kind.

"Fine. Give me a minute." Leslie wiped her face.

Damn. Christine must've eavesdropped on every word. She snaked quietly back out of the room through the cracked door before Leslie exhaled and again spoke.

"I should've screamed. Maybe the woman would've heard and helped us. But I was too scared. We crept to the dark living room and searched the floor for anything we could use as a weapon, but...he must've heard us. The other footsteps went out the door. When the front door slammed closed, his footsteps pounded across the creaky upstairs. We both scurried and crouched in the shadows.

"The basement door shot open. We were both afraid to breathe. He stalked down the stairs, flicked on the hall light, then kicked open the door where I'd been held. Then he did the same to Anne's. He stopped in the hallway. Only a few feet from us. The hall light shone behind him, making him look even more intimidating.

"Anne crouched beside me and pointed at a gasoline can. Light from the hall illuminated a rotten board sitting under a shelf. Problem was, it was on the other side of the room."

Leslie could still *feel* the sound of his voice in her bones. She'd played that particular track repeatedly in her mind. It was ingrained inside every nightmare she'd had since that day.

"He called out and said, 'There's nowhere to go. Come on, Annie, come out. Let's talk, honey.' It was like we were inside a horror film. My legs shook so hard, I couldn't move.

"Anne tapped me. When I twisted to face her, I'll never forget...her whole outlook had changed. Her demeanor turned from fear to fury. Her fists were balled. She didn't look like a terrified, abused, half naked girl anymore. She looked like a tiger, crouching, ready to attack and rip the jugular out of her next victim. It was odd because normally, Anne didn't have an aggressive bone in her body. It filled me with hope.

"I borrowed her brave. With gestures and signs, we made an unspoken decision. We'd count to three on our fingers and attack.

Together.

"We counted to three and darted out of the shadows, knocking all three of us down. But he was stronger than both of us."

Leslie raised her hand and touched her face.

"He reared back and punched me square in the eye. Anne scurried next to him and clawed at his face. Still lying on his back, and bleeding, he spun and wrapped his legs around her middle to hold her. Then he held her wrists. She screamed and thrashed but couldn't get away.

"I scrambled to my feet, one eye already swelling shut, and snatched the board from the other side of the room. Running back, I swung. Hit him square on his chest. He rolled to the side, coughing. But he still had a hold on Anne.

"Rearing back, I got one more good swing of the board and hit him square in the face. It stunned him enough for Anne to wriggle free. She stood and kicked him in the groin. I got in another two hits to his head, before blood spurted out of his forehead. His eyes rolled into the back of his head."

"What happened then?" the detective asked.

"I didn't want the bastard to be able to do this to someone else, so I..." Leslie paused. A scraping noise directly behind her caused her to spin around.

She gasped and hit the floor.

Chapter Twenty-Eight

Were it not for the musty stench of moldy wood paneling, she might have believed she was dead. The smell didn't go with the whole Heaven or Hell idea.

Leslie sat, head down, in a hard-backed chair inside a mostly dark room. She cracked one eye open. Small triangles of light came into view like night lights. But hardly any sound. Her brain was groggy, and her heart pounded in her ears.

Her mind was alert enough to understand that her movements had to be invisible. From somewhere in the shadows someone breathed, shallowly.

She moved her fingers first, in careful, calculated movements. Both hands were tied behind her back. Slow as a slug, they rubbed a slick cord that slithered between her fingers. Plastic. Tugging was useless; it wouldn't give or break.

She rolled one ankle to the side barely a half an inch. Couldn't do that either. Her feet had to be tied with the same cord. Her lower lip was numb and protruded. Slowly, she raked her tongue over it. It was at least two sizes too big. That evil bitch Christine Langford put a cloth to her mouth and nose. She must have hit the ground.

Leslie cracked the other eye open and scanned what she could without moving her head, careful not to make any sudden movements. The floor beneath her chair was old, worn-down, planked wood. A yellow light shone behind her. Maybe a small window or a bedroom light, but she couldn't move a muscle to see. Maybe nighttime, but she couldn't tell. Her shoes had been changed. That was odd. Her clothes had been changed too. A green shirt, jeans, and tennis shoes.

Screwing her eyes shut, it hit her. She wore the same outfit Anne had on the night they were drugged. The shoes were Anne's. Leslie was sure of it. Her body quaked. She struggled to stay quiet and still. Quick footsteps padded behind her. Her heart pounded. Prayer. God please help her. And please let Charlie be alive.

In another room, a woman's voice pierced the darkness. "I brought you what you wanted. Now, let Charlie go. The deal was if I brought you the girl, you'd let him live." As usual, Christine Langford was spouting orders.

"You don't get it, do you?"

The sound of Jase's voice alone caused her heart to race. Hot tears pooled in Leslie's eyes.

"I killed two birds with one stone here, precious. I got my Anne back, and my pal Skip here, well, his payment is to have a hot Hollywood starlet in his bed. You're the pawn in the middle. Killing Charlie in the mix is a bonus."

"You piece of—" A sharp buzzing sound interrupted Christine's tirade. Then the thud of a body hitting the floor made Leslie wince. A different man's low laughter rang out.

"I told you." Jase laughed. "You should consider using it. All my old equipment and bindings are in the back of the van. She'll be begging you before it's over."

The next sound was a body being dragged across the floor. Then a door slammed.

Leslie's eyes, wide open now, squinted. What was the shape in front of her? A chair faced her—with a body in it, slumped over like her. Had to be Charlie.

Footsteps made her freeze. This time they crept close behind her, stopped, then darted away. It sounded like bare feet tiptoeing on hardwood. That wasn't Jase. Felt female.

Turning her concentration back to the chair in front of her, she pulled her body toward it. Just a few inches closer and she might make out the face. As she moved, her chair squeaked, and she froze.

No movement or sound came from behind her, but she knew…knew he was there. She sensed eyes boring a hole in the back of her head.

The lights increased slowly as if she was on a stage. Wood paneling came into view and surrounded them. Just ahead, in what looked like the living room space, green shag carpet clung to the floor in patches as if someone was rehabbing the house then stopped.

The other chair had a clear tarp under it. The sandy-blond hair of the man she loved hung down, covering part of his face. He was slouched forward as far as the cord securing him would allow and even in the hazy light, she could tell someone had beaten his beautiful face.

~ * ~

Jason couldn't take the wait any longer. Impatient, like a vulture waiting his turn to feed, he looked down at his trembling hands. He'd waited for her for so long. Oh, he'd punish her for running from him. But the other part of him wanted to take her in his arms and take her to bed.

Children would finally be an option. He'd never leave her or them. He wouldn't be anything like the drunken whore. He'd be an exceptional parent.

In Anne, he found a woman pliable enough to keep in line. Unlike his father, who couldn't keep his wife in line. His heart raced as he stalked closer. He'd color her hair back to a strawberry blonde again, exactly like his mother's. Dark hair didn't suit her anyway. She'd need the exact strawberry hair she had the night they met.

"Anne, honey, time to wake up," he sang as he walked around her. "I want you awake enough to watch."

He was giddy, laughing to himself. Anne's hair covered her face, but he knew she was awake. Walking around Charlie's chair, he watched her…his Anne.

He kicked Charlie's leg. "Hey, dickhead. Wake up!"

~ * ~

Leslie willed Charlie to stay down. Head still tilted toward the floor, she searched the room for anything to help. Something shimmered in the low light on the dining table. A mirror maybe? Wait. Too thin and long to be a mirror. A knife? Jesus, a long damn knife. Way too small to call it a pocketknife. A dagger?

Jason reached forward from behind Charlie's chair and snatched the front of his hair. As Jason lifted Charlie's head, his face came into view. One eye was swollen shut, and the other one was almost closed.

She wanted to hurt Jason. Charlie's better eye twitched. Was he out or pretending to be? The crack of Jason's knuckles on Charlie's cheekbone took her breath. He still didn't move.

"You think you can take whatever you want, 'cause you're Charlie fucking Erickson? Slick bastard. You thought you could touch *my Anne* and not pay the ultimate price? You'll die today, hot shot. I should have killed you in high school, prick. Get ready to meet your maker."

Jason strutted over and took hold of the shiny dagger from the table. Spinning back around, he stalked to Charlie, turning the hilt of the knife repeatedly in his hand.

Leslie couldn't wait any longer. She had to face him and give Charlie time to wake up. Raising her head caught Jason's gaze and distracted him. He stopped in his tracks and smiled. He moved like a big cat over to her, laid the large knife down at her feet, then knelt.

"Anne! You're awake! I've missed you so much," he gushed, crouching in front of her with hands hungrily rubbing her hips and the tops of her thighs.

Her stomach churned. Bile rose in her throat. Vomiting on him wouldn't slow him down much. She'd tried that tactic once.

He must've heard her rumbling stomach. He leapt to his feet, then tucked a lock of hair behind her ear. In an erratic move, he spun around behind her. She willed herself not to shake. He scooped up a ponytail sized wad of hair and yanked her head up to face him.

"I miss your long, honey-colored hair, Anne. You'll grow it out and we'll color it back golden before we leave the country."

"Sure." She was proud of herself. Her voice didn't quiver like she assumed it would. He had to be pushed, but slow. "Why am I tied up, Jason?"

Even looking at him from upside down, she knew she struck a chord. Muscles in his jaw tightened and his face contorted. He released her hair, then bent over and picked up the knife. Tossing it in the air, he flipped and caught it like a teenager.

His head cocked to the side, he answered, "So you never run again. And so you have a front row seat to Charlie's death!"

He pointed the knife at Charlie, who looked as though he was still unconscious. "Your punishment for touching him is to clean up the blood when he's dead. Then it's immediate training."

Her eyes narrowed. He smiled. "Let's just say, I've mastered the art since you've been gone. Tested my brand-new rig on a local whore. Works like a charm. It's waiting for you. You'll be so well trained you'll strip for me, tie yourself up, and beg me to take you."

Jason scraped the tip of the knife across her chest, circling her chair. It didn't cut, but it stung. Charlie's feet moved under his chair, only an inch, but she noticed. Good, he was awake. Her plan was formulated, but to pull it off she had to wait until she pushed Jason off balance.

He resumed his monologue. "Anne, running from me, well, it tainted me. Another trained whore will come with us, so I don't get bored. We'll be long gone from here when they find Charlie's body." He laughed to himself. "The best part is they'll assume Christine did it before she took her own life. Wraps it up nice for the stupid bitch detective."

He paced, turning the hilt of the knife over and over in his hands. She needed to strike.

"You realize I'm not Anne, right?" Leslie announced, matter-of-factly, interrupting his musing.

Jason stopped mid-stride and turned to stare. "Really? Pray tell, who are you, then?"

186

"Linnie," she announced. "Remember me?" Hatred boiled inside her. Pulling and tugging at her restraints, she continued, "You know...Anne's twin? The other girl you drugged, raped, and beat that weekend at Cal State? Remember arguing with me when we left the bar about the way to our dorm? You and I both know Anne was already passed out, so there was no way for her to know that little fact."

When his face scrunched up, he touched his temple as if remembering made his head hurt. Leslie caught sight of a tremor that rocked Charlie's body. He now knew. Knew she'd been tortured by Jason. Charlie would never look at her the same way again. A sob bubbled up, but she'd be damned if she'd stop now.

Jason's eyes widened. He pointed the knife at Leslie. "You're lying, Anne. I'd know you anywhere."

"Anne's dead, Jason." His face fell, and she persisted, "She died in 2012. Breast cancer, just like our mom. She didn't love you. You've convinced yourself she did, but she didn't even know you until you kidnapped and raped us."

A pained look crossed his face. He gripped the sides of his head. Soft footsteps again padded behind her. Someone else was inside this place.

She glanced over at Charlie. One blue eye bored into hers through the swollenness of his face. Pity crossed Charlie's face. Her heart dropped. She had to push harder. Relive it all again, to save those she loved.

If it was possible, she hated Jason even more for making her recount the abuse in front of Charlie.

Anger permeated her body and hit her like a wall. She yanked at the cord tied around her wrists as she spoke. "Remember being hit in the face with a board?" Jason examined her, murder in his eyes as she prodded him, "I hit you first, but Anne hit you several times, too. I bet you didn't pee for a week."

In a flash, he stomped over and punched her, square in the mouth. Charlie sprang forward, still tied to the chair, and knocked Jason to the ground. He scrambled up, still clutching the knife. "Now you've done it, dickhead."

Charlie backed up as far as he could, head swiveling from side-to-side, looking for something to use, but he was helpless without his arms.

As Jason stalked Charlie, Leslie ripped the skin on her wrists, pulling free of the cord. Feet still bound, she lunged, knocking Jason down as she fell on top of him.

Her shriek filled the room. The knife punctured her stomach.

Jason stood, then rolled her to her side and carefully pulled it out. True grief and sadness lined his face. Blood poured out, soaking the shirt he put on her.

Charlie shouted as he flung his body at Jason. The force of the men hitting the floor sent the knife skidding into the kitchen. Charlie head-butted Jason, stunning him. The wooden chair he'd been attached to broke away, but Charlie's hands were still tied behind him.

Jason shook his head, slow and deliberate as if to say, he'd screwed up then pinned Charlie to the floor. He kneed Jason in the stomach a second before his former friend punched him hard in his unprotected face. Jason scrambled back to sit on top of Charlie. His hands wrapped around Charlie's throat.

Leslie rolled to her belly and pushed her body with stiff arms. She had to move. Had to save him. Her legs wouldn't respond. She must've lost too much blood. She dragged her body toward him with her arms, but she moved too slow. Charlie would be long dead by the time she got there. Tears welled up and her arms burned. She had to crawl faster.

A shadow fell across the floor in front of her. She froze, then twisted her head, tortoise-like, measured and deliberate. The hall light outlined a petite woman in a torn maid's uniform. She held the knife in a stabbing position. It glinted as she crept toward Leslie.

Fear gripped her like one of Jason's electrical currents.

Was she in league with him, sent to finish her off? Or worse, kill Charlie?

Leslie strained to move her legs, but they still wouldn't respond.

She spun on her back, like a dog, hands up in surrender. As the woman stalked closer, their eyes locked—and she knew. Knew the woman wouldn't hurt her. She was familiar with that haunted look. She and her sister had the same look for weeks after their ordeal. It was terror mixed with vengeance.

Only this woman's eyes were one hundred percent vengeance.

Jason had Charlie's shoulders pinned with his knees. His hands squeezed tight, forcing life out of Charlie's body. Gurgling and gasping, he struggled, but without his hands he had no defense. His writhing slowed.

Without a word, she willed the woman to walk faster. Do whatever she was set in motion to do, but hurry.

The woman stepped over Leslie, and stretching high, stabbed Jason from behind, quick and repeatedly. Her scream pierced a mainly silent scream.

She embodied every woman's revenge after surviving abuse.

She stood above the men and had gotten in about five good stabs when Jason slithered off Charlie, screeching and writhing. Charlie rolled to the side and gasped for air.

Leslie closed her eyes as the woman chased Jason and continued to jab the knife into the chest.

No matter the heinous atrocities he committed against her, her sister, and apparently this woman, Leslie couldn't witness his gruesome death.

All noise ceased in the room, except the woman's labored breathing as she finished the job. After a few minutes of rhythmic puncture sounds, the back door kicked in. Leslie opened her eyes to see armed police in blue uniforms burst through the door.

Detective Majors followed. And last in line was a disheveled, black-eyed Christine. She attempted to run past the officers, but they weren't having any part of her corrupting the crime scene. They shut her down, but demanding as usual, she yelled for someone to call an ambulance.

Yes, put Charlie in an ambulance. Make sure he's okay. Leslie's mind fuzzed.

Her jaw ached and the term "stabbing pain" took on a whole new meaning.

The officers secured the knife, handcuffed the woman, then secured the scene before allowing paramedics inside. Wide-eyed and sobbing, the woman spoke in rapid-fire Spanish. Two officers and a detective took her to the kitchen for questioning.

Paramedics swarmed Leslie. As if she were in disembodied form, she saw Detective Majors kneel and cut Charlie's cords. He scrambled to his feet as the paramedics strapped Leslie onto a gurney.

Her toes and fingers were frozen. Blood felt as if it was draining like water out of her body. She'd be dead soon. The liquid iron stench of her own blood made her want to vomit. Only she'd have to unhinge her swollen jaw to do it.

She only wanted to sleep. Then she thought of Nate. Aunt Reva would take care of him, wouldn't she? Of course she would. She loved Nate. Her heart rate began to slow. Without the threat of Jason killing Charlie, and knowing Nate would be fine, she gave herself permission to sleep.

Charlie was alive. Nate was safe. And that's all that mattered.

~ * ~

Charlie stumbled to his feet. His body ached, and his face was as tight as an overfilled balloon. Two sets of paramedics swooped in.

One team loaded a semiconscious Leslie on to a gurney while the other ordered Charlie to stop moving so they could evaluate his injuries.

He growled and pushed past them. He didn't need them. By the time he made his way around the people in the tiny living room, the paramedics had stopped Leslie's bleeding and started an IV. She'd slipped unconscious before he could talk to her.

Detective Majors grabbed Charlie's arm, pulling him out of their way, so the paramedics could push the gurney through the house toward the waiting ambulance. One cantankerous woman paramedic wasn't taking no for an answer. She walked up and swabbed Charlie's cuts.

When he turned to glare, she glared right back—letting him know she wouldn't take his shit. He nodded, and turned away, his gaze trained on Leslie as they hoisted her body into the ambulance, and secured the gurney before hooking her up to tubes.

A scratchy lump in his throat moved as they shifted her lifeless body from side-to-side. Detective Majors touched his arm and he turned.

"You all right?"

Charlie nodded, unable to speak. His mind was keyed up and ready to kill. He could have bitten through glass. Christine stood across the room talking like she was on set, casually, with two detectives as if she'd done nothing wrong.

His fists balled. He'd heard the tail end of Jase's conversation. She was an accomplice to kidnapping. They needed to lock the sick bitch up.

Detective Majors followed his line of sight. "She saved you."

When he spun around and leveled a look that said she was batshit crazy, she nodded to make her point and said, "Both of you. Her attorney is on his way now. She apparently kicked Skip in the balls so hard, it put him in the hospital. Then she found me.

"It was a godsend. We were following the wrong lead—one of many pieces of real estate Jason had purchased in the last two years. She brought us here, to you. This isn't a property he owns under his real name and we hadn't uncovered this alias yet. We'd have never found you in time, had it not been for her."

Charlie stared. He could've forgiven her if she'd only been responsible for helping them take him. But Leslie? She'd never done a thing to Christine. And worse, Christine probably knew she was handing Leslie over to her worst nightmare. No. He'd never be grateful to that bitch.

An older paramedic climbed into the ambulance. He checked

hoses and cords for placement, then laid a caring hand on Leslie's head. Charlie kept watch on Leslie and listened. Detective Majors resumed, "Jason blackmailed Christine into bringing Leslie to him or you'd die. She only had a few hours to hatch a plan and get Leslie here—to save you."

The coroner bent over Jason and snapped pictures. Charlie ambled back through the house and stopped. As they zipped up Jason's body bag, a million feelings slipped through him—hatred and sadness topping the list. Blood was everywhere. Jason's and Leslie's. The sickly metallic smell permeated his nose. How could he have been so blind? He remembered. She'd tried to warn him.

Turning back to Detective Majors and the paramedic who followed him, he cleared the lump from his throat and pointed toward the ambulance. "I'm riding with her."

The detective raised both hands in the air. "Nobody's stopping you. I'll meet you there and get word to your parents."

Charlie hobbled over and pulled himself into the ambulance. Tears stung and fogged his vision. Paramedics resituated Leslie's monitors, checked vitals then inserted another tube into her arm, hooked to a pouch of blood on a pole.

The bandage they'd applied to her side seeped red. How much blood had she'd lost? God. She'd become more than a girlfriend. She'd become part of him. A part he couldn't live without.

He loved her. And he hadn't told her.

Charlie clutched her cold, pale hand into his and kissed it. The back doors of the ambulance shut, and sirens wailed as they rushed her to the nearest hospital.

Kissing her hand once more, he begged God not to take her.

Chapter Twenty-Nine

A piercing siren.

Leslie didn't remember hearing much before the darkness grabbed her, but she'd heard that.

Perfect. She was dead. Opening one eye, she was blinded by a bright light glaring on white walls, floors, and ceiling. She couldn't be in Heaven. God knew she didn't deserve that.

She struggled to focus. A beeping monitor indicated she was in a hospital. A way-too-bright hospital at that.

She wore an all-white gown, covered by a white sheet and blanket. One purple sock decorated with pink pigs stuck out from the blanket. She wiggled her toes and stared at them for a full minute. As her eyes focused, the red and yellow splotches on the white wall resolved into flowers in a glass vase. They rebelled against the white color scheme of the room.

Pain stabbed at her side when she turned her head. Okay, not Heaven. There's no pain in Heaven, right?

Sun glinted off a picture on the nightstand, too. She squinted, and the frame came into view. The picture of her and Charlie's mom, the day they first met. A lump formed in her throat.

A nurse walked in. "Hi, honey. You're awake. You gave us a scare. How ya feeling?"

Her delicious southern drawl meant Leslie was still in Tennessee. Her mind struggled to remember why she was there. "My side hurts. What day is it?"

Her throat felt scratchy, and her voice sounded like someone else's, but her mind was finally awake and sharp as a razor.

"Tuesday," the nurse replied absentmindedly, checking a monitor.

"Tuesday?" Aunt Reva must be worried sick. Hopefully someone contacted her.

Leslie bit her lip. *Nate*. He'd be pacing the floor and having meltdowns by now. She had to get home. As soon as she began pulling at cords, another nurse trotted into the room and sent the first nurse out to fetch a doctor. Woman number two was large and in charge. In a flash, she pushed a button on the wall, grabbed a blood pressure cuff, then took control.

"Calm down," she said, quick wrapping the cuff around Leslie's arm. "Miss Carroll, we're alerting your family and the surgeon you're awake. I believe he's on this floor and will want to come and check your stitches. Does anything hurt?"

"I don't have family here. Wait... Surgeon? What surgeon?"

The nurse's face was kind, but weary. Her stance said *don't mess with me* as she leaned over and took Leslie's temperature. She pushed against the bed with her hands to lift her body to a sitting position. Pain took her breath away.

The nurse laid a heavy hand on her shoulder. "Now, honey, you gotta lay still. You came in with a stab wound. Punctured your spleen, and it had to be removed. Other than that, you've been in and out of consciousness for the last twenty-four hours. Darlin', this is the first time you've made any sense."

"Some California detective has been up here a few times. She's asked for one of our psychiatrists to come up and speak to you when you woke." When Leslie leveled a look at her, she added, "Standard protocol."

"I don't need a shrink," Leslie spat.

"Couldn't hurt," Charlie said, his voice cracking at the end.

He stood in the doorway, his chest heaving as if he'd run from the other side of the world. His swollen face had shrunk back down, closer to its normal, handsome size. Both eyes had a purple hue underneath, though. All the same, he was alive. She could breathe.

Charlie's stare never faltered as he walked toward the bed. What was in his eyes? Disgust? Pain? Or worse, pity? As he reached her, he eyeballed the nurse. She took her time, not taking the hint. When she finished, she leaned over the bed again and placed a hand on Leslie's forehead in a kind, motherly way. Then she shot a warning to Charlie before she left—he was not to squeeze or hug the patient.

Leslie couldn't bear his eyes on her. She stared out the window. Couldn't face him. He knew.

Knew she'd been savagely raped as a teenager. Her virginity taken because of one stupid decision. He knew she was broken, and nobody could put her back together again. Why was he still there and what kind of an idiot would he have to be to still want her?

He sat on her bed then busied his hands—at first by wringing them, then sitting on them. His face was conflicted as if he wanted to touch her but was afraid to. He opted briefly for her hand, but she couldn't look at him.

"Look at me," he said. When she didn't, he begged, "It's important."

Reluctant, she turned.

"Your socks." He nodded toward her feet.

She followed his stare, wiggling her toes again.

"They're compliments of Sissy. She didn't like the fact the hospital put you in all white. Said you looked dead. Before we could stop her, she pulled those out of her bag and shoved them onto your feet."

"Your family was here?" Her voice was laced with more emotion than she wanted.

"They're not just *my* family anymore."

No strength in the world could've stopped her tears.

Charlie leaned over her and kissed her hair. "Shh, it's over. I promise, nobody will ever hurt you again."

Leslie shook her head and released his hand. "It'll *never* be over." She raised her voice as she said, "I'll *never* get past this, don't you see? I'm not the girl for you, Charlie, I never was."

Charlie stared as if she'd lost her mind. "Leslie—"

"It's Linnie, Charlie, not Leslie. Leslie was my mother's name."

"Linnie," he echoed, thoughtfully.

She took a ragged breath. "My dad was a judge appointed by the governor, but up for re-election. He was revered by the majority for his conservative and religious background but ran against a flamboyant liberal who lived to slander him. After…after *it* happened, Anne and I ran back home. Anne ended up pregnant, so we had to tell him. He was angry and disappointed—not only at the situation, but that we didn't report it."

Linnie's throat was dry. She couldn't tell if she was dehydrated because of her ordeal or if her throat was holding back tears. The constant pain in her side and in her heart kept sidetracking her thoughts.

She took a shallow breath and stared up toward the ceiling, regaining her train of thought. "We couldn't ruin his career. It was all he had. Anne couldn't bear to abort the baby, even after her initial checkup revealed undiagnosed stage IV cancer. She was stubborn. Wouldn't even talk about chemo until after the baby was born. He might have been unplanned, with a psychopathic father, but she couldn't murder an unborn child.

"Toward the end of her life, my dad pulled in favors and committed the only unlawful act of his career. He had my social security number, my looks and my records changed into my mother's name, so if our abuser ever went looking for either my sister or me, he wouldn't be able to track either of us. Anne wasn't expected to live much longer, and I'd be someone else."

She snuck a glance at him. Charlie's mouth hung open. The intense pain in her heart overshadowed her stab wound. She'd lied about everything: what kind of person she was, Nate, her identity, everything. By the look on his face, he hated her for it, she was sure. Linnie sucked in a sharp breath and braced herself, memorizing his face.

"My sister and I even pretended to be a lesbian couple when she had Nate to get both names on his birth certificate." Linnie chuckled despite herself. The sheer absurdity of it. They'd been so young and so stupid.

"Nate's not your biological child," Charlie whispered. His face searched hers as though unanswered questions were now piecing together.

"No, but I've raised him. And he's definitely mine now that both his parents are dead."

~ * ~

The room spun. Charlie's mind raced as pieces of her story clicked into place.

Her eyes and body language seemed defensive. Like she expected a fight, or maybe she was angry. Angry he hadn't saved her. That regret had haunted him every minute since the attack. He shook his head to concentrate.

Nate wasn't hers. She'd raised a boy with autism entirely on her own, and he wasn't even her child, but her sister's. He was in even more awe of her than ever.

But she said she'd never get over it. And she wasn't the girl for him. That stung deeper than he imagined.

Three doctors came into the room. They asked him to leave if he wasn't family. Leslie, Linnie, didn't bother to tell them otherwise, so he stood, slowly as if he was in a trance, and left the room. He meandered back down the hallway toward the waiting room, defeated. How could he convince her she was all he ever wanted?

As he crossed the threshold into the waiting room, Christine picked at her fingernails, staring at the carpet by the coffeemaker. She looked like hell. He had hours of waiting time to mull over how he felt about her.

He walked over and poured two cups, then handed her one. Her black eye gained more purple rings, her hair curled in unruly waves, and she wore sweats, of all things. Nobody recognized her like this.

Christine accepted the cup. Her hands shook. After a moment, her voice hoarse, she spoke. "I have no idea what to say. 'I'm sorry' doesn't seem to be enough. I thought I was doing the right thing to save you, but I had no regard for her life at all. I viewed her only as competition. I'm a screwed-up piece of work, aren't I?"

He nodded and sipped his coffee.

"She's been through some pretty scary shit, hasn't she?"

He nodded again.

"Listening to her recount the abuse to the detective, I almost backed out. I couldn't imagine putting her in the same room as that psychopath again."

Charlie almost spat out his coffee. He jumped up. *The detective. She'd have the recording. He could tell Leslie...crap, Linnie—he could convince Linnie he knew everything and loved her anyway.*

Without another word, he tossed his full cup into the trash and trotted toward the hall. Christine stopped him.

"Charlie?" He turned, expressionless. "Do yourself a favor—sell your house. She's not gonna want to live there. Trust me." Christine picked up her purse and left.

As he ran toward the elevator, he pulled out his phone and dialed Detective Majors' number. Three rings, and she answered. "Charlie?"

"Detective, I need a favor."

"I wondered when you'd put it all together. I can't help you. Not without her permission."

"Shit. Stand by your phone; she'll be contacting you shortly." Charlie hung up.

His plan ran through his mind as he rode the elevator. He scrubbed his face with his hands. Could he pull it off? It'd be the hardest thing he'd ever done. God this was gonna kill him. He'd have to put her on the defensive and push her. And use his acting skills to make her believe he was selfish enough to walk away. Deep down, he knew she believed she was unworthy of love. Guilt held her back. He was sure of it. He took a deep breath and walked into her room as the doctors left.

Leslie—no, Linnie—was rolled toward the window. He stood next to the bed. She didn't move. "Nothing left to say, Erickson. Go home to your family."

He crossed his arms and planted his feet. "I can't."

~ * ~

Linnie turned her head and stared. She didn't want to do this. She felt defeated, but angry too. Not so much at him, but how much does one person have to lose over one mistake? Hadn't she sacrificed enough? She didn't want to see the pity in his eyes. Couldn't he just concede, they weren't meant to be and leave? She'd have to make him go. She knew that now.

"Why can't you?" She snapped.

"Because we're not finished yet."

"Impossible." She scoffed and rolled again toward the window, then spun back, suddenly angry. "Did you hit your head or something? What in the hell is wrong with you? You heard what happened. You know that he…" her voice trailed off.

"—no. I don't know what happened. I know part of it, and all the lies you fed me."

Linnie glared at first, then conceded. She had lied to him and everyone she knew. She had no defense there.

"Listen to the recording. I'm sure detective Majors would be more than happy to let you hear all the details. But after that…we're through."

Charlie grabbed a chair, spun it around and sat with his chest against the back. His face registered rage.

"After everything we've been through, you still don't trust me." His voice shook with anger.

Linnie reached for her phone, typed a message to Detective Majors then threw it at the foot of her bed.

"There. Call her. Listen to the whole damn thing. I don't care. This isn't just a state of mind, Charlie. I can't love you the way you need to be loved." She stared at her fingers. "I'm damaged. And I don't have it in me to be fixed."

Her voice failed her, cracking at the end. She felt the full weight of what she was giving up. But she couldn't allow him to be tied to someone not whole. "You don't even know the half of what he did. Forget about us. Move on. I'm not in love with you."

Her gut twisted. Letting him go was selfless, she told herself. The right thing to do. Save him. He could have a family, babies…a happy, normal life without her. She'd survive. She always had.

She didn't deserve the happy ending anyway and she knew it. Her stomach heaved. If she could've thrown up right then, without feeling weak, she would've. She just told the man she loved she didn't love him.

His eyes registered sadness, but his jaw was tight and angry. "Is this because I couldn't save you?"

She looked at him like he had three heads. Then the lightbulb went off. "Maybe. Maybe I expected you to be the hero like in one of your movies."

"And I expected you to be honest, and not just with me, but with yourself. Your sister died. I'm sorry that she did, but it wasn't anyone's fault. Cancer took her, not you. And you're right, you can't love me the way I need to be loved. Not until you forgive yourself."

"Get out!" After raising her voice, she turned her back on him.

Her heavy-set nurse pushed open the door and glanced from Linnie to Charlie. Hands on full hips, she glared at Charlie like she could take him out.

"Look at me." When she refused he repeated it louder and firmer. "Look at me."

The nurse at the door stomped one foot, then huffed, letting him know she was about to intervene. Linnie obeyed, rolling over slightly, then glared at him with puffy, wet eyes.

He pointed a finger. "I'm not giving up—don't you *dare* give up either." Charlie spun, and shot a look at the nurse, who stood at the door, poised to take him out.

"Erickson…" Linnie squeaked. He stopped and turned. "I'm finished. Don't *ever* come back." She turned away as he stormed out.

Chapter Thirty

Filming was postponed indefinitely. Charlie's entertainment attorney filed a motion allowing him out of his contract, citing PTSD. In truth, his heart wasn't in it. Not without her. And they couldn't pay him enough to do it with Christine.

Yes, she'd saved them, but only because she put the only woman he truly loved in danger.

Charlie went into hiding. Back to the only place his life made sense—home. At first, he slept. Slept for days longer than he ever slept before. His mom hid her worry by cooking nonstop. All his favorite foods were stockpiled when he woke.

Days passed. He busied himself with a punch list of projects his dad had been putting off. He took the Christmas lights down, built new tool shelves, ran the tractor, and constructed a roof over his mom's chicken coop. Work began every morning around five. At lunchtime he sat only long enough to eat, then he'd work until dark. He didn't think about Hollywood, or films, or his money.

But he never stopped thinking about Linnie. How he missed her snark and her laugh. It punched him in the gut remembering the pain in her eyes. He smiled. She'd been so brave as she fought Jason to try and save him. She did more for him than he could do for her.

His only contact with the outside world was Kat. She agreed to cover for him until he got his mind straight. He turned off his cell and never took it with him to the barn. At first, he felt naked without it, since he'd taken the damn contraption everywhere for so long.

It took a few weeks but breathing became easier. If he concentrated on physical labor, he could get out of his own head. And maybe close the gash in his heart.

Right at dusk, as the sun was only a spot left on the horizon, Charlie was about to knock off for the night when his mom walked into the barn.

"Charlie?"

"Yeah, Mom, in here," he called from one of the horse stalls.

"What're you doing?" she asked, standing on tiptoes looking

over a half wall.

"Fixing loose boards."

Pat followed him with her gaze and chewed on her bottom lip. Something was on her mind. He'd avoided an interrogation, but now, it was unstoppable. He nailed the last board then crouched, gathering wayward nails and screws and placing them in his dad's bag. He looked up. Her face was pleading and yet worn with sadness at the same time.

"You okay?" He stopped moving.

"Not really, son."

When he stood, she elaborated. "You'll experience it one day with your own kids, when they're grown. You stand by, helpless, as your child shuts down, and there's not a damn thing you can do about it."

She searched his face.

Charlie zipped the bag and hoisted the strap over his shoulder, then picked up the hammer and drill and tamped the hay down with his boot. Anything not to meet her eyes. He had walked barely past her, when she spoke.

"Charlie, stop. Look at me."

He obeyed.

"Tell me what happened with you and Leslie—I mean Linnie?"

He walked out of the stall, past his mom and placed the tools on his dad's work bench. His back was toward her. "Not much to tell, Mom. She doesn't love me, that's all."

He dropped the nail bag inside the box, where it always sat.

"Charles Thomas Erickson, that is quite possibly the dumbest thing I've ever heard you say." Pat folded her arms across her chest and huffed.

He spun, just as angry. "Why? She said it herself. She can't love me the way I need to be loved. She said she wasn't the girl for me, and she'd never be able to get past what happened to her. She told me to leave and never come back." He sucked in a shaky breath and added, "She said she wasn't in love with me."

His mom let out a long breath then sat on the bench next to the stall. She patted the seat next to her, but he shook his head. Then she said, "Boy, listen to me. We women are crazy creatures. Most of the time we say exactly what's on our mind *at that moment*, only to regret it the very next. Your dad said Linnie was abused by Jason, and you wanted to know the things he did to her. Why would you want that, son?"

He took a deep breath, then changed his mind and sat next to her. "I wanted to tell her I knew everything, and I wanted to be with her anyway. I needed to be able to chase her nightmares away. She gave permission for me to listen to it, but I never called the detective back. Never listened to the tape. I realized that it didn't matter what happened to her before."

Pat sighed. "So, have you changed your mind?"

Charlie pondered the question. "I still want her, more than ever," he said quietly. "But I couldn't save her. My hands were tied behind my back. She was bleeding and...all the fame, the money, the movies... I thought I was so powerful. But I couldn't save her." He looked down at his boots. "She looks at me differently now."

Pat put her hand on his arm. "Those are *your* feelings, son, not hers. She doesn't hold you responsible for that night, I'm sure of it. I bet she's kicking herself for telling you not to come back. No doubt she said it out of fear or guilt, and she's regretting it now. She probably thinks you listened to the tape and now you don't want her since you know her abuse."

Charlie's head snapped up. "Why would she think that?"

His mom cocked her head to the side. "Son, she gave you permission to listen to her statement, right?"

"Yeah."

"Then you left?

"I had to, I—"

"She hasn't heard a word from you since. If you were in her shoes, what would you think?"

He ran his fingers through his hair, then dropped his face into his hands. "What if it's too late?"

Pat stood. "Charlie, honey, listen...if she's your future, you need to stop feeling sorry for yourself and go talk to her. You're never gonna know the truth, until you do."

He sat in silence then made up his mind. He stood and squeezed her tight. "Thanks, Mom." He flashed her a real half-smile—the first in weeks.

"Anytime, son," she said, flopping back down on the bench and smiling up, like she was thanking God.

He marched toward the house and straight up to his room. When he turned his phone back on, he'd missed a host of calls and texts, but none from Linnie. He let out a defeated breath and deleted all, except one. It was from Detective Majors and it read: "*Charlie, it's Michelle. I'm sending you a five second sound bite from my conversation with Leslie. Please do yourself a favor and listen to it.*"

Charlie clicked the button and listened. His legs carried him out his bedroom door and down the stairs two at a time before he even realized it. Charlie ran from room to room. "Dad? Hey, Dad, you in here?" he yelled.

Sissy and his dad sat in the den playing checkers. Tom stood, looking startled. "Charlie, what's wrong?"

Charlie strode toward his dad, smiling from ear to ear. "Remember how you and I plotted out part of the property last summer, those thirty acres I wanted?"

"Sure, son. Why?"

"I'd like to write you a check…today."

His dad beamed. He'd made it clear he'd wanted nothing more than to have his son home. "We can clear part of it this afternoon if you want?"

"Sounds perfect, Dad."

Chapter Thirty-One

PRP sent a massive bouquet of flowers to the ICU and an ugly termination letter to Linnie's home. They couldn't employ her until the little issue of her fraudulent social security number/name fiasco was resolved. A small piece of light green stationary was tucked neatly inside the letter. Scrolled handwriting indicated they'd gladly take her back when the misunderstanding was cleared up.

It was unsigned, but she knew Mr. Miller's handwriting.

Nate, thank God, never got sick while she was in Tennessee. The nebulizer, it seemed, stopped whatever virus had started. And her second flight—this time on a commercial airline—wasn't nearly as scary as the first one, for several reasons. Her stitches were taken out and her incision was tender, but healing. It'd take much longer for her heart to heal.

Charlie hadn't called or texted since she told him to leave. And that, she was positive, was for the best. He probably listened to her abuse and ran for the hills. Who wouldn't?

She spent the last few weeks talking with the shrink the hospital appointed, everyday both in person and over the phone. Slowly, the psychiatrist was convincing her that none of her suffering was her fault. And neither was her sister's death. Charlie had been right.

At the end of her first full week back in California, she got up and took Nate to school. Her body was sore, but she had an appointment with an attorney downtown to fix her identity. He'd known and respected her father. His plan was to cite extreme abuse and terror as their reason for skirting the law.

She'd miss the name Leslie. Sitting in her Bronco at the light, she remembered how Charlie had said it the first day they'd met. Thinking about his smooth voice and the way his eyes danced with laughter, usually at her, caused her chest to tighten.

The more she told her brain not to think about him, the more the memories flooded back. The dressing room, holding hands in front of the producers, the twenty questions plane ride and the riverboat.

She'd driven him away, hadn't given him a choice to stay and fight. That might be the one decision she regretted for the rest of her life.

The Bronco groaned into a parking space. Summer was rolling in fast. Heat rising off the pavement made her wish she'd worn something other than her white cotton dress. Taking the hardtop off with a dress on was no easy task. But she could do it. No need to hide any longer. Her monster was dead.

Linnie tossed the keys into her purse and strolled down the sidewalk toward the old stone courthouse. Her hair blew in the breeze and more than once she had to catch her dress from flying up. Once inside the building, she navigated through security and headed up the wide, curved stairs to the fourth floor to meet her attorney.

On the second-floor landing, a crowd huddled together. She sidestepped to see a white-gowned bride and her black-tuxedoed groom posing for pictures. The young woman glowed, and her new husband grinned ear to ear. Most of the crowd continued upstairs. But not Linnie.

She couldn't rip her attention away from the sweet couple. Stupid tears stung her eyes.

For the first time in her life, she could envision being the bride. She could let go of her past and love someone else unconditionally. The truth was she'd sent away the only person who made her heart sing. Turning, she trudged up, hanging on to the rail with one hand and swiping tears with the other.

On the third floor, heading up with her head down, a woman ahead of her called out, "Leslie…ah shit…Linnie, hey, Linnie."

Detective Majors walked down toward her and stood tall on the stair above her. They shook hands. "How are you?" the detective asked with serious, narrowed eyes.

"I'm healing pretty well." Linnie looked down at her shoes.

"Hmm."

"What?" Linnie noticed the tips of the detective's lips curled into a wry smile.

"I can always tell when you're holding back. I knew it the first time we met." She wagged a finger. "I couldn't tell what you were lying about, but something was off."

Linnie laughed. "And I thought I was so slick."

The detective laughed, then turned serious, cocking an eyebrow. "You never answered my last question."

Detective Majors was way too curious to let it go. Linnie knew the question would come back up. "What did I do to Jason after we knocked him out with the board? Off the record?"

"Of course."

Linnie sighed. "I took the gasoline can and poured gas on the walls, found a lighter in his pocket then I torched the house."

"Oh my." The detective glanced around scratching the back of her neck. "I'm gonna pretend I didn't hear any of that. Wait... Jason was unconscious at that point—how'd he get out?"

"My too-kind sister." Linnie shook her head. "She couldn't stand the idea of killing anyone, so she made me help her drag him outside before I lit it."

"I see." The detective's head tilted to the side. "So what happened with you and Charlie?"

Damn, the interrogation continued. She glanced at her watch. She didn't have the time or desire to rip back open this scab. "He's gone," Linnie stated plainly. *Please God, don't ask me to elaborate. Too soon and too raw.* Detective Majors raised her eyebrows, prodding her to continue.

"I told him to leave and he did."

Detective Majors moved close and whispered, "He's closer than you think."

Linnie turned. Charlie's smile lit up his tanned face when their eyes met. She couldn't breathe. He trotted up the stairs toward her, holding a small bouquet of yellow flowers. His stare never wavered, as if she were the only person in the building.

His Hollywood was showing, in a crisp white shirt and tailored black pants. This time, she wanted to swoon. Gasps from onlookers who recognized him confirmed it.

He took all the air from the room and yet somehow brightened it.

Detective Majors squeezed Linnie's arm before departing. "Grab hold—you deserve happiness."

Linnie shot her a tight smile and turned back to face him. Butterflies danced in her belly.

"Hello, beautiful." Charlie's voice was laced with emotion, husky and low. He stood on the step below her, making them the same height. Leaning in, he kissed her on the cheek. The normal urge to back away didn't come.

"Thanks," she stammered. "You're...very tan."

She could kick herself. Of all the things to say to this man she loved. And that's what came out?

He chuckled, turned serious, then cocked an eyebrow. His face was so close she could smell his minty breath. "You're an awkward compliment-giver."

Linnie laughed—a hard, real laugh. Enough to make her incision pinch, but she ignored that pain. He hooked his arm around her waist gently and pulled her to him. She placed her hands on his chest. God, she missed him. "Been clearing land for our new summer house on Mom and Dad's farm."

"Erickson, what are you…wait, what? *Our* new summer house? What do you mean?" People stopped to stare.

"I'm talking about loving you, Linnie. Like I have from the first moment I met you. You've become my world. Nothing else matters if you're not in it."

He'd said her real name.

She'd dreamed of his smooth voice pronouncing her name. Closing her eyes, tingles spread through her body. When she opened them, he reached into his pocket with his free hand and produced a tiny box. Her knees wobbled. She was sure most of the blood drained from her face into her toes. Thank God he still had a hold of her.

"Before you say anything," he whispered, "I want you to know…I have all the information I need about your ordeal."

When she glanced down, he paused and tilted his head until her eyes met his again. "I only listened to the first five seconds. Only the part of the recording where you said you were in love with me. It was all I needed to hear."

Her lips curved up on their own and her eyes filled with tears. His turned misty too and his voice quivered. "The way I see it—you're the same innocent girl I met in the dressing room. None of it was your fault. I want you for the rest of my life. I'll do everything in my power to keep you safe. It'll be my mission to make you, Nate, and anyone else who comes along—happy."

Charlie handed her the box. "Marry me."

It wasn't a question.

Opening it with trembling hands, she stared at the sparkling ring inside. When she didn't answer right away, Charlie cleared his throat. She glanced up.

His eyebrows shot up, humor dancing in his eyes. "I don't have a plan B, Miss Carroll. And I'm not leaving here without you."

Linnie surveyed the face she loved, then bravely did two things she'd never done before. Lifting a hand, she placed it on Charlie's cheek and initiated her first real kiss.

Then she said yes.

Acknowledgement

There are a host of people to thank. Were it not for the tireless efforts of a handful of friends, fellow writers, beta readers, and my awesome BBR launch team, this book would be nothing more than a lonely file on my computer, so thank you—you know who you are.

I especially want to thank Nikki, Kat, and Cassie at Champagne Book Group for having faith in my story and showing me the ropes of traditional publishing. Also, to Ellie Maas Davis, my first ever hired editor—thanks for the tough love, I needed it. And to Deb Rhodes, my friend and beta reader who not only read my stories and encouraged me but became a good friend in the process. I wouldn't have half the confidence I have as a writer without you, Deb, thanks!

And lastly, to my family—Seth, Sam, Shane, Sean, Sonny, and especially Stacy. Thank you for loving me and tolerating all the time away from you to play with the characters in my head.

About the Author

Kelley Griffin is a closet romantic suspense author, teacher, mom to five sons, wife to a Marine, and southerner by common law. GO VOLS! She's blessed to be surrounded by testosterone, laughter, and family every day. When her characters fall, embarrass themselves or bumble into a scene, you know it's something she's either experienced firsthand or accidentally caused.

Kelley loves to hear from readers. You can find and connect with her at the links below.

Website/Blog: www.kelleygriffinauthor.com
Facebook: https://www.facebook.com/KelleyGriffinAuthor/
Instagram: https://www.instagram.com/kelleygriffinauthor/
Pinterest: https://www.pinterest.com/kgriffin98/
Twitter: https://twitter.com/AuthorKTGriffin
YouTube:
https://www.youtube.com/channel/UCkW4a7FCS5nKzB6MzKIf6Gw?
view_as=subscriber

~ * ~

We hope you enjoyed *Binding Circumstance* as much as we did. If so, , please write a review, tell your friends, or go check out the other terrific offerings at Champagne Book Group.

~ * ~

Turn the page for a sneak peek into *Cold Sweat*, book 1 of the romantic suspense series, Heart & Endurance by J. S. Marlo.

Cold Sweat

Blistery fire, Hope. What possessed you to name your father?

The name of her father belonged on Hope's birth certificate. Nowhere else. Colonel Amelia Matheson had seen to it, or so she'd thought.

Her daughter's biography, which Amelia would never have authorized, was posted on the team's website along with the life stories of the other biathletes. The only person who could have written and submitted the article was Hope.

Sometimes that only child of mine is as infuriating as her father had been.

Amelia was tempted to ask Hope's coach to take it down, but the request would raise questions. A silent sigh expanded her ribcage. After eighteen years, she was tired of the truthful lies, though she only had herself to blame.

With any luck, no one will read it. Regardless, her feisty daughter would still get an earful when she called from Montana tonight. She'd better wear her transmitter.

A knock on her door ended Amelia's broodings.

"Come."

Captain Garner stepped into her office. When he closed the door behind him, Amelia braced herself for more bad news.

"Yes, Captain?"

With his hands behind his back, the junior officer came to stand at ease in front of her desk. A beautifully handcrafted desk buried under a mountain of paperwork.

"We have two problems, ma'am."

Back in her younger days, Amelia had loved handling problems, the bigger the better, but since she got stuck behind a desk, problems had multiplied at a higher rate than solutions had surfaced. Her body and her mind screamed for action. Accepting her latest promotion had been a mistake and filling in for Colonel Lewis until her position at the Pentagon became official had been an even bigger one. She belonged in the field searching for answers, not in an office waiting for reports.

"What problems?" She kept her frustration wrapped under a cool and professional demeanor.

"The body of a young woman was found in Major Elliot's cottage in New Hampshire. She was in one of the guest bedrooms dressed in a nightgown. Preliminary report indicates she's been dead at least two weeks. No name or cause of death yet."

According to his exemplary service record, Major Charles S. Elliot owned a private medical practice in North Carolina. He was one of many military doctors who provided medical care to the civilian population in his spare time.

The cottage in New Hampshire is a long way from the private clinic in North Carolina.

It baffled Amelia that in fifteen years, Elliot's behavior or evaluations hadn't shown he was prone to negligence. Had the doctor been incarcerated instead of being remanded to house arrest, he wouldn't have escaped, and that young woman might still be alive.

If the victim is one of his civilian patients, the media will have a field trip with the story.

"Was Elliot apprehended by the local authorities?" Not territorial by nature, Amelia didn't care who arrested the fugitive as long as the bloody trail ended. Getting the job done was more important than receiving credits.

"No, ma'am, and that's the other problem." Not one to be easily intimidated, Garner looked her in the eye when he spoke. "A male nurse was arrested last night for administering an unapproved drug to a female soldier. The victim developed an adverse reaction similar to the one that killed Major Elliot's three patients. A look at the nurse's schedule showed he'd also tended to those patients within twenty-four hours of their death. The charges against Major Elliot haven't been dropped, but he's no longer the only suspect."

Wonderful.

A month ago, Elliot had escaped custody while awaiting his court-martial for negligent homicide in the death of three patients. If he were innocent, he'd chosen the wrong month to take a hike and hide a fourth body in his cottage.

"Regardless of his guilt or innocence, Major Elliot is AWOL since November fifteenth. Our job is to track him down and bring him back. The lawyers can figure out the rest."

~ * ~

The snow glistened in the early morning sun and the air sparkled with tiny crystals, changing the mountains into a picturesque Christmas card.

Quest loved the serenity and beauty of winter with as much passion as she loved skiing and shooting.

Her skis glided on the trail, packing the fresh snow into two parallel lines every time she raced down a hill and adding crisscross design to every slope she climbed. Ahead of her, a cute blond guy with dark brown eyes and a smile that could melt a glacier, groomed the trail. The vibrations of his machine sizzled through Quest's body, but as the distance between them grew farther, the sensation faded away.

Her rifle bounced on her back, unloaded, a comforting ally in her silent world. Alone on the trail, Quest didn't bring any ammunition for target practice and didn't wear her transmitter. Later on, once she rejoined the other athletes, she would rectify both situations.

To give her brief reprieves from the white noise she must tolerate in order to hear, Coach Goldman had requested special accommodations. Thanks to him, Quest had been granted permission to train in the early morning solitude of the sleepy mountains, outside the normal hours of operation. She appreciated the consideration.

As she ventured deeper into the forested area, the naked trees cuddled closer against the evergreens, blocking her view of the valley below.

Being invited by her coach to the altitude training camp at Snowy Tip had been a dream come true. Convincing her mother and grandfather to let her take the year off and postpone her entrance to Princeton University in order to train full-time for the Olympic trials had required grueling efforts and perseverance.

White clouds formed around her mouth with every breath she took. After two months in Montana, her lungs had adapted to the lower atmospheric pressure. She no longer felt the effect of the altitude. The trials were three weeks away. She was as ready—mentally and physically—as she'd ever be.

Beads of perspiration trickled between her shoulder blades, quickly whisked away by the microfiber undershirt she wore like a second skin. Every piece of clothing and equipment played a role, down to her gloves from which she'd cut off the tip of the right index finger to better feel the resistance of the trigger when she fired.

The flat section ahead curved around a frozen pond. Red markers delimited the perimeter of the ice surface in case some skiers were tempted to cross over.

A yellow light reflecting over the white blanket of snow caught Quest's attention. Pausing, she looked behind her. Two snowmobiles were headed in her direction. The last one pulled a rake on the ground, mimicking the grooming effect and erasing her ski tracks. Puzzled by their presence on the trail, she moved to the side to let them pass. As they approached, they slowed down, stopping a few feet away from her.

Despite the cold and wind, the ski masks covering their faces weren't common attires among the maintenance crewmembers. One driver stood up. Big and stocky in his black snowsuit, he looked more like a man than a woman.

Trying her best not to appear intimidated, Quest glanced back and forth between the two of them as she tried to decipher which one led the pack. "Is there a problem, guys?"

The lips of the closer individual moved. "Hope Craig?"

Only strangers—and her mother—called her Hope. "Who wants to know?"

He pulled a gun on her. "No reaching for your rifle. You're coming with us."

~ * ~

For their guests' enjoyment, Scarlet Vacation Resort offered miles of private trails winding through the mountains. The red iron bridges along the trails, a trademark of the resort, added a touch of color to the wintery landscape.

Sheriff Richmond Morgan and Deputy Gil Thompson had been hiking since dawn searching for a specific red bridge. In the photos in Rich's pocket, the bridge overlapped a stream, guarded on one side by trees and on the other by a steep, rocky wall.

In the last month, someone had snapped compromising shots of Senator Craig Norman while he vacationed alone at the resort, but the senator hadn't deemed it important enough to notify the authorities he was being blackmailed until last night.

Rich pulled the first photo from his jacket and compared it to the actual landscape.

Some twenty feet ahead, a red bridge overlapped a snow-covered stream. In the morning sun, shimmering ice filled the crevasses in the rocky wall and fresh snow weighed down the branches of the evergreens.

Despite the artistic differences crafted by the weather, Rich was confident he stared at the same bridge from the same vantage point.

"Look at that. The bridge does indeed exist."

"That's a shocker." A cocky grin split his deputy's face. "We're just missing the senator and his black beauty cuddling by the railing."

Senator Norman was married with five kids. His wife of

twenty-seven years had olive skin, not dark chocolate like the beautiful woman in the photo.

Scanning the surrounding area for a suitable place to hide and snap, Rich found none.

"The senator vaguely remembers taking a friendly walk with a dark-skinned woman he ran into on the trail. Nothing more. How did Norman not see the blackmailer snap the pictures?"

"Maybe his eyesight is as faulty as his memory, Sheriff. Or maybe he was too busy enjoying his new *friend's* curvy attributes to notice, or care."

The politician didn't strike Rich as the careless type. "Something in this story doesn't add up."

In a bid to avoid political embarrassment and protect his marriage, the senator had paid the blackmailer fifteen thousand dollars for the suggestive snapshot despite claiming it was fake. Two weeks later, a second picture, more provocative than the first one, had landed on the senator's desk. The two hundred per cent increase in price had rattled Norman. He'd sent another fifteen thousand and begged for a two-week grace period in order to raise the missing thirty thousand dollars. Surprisingly, the blackmailer had agreed and Norman had contacted the sheriff's office.

The FBI should be handling this investigation, not me. As a former federal agent, Rich had suggested that much, but for reasons Norman didn't or wouldn't share, the senator had ordered him to conduct a discreet investigation without involving any other agencies.

Rich pulled out the most recent snapshot.

Snowflakes dotted a gray, teal, and purple snowmobile parked near the same red bridge. Straddled over the seat, the senator hugged a youthful-looking blonde sporting nothing more than a pair of black boots and a pink hat with a purple pompom.

According to Nathan Ford, their civilian computer technician who doubled as a photographer in his spare time, the pictures were real. No retouch. No Photoshop.

"You have to give it to the senator, Sheriff. He's trying his best to keep Snow Bunny warm."

The blonde girl didn't look any older than the senator's children. If she was underage, Norman had bigger problems than worrying about losing his wife or his career.

Rich gave the pictures to his deputy. "I want that girl's name and age. Go back to the office and take Eve with you. She needs to see some action before she develops cabin fever."

* * *

Cold Sweat
J. S. Marlo

Can they conquer the mountains and the past in time to save Hope?

Seventeen-year-old Hope Craig is deaf and training hard to make the biathlon Olympic Team. When she is kidnapped from the groomed trails and taken to a remote cabin in the mountains, she must battle more than the elements to survive.

On the hunt for her daughter's abductor, Colonel Amelia Matheson enlists the help of Richmond Morgan, a local sheriff who once hurt her. To find Hope, Sheriff Morgan and Colonel Matheson must untangle a web of secrets, including their own.

Using her wits and skills, Hope sets out to escape the mountains and save the man her mother had sent to rescue her—a man who is not who he appears to be.

Cold Sweat, as well as *Thin Ice*, book 2, and *Hot Water*, book 3, are available at all major retailers

~ * ~

Made in the USA
Middletown, DE
03 October 2021